Praise for Eve Vaughn's *A Night To Remember*

"...a titillating romance packed to the rim with scorching love scenes and emotional journeys...For a heartfelt tale packed with a bit of spice, make sure A NIGHT TO REMEMBER is in your reading arsenal this fall."

~ Amy Cunningham, RRT Erotic

A Night to Remember

Eve Vaughn

A SAMHAIN PUBLISHING, LTD. publication.

Samhain Publishing, Ltd.
2932 Ross Clark Circle, #384
Dothan, AL 36301
www.samhainpublishing.com

A Night to Remember
Copyright © 2006 by Eve Vaughn
Print ISBN: 1-59998-354-0
Digital ISBN: 1-59998-076-2

Editing by Angie James
Cover by Scott Carpenter

First Samhain Publishing, Ltd. electronic publication: October 2006
First Samhain Publishing, Ltd. print publication: January 2007

Dedication

To a woman who has taught me courage against the face of adversity. Love ya, Mom!

Prologue

One year of wedded bliss! Charlie hummed to herself as she danced around the kitchen, preparing Paul's favorite dish— steak and garlic mashed potatoes. This night had to be absolutely perfect. A smile touched her lips when she remembered waking up in his arms that morning.

"Good morning, peanut. Happy anniversary." Paul had leaned over to kiss her gently on the lips, running his hand along her body in a light caress.

She moaned in delight, returning his greeting. "Good morning, handsome. Happy anniversary, baby. Did you know that it's a crime to look so damn fine this early in the morning?"

"If that were true, you would have been arrested a long time ago."

His retort brought a smile to her face. Paul had the ability to make her as giddy as a schoolgirl with his smooth words. "How is it that you always manage to say such nice things to me?" She had wondered what she had done right to deserve such a wonderful, gorgeous husband like Paul.

She touched his face, running her fingers over his morning stubble. Charlie adored his warm, light brown eyes, dark brown skin, kissable lips, and a smile that made her heart melt and vaginal walls tighten with need.

They'd met when he had come into the accounting firm she worked for to have his taxes done. It was love at first sight, and they were married within a month. Though it had been a whirlwind affair, she never regretted for a moment surrendering so completely to their love.

Their eyes locked and his knee nudged her legs apart. Charlie sighed when Paul slowly slid his cock into her wet, ready channel. "Oh, baby," she sighed as he began to move inside of her with sensual strokes.

He kissed her neck, whispering words of love. Charlie clung tightly to him. "I love you so much, Paul," she whispered, becoming lost in her desire for him. Nothing else existed except she and Paul, and nothing felt more right than being in the arms of the man she loved on their wedding anniversary. The year had gone by so fast, and she looked forward to spending many more with him.

The rhythm of his delicious thrusts sped up. "Oh God, yes, Paul!" She cried out as he slammed into her.

"Whose pussy is this?" He demanded, pounding her pussy with a savage frenzy.

"Yours! Only yours!" She tilted her hips to meet his dick, thrust for thrust.

"Damn right it is, girl. Oh God, peanut, what a sweet pussy you have."

He knew it drove her wild with lust when he talked dirty to her. The heat of their passion for each other burned so strong, it threatened to consume them both. They made love for what seemed like hours until they both reach their mutual peaks, screaming out the other's name.

They had lain in each other's arms afterwards, both wishing they could stay like that forever, but Paul had to go to work at the fire station. Charlie worried about Paul risking life and limb to put out fires. Every time he donned his uniform, she made him promise he'd come back to her. Paul usually laughed and assured her he would be okay.

"I will never leave you, baby. I will be here for you," was his usual reply.

After making love, Charlie showered with Paul and saw him off. She had opted to take the day off so she could prepare the house for when he got home. First she scrubbed their house from top to bottom, then threw rose petals in strategic places, and finally placed scented candles in every room. During the day, a huge bouquet of flowers was delivered to her. It was just like her husband to be so thoughtful.

She was nearly finished fixing dinner when the doorbell rang. Paul must have forgotten his key again.

"Just a minute," she called out.

Charlie dashed to bathroom to check herself out. She knew the pink teddy she wore looked great against her dark skin. Paul's socks would be knocked off. Maybe tonight would be the night they'd make a baby. The doorbell rang again, a little more persistently this time.

"Hold on, Paul, I'm coming. She ran into the living room and pulled out a Teddy Pendergrass CD. Now they could really get the party started. The doorbell rang again just as she opened it.

The wide smile pinned to her lips fell. Standing at the door was the fire chief. Charlie's heart stopped. Something was wrong. Terribly wrong.

Chapter One

"Well, baby, I've made it through another day without you. I miss you so much I physically ache." Charlie spoke softly to the photograph that she held in her hand. "I don't know how I made it through this past year without you, and I sure as hell don't know how I'll make it through another." Her chest was tight with grief. "You promised me that you would always be here for me. You promised me that you would do everything in your power to make me happy. Well, I'm not happy. I need you, baby." She broke off with a sob. "Oh God, Paul, I'm so very unhappy."

She glanced up from the photo to see the sympathetic looks from the onlookers sitting around her, and the speculative gleam in the bartender's eyes. Let them look. She didn't know any of them from Adam. They couldn't possibly understand her pain. She turned her attention back to the photograph she held.

Taking another swig from her whiskey glass, she fought to keep the tears at bay. She winced as the warm amber liquid burned a trail down her throat. This was her fourth glass. She couldn't stand the stuff, but it helped to numb the pain she felt inside.

Why did I come here tonight? Her eyes began to water yet again.

She dug into her purse in for a tissue, already knowing the answer to that question.

Tonight was the loneliest night of her entire twenty-eight years. Charlie couldn't spend another night in her empty house, especially on this particular date. She should have been celebrating her two-year wedding anniversary; instead it was the anniversary of her husband's death.

"Oh, Paul. You broke your promise to me," she whispered to the picture as if it would answer back. Paul's image stared back at her, unmoving. His warm brown eyes contained a hint of mischief. The huge smile on his face tugged at her heartstrings. His smooth mahogany skin made her fingers itch to touch him one last time. Paul had often been likened to Denzel Washington when described, but in Charlie's opinion, Denzel had nothing on her man.

Besides from being incredibly good-looking, Paul had been the most unselfish, caring human being she'd ever met. He had been a good husband and treated Charlie like a queen. Everyone who'd known him loved him, and Charlie had loved him most of all.

There was nothing Paul wouldn't do to help out his fellow man. He had been the type of person who would give the very shirt off his back to a person in need. He would lend his last dollar if he had been asked. Charlie sighed, thinking it was his willingness to help others that got him killed.

Paul had been a fireman, and according to eyewitnesses, he had run into a burning house to save an elderly lady trapped inside. Everyone around had told him how hopeless the situation was, but Paul would not listen. As he was coming out of the house with the victim in his arms, a beam collapsed over Paul, but not before he threw the rescued woman to safety.

He'd died a hero.

While Paul lay dying, Charlie had been home, cooking a special dinner for their first wedding anniversary. When she'd answered the door and received the fateful news, Charlie wanted to die as well.

She'd gone into a deep depression, causing her family great distress. Each night after Paul's death, Charlie would curl up with his favorite T-shirt and cry. That particular shirt had been such a bone of contention between the two of them since they had been married. It was from Paul's alma mater, the University of North Carolina. She had hated it, because she had gone to UNC's rival school, North Carolina State.

Seeing him in that Carolina blue monstrosity, with the huge ram and the Tar Heel symbols, made Charlie grind her teeth. A shiver ran down her spine as she thought about an awful row his shirt had once caused. Now she would have given anything to see him wearing the damn thing. He could wear it every day if he wanted, just as long as he was alive.

Charlie had taken a leave of absence from work for a couple of months before she was able to face the world again. When she did eventually emerge from her cocoon of depression, she threw herself into her work, spending as much time as possible in the office. Often she'd return home only when exhaustion overtook her.

Unfortunately, work didn't help her with the solitary nights. She couldn't sleep in their bed anymore, preferring the guest bedroom. Sleeping in the empty king-size bed they once shared reminded her too much of their steamy nights of passion. Paul had been an excellent lover. He knew just how to touch her, lick her and fuck her. Charlie sighed heavily as she remembered the naughty things he would say to her in bed.

What a sweet little pussy my baby has, or *girl, you are the best ride that I've ever been on.*

It wasn't even the physical side of the relationship she missed the most. It was his scent, the way he would wake her up every morning with a kiss, and the way he would rub her shoulders when she was tired. Hell, she even missed his silly nickname for her. Paul called her peanut, a play on words due to her unfortunate name.

He had been a good listener and confidant. Charlie could tell him anything. They laughed together. They cried together. They shared in each other's failures and triumphs. He was her best friend.

And now he was gone. Some anniversary this turned out to be.

Her parents had invited her over for dinner tonight, and a few of her friends had done the same, but Charlie declined their invitations. She didn't want to be around people who felt sorry for her. That was the last thing she needed right now.

Tonight she wanted to get thoroughly drunk and not remember how much Paul's death still ripped at her insides. She didn't want to think about how a part of her was missing. A tear escaped the corner of her eye before she could catch it.

଼୨ଓ୪

Jake Fox had thought his clients would never leave. He sat at his table, taking another sip of beer. He loved his job, but hated the business dinners and traveling from city to city. Usually his vice-president handled the schmoozing while Jake ran the show from behind the scenes, but Steve was on a long, well-deserved vacation. Jake wished he were on the beach right now. He needed a vacation, but things at work were just too hectic at the moment.

Tonight Jake had wined and dined potential clients for MBF, who were probably more trouble than they were worth. For months, these people had given Jake's company the run around, and after intense negotiations, there was finally a light at the end of the tunnel. Thankfully, they signed the contract he'd offered and Jake was now able to breathe a huge sigh of relief.

When the last the of Banner group finally left, Jake decided to hang back and have another drink. Dealing with Joe Banner, the group's CEO, had been quite a trial. Whoever came up with the slogan "The customer is always right" should have been shot. Brown-nosing was not Jake's strong point.

When he looked over, he was relieved to see she was still there. The woman at the bar had caught his eye the minute she walked into the tavern. His table was close enough to the bar for him to sneak a peek at her every so often during dinner. It was because of her that he'd been able to make it through the evening with his clients. When Joe Banner would start to irritate him, Jake's gaze would stray toward the mystery lady's direction.

She was certainly an interesting person to watch. Something was obviously bothering her, however, and it seemed as if she were talking to herself. He couldn't quite make out the words, but whatever they were they couldn't be happy ones. Perhaps she had been stood up. For the life of him, Jake couldn't rationalize why anyone would want to break a date with someone so lovely.

On impulse, Jake signaled the waitress to his table. "Do you see the pretty lady sitting over there at the bar?"

"Yes, what about her?"

"I would like to have her tab placed on my bill."

"Sure, whatever. I'll let the bartender know." The waitress smiled.

It bothered him seeing a beautiful woman in distress, but if he were being honest, it was her beauty more than her distress that caught his eye. There was no doubt about it. She was sexy-as hell. In fact, she had to be one of the sexiest ladies he had seen in a long time. Lowering his lids, Jake casually studied her through his lashes.

Her skin was a rich milk chocolate, so smooth in appearance; his fingers tingled with the need to touch it, if only to see if it felt as soft as it looked. Her face was not beautiful in the classical sense, but she was stunning nonetheless. She wore her dark hair pulled back in a tight ponytail, making him wonder what it would look like hanging loosely around her shoulders.

Dressed casually in a pair of jeans and a tight black silk top, she still managed to look elegant. Jake could tell she wasn't wearing a bra because he could see the outline of her nipples poking through the glossy fabric. His mouth watered as he imagined what those hardened little peaks would look like exposed to his gaze. He bet they were dark like blackberries. He wondered if they would taste as sweet.

Two things in particular stood out on this woman: her lips and ass. Her lips were larger than average, even for a black woman, however they had the well-shaped bee-stung look that Hollywood actresses paid thousands of dollars to achieve. The kind men fantasized about kissing. They looked soft and welcoming. Just above the corner of her top lip there was a heart-shaped mole emphasizing the sexiness of that generous mouth.

Damn, I wouldn't mind tasting those lips.

As enticing as her lips were, his eyes wandered to her other prize—that ass. It was high, round, and accentuated by her tiny waist. A certain Latina singer would have been jealous had she seen this woman. Jake could feel a stirring in his pants as erotic images popped in his head. He imagined his cock sliding into her pussy from behind with his balls pounding against the round globes of her backside, and then he'd take his prick, dripping with her cunt juices, and slide it into the tight forbidden hole between her cheeks. He couldn't shake the image from his mind.

In normal circumstances he would have gone over to her and introduced himself, but he knew he had to catch an early flight back to Washington, D.C., the next morning. Jake hated being away from his office for too long. He sighed before finishing his beer. It had been a few months since he'd had some pussy and his need was never more evident than it was now.

Ever since his break up with Diane, a hot redhead with a body that did not quit, he'd been celibate. Diane was a nice woman, but she was extremely clingy and a bit on the mercenary side. He knew it was probably his fault for choosing the kind of women who would eventually want more than he was willing to offer, but damn it, at thirty-three he was entitled to a bit of fun after all the hard work he'd put into his company.

From the moment he'd left college, Jake had put most of his time and effort into building his now successful software business. Starting out with just himself, he eventually brought his best friend Steve on board when things began to take off. Steve happened to be a marketing genius, and now his company was thriving with nearly three hundred employees.

Jake had worked hard to get to where he was, and in the past few years, he'd enjoyed sowing the wild oats he missed out on in his early twenties. Was it too much for a woman to understand he wanted sex with no strings attached? Or at least for now. He'd always been up front at the beginning of a relationship about not looking for a long-term commitment. His girlfriends, however, always seemed to think they were the one who could change his mind.

Jake was the first to admit he was a bit spoiled when it came to women. From a young age, they had always thrown themselves at him. He never really knew why, but it simply happened. Without conceit, Jake knew he was attractive to the opposite sex, but it wasn't something he dwelled on. Having been raised by a strong and loving mother, he appreciated women in all shapes, sizes and colors. He lived by the adage that variety was the spice of life.

He did however, have a soft spot for beautiful black women. When he was twelve years old, he shared his first kiss with a black girl. She had been his first crush. Angela was her name. He remembered following her around like a puppy dog and carrying her books between classes. Jake had been heartbroken the day she had to move away when her father was transferred due to a promotion. Not since then had his heart ever been engaged in a relationship. He did care about the women he dated, but love had never been involved.

He knew his parents wanted him to settle down and start a family of his own. His mother was the most vocal about his single state. She constantly lectured him on the joys of being a father and having a family. Jake was sure his mother would have been happy if he settled down with a Martian at this point. There would come a time when he would meet someone he couldn't live without, but until then he would have some fun.

ഇരു

Charlie signaled to the bartender when her glass was empty. The big bald man gave her a wary look before coming over. "Can I get another whiskey, please?"

"I don't think so, ma'am. I believe you've had enough, and if I may be so bold, I suggest that you check into the hotel next door if you drove yourself here." He frowned with a shake of his head, giving her the you've-had-enough-to-drink-for-tonight look. "You've been talking to yourself practically the whole time you've been here. My conscience won't allow me to give you another alcoholic beverage."

Charlie would have gotten angry at his presumption but her lightheadedness got the better of her. Besides, sitting alone at a bar was downright depressing. The idea of checking into the hotel became appealing since she didn't want to go home.

"Okay, Mac. If you say so." There was no point in arguing. The man was only doing his job. She reached for her purse to pull out her wallet.

"It's okay, miss. It's been taken care of."

Charlie looked at him, wondering if she had heard him correctly. "What do you mean?"

"Someone has taken care of your tab."

"Oh, that's nice. Who was it?" she asked, curiously looking around her.

"The gentleman over to your right." Mac pointed in the direction of his gaze for her.

Charlie looked to see where Mac was pointing. She nearly fell off of her stool when she beheld her benefactor. Sitting alone at a table was one of the most handsome men she had ever seen. He looked as if he'd just stepped off the cover of *Gentleman's Quarterly* magazine. Not bad for a white boy.

She had nothing against white men, but she had always preferred dark-skinned black men like her husband. Not many men of other ethnicities had ever turned her head the way this one did. Charlie had to admit if she had met that Mr. Universe a long time ago, she wouldn't have been averse to getting to know him better.

The room seemed to spin and her pulse raced, probably from the alcohol. She turned her back to him so he wouldn't catch her staring. Once her heartbeat was under control again, she snuck another peek at him. This time, he was looking back at her. Their eyes met, and she couldn't look away even if she wanted to. His magnetic gaze held her.

He was the epitome of drop-dead gorgeous. From what she could tell, his body was long and lean. Even from his sitting position she could tell he had an athletic build, which wasn't disguised by the suit he wore. His wavy brown hair touched the collar of his jacket. It was worn longer than the current style, but it looked good on him. A stray brown lock fell carelessly over his brow. His chiseled features reminded her of the statue David. Ice blue eyes seemed to be undressing her.

He smiled at her, showing even white teeth. Even his teeth were perfect, damn the man. She shook her head, coming out of her trance. What was she thinking? She had no time for some two-bit Casanova right now. He wasn't Paul and no one could take her husband's place. Charlie politely smiled back at the gentleman who had fixed such an intense stare on her, before turning back around.

"Okay, Mac. It's been a lovely evening." She smiled at the bartender before getting up.

"Aren't you going to go over there and thank him?"

"I didn't ask him to pick up my tab. Before he leaves, thank him for me."

Mac just shrugged. "Whatever."

Charlie wasn't in the mood for the kind of attention the man's look offered right now.

ഇരു

Jake sat tensely as he watched his mystery woman walk out of the bar. When his eyes had locked with hers, he'd felt a jolt of something he'd never experienced before. Little beads of sweat formed on his brow. It couldn't have been just sexual.

I must be crazy.

There was no way he could feel such a strong connection for a woman he had seen at a bar, no matter how beautiful she was. Even though Jake was a strong believer in fate, the fact that she had barely acknowledged him indicated it was not meant to be.

Besides, he was only in town for one more night. This sudden burst of feeling at one glance was obviously just lust. He needed some pussy and he planned on pulling out his little black book the minute his plane landed in D.C. tomorrow.

ഇരു

"What do you mean you don't have any rooms?" Charlie asked in dismay. The poor front desk agent looked at her with pity.

"I'm sorry, ma'am," he said. "The convention has the hotel booked. Let me see if the other hotels in the area have anything available."

Charlie waited impatiently while he made the phone calls, angry at herself for being in such a situation.

Charlie couldn't trust herself to drive home. She didn't feel drunk, but she always got a little dizzy when she drank. It would not be ideal to drive a vehicle in her condition. The prospect of spending the night in her car was unappealing, but she didn't really have a choice.

That's what you get. You just had to bring your sorry ass downtown and get sloshed; now you're stuck here.

Calling her parents was out the question. She could just imagine what they would say if they knew how much she had drank. Her best friend, Laura, was out of town so Charlie couldn't call her either. There was no one else she felt comfortable enough to contact in her present condition.

She could have called a cab, but she didn't want to leave her car behind. It would be such a hassle to call a cab to take her home, and then call one in the morning to bring her back to her car. It was probably lazy of her, but nonetheless, it wasn't an issue she wanted to deal with. It was beginning to look like she'd be sleeping in her car tonight after all, if the agent couldn't find her other accommodations.

"Ma'am?" The desk agent interrupted her thoughts. "I'm sorry, but the other hotels are booked solid as well.

"Great, just my luck. Thanks for checking anyway." Charlie turned away from the front desk only to run into something that felt like a brick wall. She would have fallen backwards if two strong arms hadn't wrapped themselves around her. Charlie looked up to see whom she had run into. Damn, it was the pretty boy from the bar. Her heart beat a tattoo against her chest.

Oh dear, I hope he isn't following me. This is the last thing I need.

"Thanks." She pushed away from him, but not before Charlie noted how solid he felt. Why were her palms suddenly sweaty and her breathing abnormal?

"Can I be of some assistance to you?" His voice was deep and as sexy as the rest of him.

"No, thank you." Charlie would have walked past him had he not been blocking her way.

"I couldn't help but overhear you at the reception desk and I think I may have a solution to your problem."

"Whatever solution you may have, I'm not interested."

He went on as if she hadn't spoken. "There's a convention in town and all the hotels within walking distance are booked solid. I was fortunate enough to get one of the last available rooms in this hotel, which just happens to have two double beds. I would be happy to share with you tonight."

"No, thank you." Her voice came out in a weak croak. She hoped she sounded firmer to him than to her own ears.

This man was obviously out of his mind if he thought she was going to share a room with him. No matter how handsome he was, he could be a sex maniac for all she knew. Ted Bundy stood out in her mind.

"Don't be so stubborn. You know as well as I do that you shouldn't be driving. Where will you go?"

He had a point, but still, how could she know he wouldn't try anything? As if reading her mind he said, "Look, I know what you must be thinking but I'm not some raving lunatic. You are a very attractive woman, but believe me, I need sleep more than anything else right now. I have an early flight to catch tomorrow. Besides, I'm placing myself in as much jeopardy as you are lady. How do I know that you won't rob me blind?"

"I am not a thief!"

"And I'm not a sex fiend. Unwilling women aren't my scene. Also, if I might suggest, you need to sleep off all the alcohol you drank tonight."

Charlie felt like a jackass. She hadn't meant to offend him; after all, he had been nice enough to pick up her tab at the bar. Charlie was generally a good judge of character and intuition told her she could trust this man. "I'm sorry. You're very kind to offer me a bed for the night. I really appreciate it."

"Does that mean you're accepting my offer?"

"Yes, I am, that is if I haven't pissed you off. I meant no harm, but you never know these days."

He smiled at her. "It's okay. Since we will be roommates for the night, you should at least tell me your name. I'm Jake Fox." He held out his hand to her.

"Charlie Brown." She took his hand and laughed at the expression on his face.

"You're joking right?" He smacked his head as though realizing how rude his question was. "Sorry," he apologized quickly.

"Don't worry about it. I get that quite a bit. Charlie is short for Charlotte, but no one but my parents call me Charlotte. Even then, they only use it when they're mad at me. As you can imagine, my parents have a twisted sense of humor." She smiled, feeling shy all of a sudden.

An indiscernible expression flickered in his blue eyes as Jake looked down at her, but it was nothing that made her feel ill at ease. He smiled back. "It suits you. Well, let's go, Charlie Brown."

To Charlie's surprise she felt comfortable with Jake. All her reservations about staying with him slid away as he led her to his room. She shouldn't have trusted this stranger on such short acquaintance, but she did. Charlie couldn't explain the feeling, but his very presence put her at ease.

When they arrived at Jake's room, he opened the door, motioning for her to enter first. Charlie hesitated for only a second. She looked at him and he smiled at her. Her heart twinged. It was the alcohol, she was sure of it.

"Don't worry, I won't bite if you don't want me to," he teased, as he nudged her further into the room.

"Well, you can't exactly blame me for being a little nervous. I've never shared a hotel room with a stranger before," she pointed out.

"Well, aren't I taking as big a risk as you are? How do I know you won't take advantage of me?"

She shook her head, seeing the playful gleam in his eyes. "Okay, you big idiot. I give. You're going to have to turn your back while I undress, though."

He pouted. "Do I have to?"

Charlie laughed wondering what she had been so afraid of in the first place. They seemed like old friends. After chatting for a few more minutes, she yawned. "I'm exhausted."

"Yes, I'm pretty tired as well. You can take this bed. I'll take the one on the wall. Is that okay with you?"

"Sure," she agreed with a shrug.

Jake walked over to his side of the room, turning his back so she could undress and slip into her bed.

"Okay," Charlie indicated to Jake after she'd gotten under the covers. "It's safe to turn around now."

Jake turned and looked at her with those arresting eyes again.

"Goodnight, Charlie." He reached down to turn off the lamp and got into his bed.

Long after Jake was asleep, Charlie lay in her bed wide-awake.

Chapter Two

Something woke Jake up. He sat up in bed, disoriented, and shook his head to gather his senses. It was still dark outside, the moonlight seeping through the curtains. Looking over at the clock on the nightstand, Jake saw it was only midnight. It took him another moment to remember he had a roommate. He soon realized she was the one who'd caused the disturbance.

Charlie wept softly into her pillow, but it was still loud enough for him to hear. He'd always been a light sleeper. Jake flipped the light switch on and slid out of his bed, unmindful of the fact he was only wearing a pair of boxers. Taking a seat next to her, he gently shook her shoulders, concern for her filling him. "Charlie, are you okay?"

She turned around then, tears clouding her beautiful dark brown eyes. "Did I wake you? I didn't mean to. I'm sorry. Please go back to bed."

"And leave you crying your eyes out? I don't think so. You were upset at the bar and it's obviously still bothering you. Won't you tell me what's wrong?" When she didn't reply, he sighed. "I won't go back to bed until you tell me. We can sit here like this all night if you want."

After what seemed like several minutes, Charlie finally spoke. "It's my second wedding anniversary."

Jake pulled away abruptly as if he had been slapped. She was married? What the hell was she doing here then?

"Where's your husband?" He felt an irrational sense of betrayal. It bothered him more than he cared to admit to know she was some other man's wife. It didn't make sense, but jealousy rarely did.

"He...he died a year ago tonight," Charlie said through held tears.

"I'm sorry." Shame washed through Jake at the brief moment of relief he felt. Charlie was obviously miserable.

He pulled her into his arms to console her. The warmth of her body against his nearly made him forget he was supposed to be comforting her. Charlie relaxed, seeming to melt as she surrendered to her apparent misery, bursting into loud, body-shaking sobs. Jake was not normally equipped for dealing with emotional females, but with Charlie, he felt protective. He wished he could make things better for her, but what could he do?

Jake tightened his arms around Charlie and began to rock her back and forth in his arms while she bawled. She clung to him tightly, releasing anguish like he'd never heard before.

Charlie cried as if her heart were breaking. Her gut-wrenching cries tore at his heart in sympathy. He stroked her hair and dropped light kisses on her head in an attempt to soothe her. He held her for several moments before her tears subsided into weak sniffles.

Jake suddenly realized she was only wearing a pair of panties. Her soft breasts pressed against his chest, her nipples burning holes into his flesh. He was also painfully aware that her lips were resting unconsciously against his throat. He could feel his body tightening in response to her nearness. If there were time for carnal thoughts to invade, this certainly wasn't it.

27

He looked down at her, noticing Charlie was unaware of the effect she had on his body. When her tongue came out to moisten her lips, the tip grazed his throat. Jake shifted uncomfortably when his cock stirred to life. More than anything he wanted to bend down and capture that pink tongue between his teeth and suck it.

Fuck!

He had given her a lecture about him not being a pervert and here he was hard as a rock, wanting her more than he had ever wanted any other woman.

As her sobs subsided, Charlie looked up at him. "I'm sorry for releasing the floodgates. I didn't mean to make you uncomfortable. You probably think I'm a big baby?"

"I don't think that at all. You have every right to be sad. Were I in your predicament I'm not sure how I'd handle it. It certainly explains why you looked upset earlier."

"But still, when you invited me to share your room tonight, I'm sure you didn't have this in mind."

"No, I didn't, but it's no big deal. It sounds like you really needed a good cry. I'm glad I was here for you to be that shoulder to cry on."

Charlie looked up at him with her doe-like brown eyes and his body tightened with need for her. Being so close to this woman was affecting his equilibrium. He wanted her. His cock was already hard as a rock. Jake only hoped he could untangle himself before she realized it.

"I appreciate your being so nice about this." Charlie shifted her weight causing her hand to brush against his stiffness. She froze.

Jake pulled away. "Look, I'm sorry. I guess it's just one of those things." He was mortified. Heat rushed to his face. He thanked goodness, the room was masked in semi-darkness, otherwise she'd see how red his face probably was. Charlie didn't say anything. She merely looked at him with her eyes full of wonder.

"Don't look at me like that, Charlie," he groaned. Only minutes before, she had been distraught. Now there was a new look in her eyes. If he weren't mistaken, it was one of desire.

"How am I looking at you, Jake?" she asked innocently.

"Like you want me." The words came gruffly from his throat.

"Maybe I do." Her response surprised him. Had he just heard her incorrectly? There was no way she'd just said what he thought she did.

"You don't know what you're saying."

She slid her finger down the center of his chest. He gasped at the blatant contact. "Please, Jake."

"Charlie, you've had a lot to drink tonight. You may think you want me now, but in the morning you'll regret it."

"Tomorrow doesn't matter. Let's just live for the moment."

"You can't possibly want this. Not now, not after having such an emotional experience." Jake wanted to give in to her more than he had ever wanted anything in his life. He could smell the faint scent of her pussy and it was driving him crazy. The very thought of burying his face between her chocolate thighs and feasting on her cunt sent spasms of delight through his body.

"I do. This is exactly what I need. Jake, please kiss me." She gazed at him imploringly. How could he deny her this? But he had to!

"Charlie, you're in no condition to ask for such a thing." Despite his half-hearted argument, his cock ached for her.

Jake's breathing grew shallow, and he wanted to push her back on the bed and fuck her until she couldn't walk.

"I know what I want. Please, Jake. I need you. Don't go back to your bed. Stay with me." Charlie batted her eyelashes and poked out her bottom lip.

Looking at those sexy lips, he did the only thing he could— give in. Jake lowered his head and tugged on her tempting lower lip with his teeth. He nibbled at the tantalizing fullness of her mouth before crushing her lips beneath his. Jake kissed her hungrily wanting to devour her. When Charlie parted her lips ever so slightly, his tongue invaded the warm cavern.

She tasted like heaven. It was unlike anything else. She was sweet, spicy, warm and cool at the same time. Just kissing Charlie made him hotter than he had ever been for any woman. With reluctance, he lifted his head for a moment. "You won't say I took advantage of you in the morning?" he asked with an uncertainty foreign to his usually confident self. Charlie made him feel like a schoolboy all over again, not knowing right from left or which way was up.

"Like I said, I don't care about tomorrow. Let's just think about tonight, and how much I want you. I know you want me, too. I saw the way you looked at me at the bar." She placed her hand behind his neck and pulled him back down to her.

Jake's head told him this wasn't a good idea, but his dick was running the show. His cock was so damn hard, he feared he would spew come inside his shorts without ever sliding into the bliss that waited between her legs.

Charlie reached out and ran her hand down the front of his boxers, making contact with his penis. "You have quite a package hidden under these boxers. Take them off, so I can see exactly what I'm dealing with," she demanded.

Jake complied quickly, practically ripping them off. He would have fallen on top of her afterward if she hadn't halted him

"No, wait. Let me look at it," she commanded softly. Jake knelt on the bed, his cock exposed to her gaze. He wasn't ashamed of his body, and the hungry look in Charlie's gaze filled him with manly pride.

"You're so big, Jake. It must be nearly ten inches." Charlie's eyes widened with apparent wonder as she licked those gorgeous full lips of hers.

"Nine and a half but who's measuring?" He grinned at her. The huge purplish head of his cock dripped pre-come—ready and waiting for her pussy.

Charlie reached out and touched it lightly. "You have a beautiful body, Jake."

He felt as if his body would melt under the heat of her stare. Jake fought back a groan.

"Beautiful," she whispered, running her fingers along his hard length.

"And it wants some pussy," he said hoarsely when she continued to lightly stroke his cock.

"Umm, I think I can help you with that." Smiling coyly, Charlie laid back on the bed.

Jake's control snapped and he covered her body, pressing her into the mattress. He kissed her, relishing the feel of her soft lips beneath his.

"Umm, I like the way you kiss, Jake." Her husky voice practically purred like a satisfied kitten's when he began to explore her body, his hands leaving no part of her untouched.

He cupped her breasts, his mouth never leaving hers. Shaping the pert globes in his hands, he squeezed them gently. Her fingernails raked up and down his back.

"Damn, you're sexy, Charlie," Jake muttered against her throat, kissing her the pulse of her neck. He made a trail of kisses along her jawline and back to her lips.

Jake was practically a stranger to her, yet he made her feel things she had thought died with Paul. She needed this. Charlie wanted to live tonight. For once in her life she threw caution to the wind, but Charlie wasn't content to let Jake have all the fun. She ran her hand slowly down his chest, reveling at the feel of his hardness beneath her finger tips. She stopped only when she reached his throbbing shaft. It was so thick that her small hand could barely wrap all the way around it. Her fingers grasped his cock and she began to pump it gently with her fist.

He moaned with apparent pleasure. "Oh God, Charlie. You don't know what you're doing to me."

Charlie knew exactly what she was doing to him. High on her own feminine power, she grew very aroused by the sight of her dark hand wrapped around his long pale rod. She didn't know something as simple as color contrast could be such a turn on.

With a groan, Jake ripped her hand away. He collected both of her wrists in one of his hands and pinned them above her head. "Any more of that and I will be finished before I even get started, sweetheart." His warning sounded rough and hoarse to her ears.

"And we wouldn't want that would we?" Charlie teased.

"Hell no! By the end of the night you'll be well acquainted with my cock."

"I can hardly wait."

Charlie squirmed underneath him, enjoying the feel of his body on top of hers. The inside of her thighs dampened from her juices. She longed to run her tongue over his tight, muscular body. She needed to feel his cock plowing into her, filling her. The delicious sensation of his body against hers slowly drove her insane with lust. "Do it now, Jake. I can't take anymore." The last time she'd been consumed with such aching heat had been with Paul. It was a deep, slow burn, which could only be quenched with his throbbing erection.

"Patience, angel. I want to taste you." His eyes feasted on the twin peaks of her breasts, making her shiver with desire. No one had ever looked at her with such fierce, possessive desire.

"Jake—"

"Shh. You're so beautiful. Coffee-colored skin, gorgeous breasts, suckable nipples. You look good enough to eat. When I saw you, I knew you had a nice body, but this is much better than my imagination."

Still holding her wrists together, he lowered his head to lap one of her highly sensitized mounds. His tongue circled her areola sending spasms of delight to her very core.

"Oh God, Jake, your tongue is magic," she cried out. Charlie bucked against him, unable to get enough of his tongue bath.

He chuckled softly before taking a hardened nipple into his mouth. Jake took his time sucking, nibbling and licking the tasty peak before transferring his attention to the other one.

"Jake, that feels so good." Her body was on fire and her pussy tingled like crazy. If he didn't screw her soon, she was going to roll over and take some of that beautiful dick he was withholding from her.

Jake worked her body into a frenzy, nuzzling his face against her globes. After he finished worshipping the taut peaks, he ran his tongue from the valley of her breasts, down to her navel.

"Please let me touch you," she pleaded trying to free her wrists, but Jake held her firm.

"Patience, Charlie. If I let you touch me, I won't be able to hold out and I want to give you a fucking you won't soon forget."

Charlie bit her lip in frustration. This was pure torture. She couldn't remember a time when she had ever been so damn horny.

With his free hand, Jake quickly disposed of the lacy panties she wore, running his fingers lightly over her fuzzy mound. He briefly tongued her navel before moving lower down her body. He released her hands as his face dove for her cunt. Charlie gripped his shoulders, digging her nails into his flesh when he kissed the outer labia.

"Hmm, you don't shave. I like that. It's much more feminine," he growled with appreciation.

With each word that he spoke, Charlie fell deeper under his spell of seduction. He parted the slick folds of her labia with his middle finger before licking her from the bottom of her sex to her clit.

He lifted her hips, exposing all of her to his tantalizing gaze. Jake then parted her rounded cheeks and ran his tongue from her puckered little bud to the opening of her box. He rubbed his thumb over the tight bud of her ass while his tongue slid in and out of her channel.

Charlie had never had her ass stimulated before. Frankly, she was not a fan of back door love, but the way Jake touched her and caressed her slowly changed her mind.

He lapped her pussy and ass with several more strokes before he turned his attention to her clit. He nipped at the tingling bud gently with his teeth, eliciting loud, guttural moans from Charlie's throat.

Damn. Jake eats pussy like nobody's business.

She wiggled uncontrollably beneath him. He gripped her thighs firmly to keep her still then fastened his lips over her protruding clit, sucking fiercely while he slid a finger into her wet opening.

Charlie was so wet, she was literally dripping.

"Damn, woman, I didn't think it was possible for a pussy to get this wet. You're full of surprises, Charlie Brown. Very pleasant surprises," he murmured against her clit.

"It's wet for you, Jake. Your tongue feels wonderful," she moaned squirming under the ministrations of his mouth. He was going to kill her with too much pleasure. Jake continued to feast on her pussy until she yanked roughly on his hair, screaming for his cock.

"Jake! Stop playing and fuck me. I need your cock right now."

"You're going to get it."

He could have stayed between her creamy chocolate thighs forever, but his cock wanted some pussy too. Jake didn't need any more prompting after her impassioned plea before he positioned himself over her, guiding his hard rod between the folds of her dripping wet box. He nearly came the moment he was inside of her. Charlie's cunt was so tight around his nine and a half inches, it felt like her pussy was made especially for him. She wrapped her legs around his waist as he began to pump gently in and out of her.

Jake felt an unfamiliar emotion when he became one with Charlie. *It's just sex, it's just sex,* he chanted to himself. Funny, but sex had never felt like this before.

He moved with slow, precise moves in the beginning, wanting to give her time to adjust to his size, but Charlie had other ideas. She set the pace, bucking fiercely against him, forcing him to pick up speed. He fucked her with everything he had in him. She felt so good he knew he wouldn't be able to hold out for very long, much to his chagrin.

"I'm coming!" she screamed.

"So am I," he grunted breathlessly.

He gripped her thighs roughly as he released his seed into her hot channel. With the last pulse, he collapsed into her waiting arms. Jake kissed her sweaty brow. Her eyes were closed, but there was a content smile on her face. He couldn't resist giving her one last gentle kiss on the lips.

"Next time, we'll do it doggy style," he whispered, positioning himself so that he held her in his arms with her bottom nestled against his now sleeping cock.

Later that night, Jake woke Charlie, his cock persistently poking at the entrance of her vagina. She opened her legs to accommodate him. He slid into her still wet opening and pumped gently from behind her. This time he took her slowly, fondling her breasts as he thrust himself inside her damp sheath. Charlie came almost at once and Jake followed shortly after. As Jake's eyes grew heavy with sleep, all he could think about was changing his flight schedule in the morning. For some reason, the thought of leaving Charlie tomorrow bothered him. They fell asleep with Jake still inside of her.

৪৩CA

Jake woke up with a smile on his face. He couldn't remember a time when he had felt so good and relaxed. His arms were still wrapped tightly around Charlie's soft, pliant body. Her head rested peacefully against his chest and the smell of their mingled sex lingered in the air. He reveled in the protective feeling she produced within him.

He was on top of the world. In his entire life, no woman had ever brought him to such an intense peak of sexual satisfaction. Nothing had ever felt so good or so right. He glanced down at her as she slept, barely making a sound with her even breathing. She looked a sleeping angel, vulnerable and beautiful.

How in the world was he going to be able to get on a flight and walk away from her? Jake wanted to know what Charlie was like when she wasn't being made love to. He already knew from last night's encounter that when she made love, she gave all of herself, her body and soul. He liked that and wanted to know more. Her sorrow and her vulnerability had touched him.

There was no way he could get on that flight. Easing out of bed, careful not to disturb Charlie, he walked over to the phone and called the airline. He didn't care about the extra cost of a ticket for changing his flight so late. All he cared about was spending more time with Charlie.

When he booked his new flight, Jake slid back into bed, eager to feel the warmth of her body against. Her back was to him and her round bottom rested snuggly against his cock, making it hard once again. Damn he was horny. He tightened his grip around her, hoping she would wake up, but she hardly stirred.

Jake wanted nothing more than to slide it between her slender thighs and take her from behind again, but he respected the fact she needed her rest. Being inside her had felt like paradise. It was so good that if she could bottle it he knew she would make millions. Just the thought of it was making him dizzy with need. Poor thing, she must have been exhausted. He wore her out, he thought cockily.

Jake dropped a soft kiss on her brow and he could have sworn a smile touched her luscious lips.

Now that he had found this treasure, there was no way in hell he wanted to let her go so easily. Granted she was obviously still a grieving widow, but wasn't a year enough time to heal?

Jake realized how crazy this all was, but he couldn't help it. Something about Charlie Brown made him react this way. He didn't know what it was. Certainly she was a beautiful woman, but beautiful women were a dime a dozen. Their lovemaking had been explosive, but that hadn't been it either. Jake was too cautious to think about the L-word on so short an acquaintance, but no one had ever made him feel like this before. He fully intended to find out what it was about this woman that made him react so strongly.

He wondered if this was the woman he had been waiting for all his life. Jake came from a very happy family. His parents were both very much in love after thirty-seven years of marriage. His older brother and younger sister were both in loving relationships.

Jake's brother, Carl, had been married for ten years with two adorable twin daughters, while his sister, Helen, had been married for seven years with four boys of her own. The running joke in the family alluded to Helen's constant state of pregnancy. Jake chuckled when he thought of Helen, affectionately called the dictator. Helen was a born mother and she doted on her boys. A stay-at-home mom, she often joked that her boys were her career.

Perhaps it was time for him to stop playing the field.

Jake never thought he would end up feeling this way. It had always been the other way around for him. The women he usually dated always seemed to want more than he was willing to give.

They would tell him they loved him after a brief romp or a few dates. Being a cynic, he would laugh behind their backs because he never believed that it could happen so easily or so fast. Now he realized how wrong he'd been.

Jake had only intended to buy Charlie drinks but, if he were being completely honest with himself, had she come over to his table, he would definitely have made a play for her, early flight or not. At the time he was sure that it was only physical.

When she had walked out the bar, he reckoned that it wasn't meant to be, but the fates smiled on him. Spotting her in his hotel had to be some kind of sign.

Charlie Brown was a mystery. Thoughts of the proverbial kids and the white picket fence had run through his mind. He couldn't help but wonder what kind of mother she would be. *Whoa, you're going way too fast.*

Jake glanced at the clock. An hour had passed since he had changed his travel arrangement and he was becoming restless. He decided to take a cold shower; otherwise he would have to wake Charlie up after all. He hoped she would be awake by the time he finished.

Chapter Three

With a content smile on her face, Charlie stretched her body leisurely. She couldn't remember the last time she'd slept so peacefully. She opened her eyes, and surprisingly enough, she wasn't suffering from a hangover. The shower was running. Charlie paused. Why was the shower running? And for that matter, where the hell was she?

Charlie looked around in a panic. What was going on here? She wasn't in her house, nor in her own bed.

"Oh my God!"

Charlie then realized she was completely nude and there was something sticky between her legs. The events of last night came rushing back to her. She recalled going to the bar to forget about her wedding anniversary then getting a little tipsy. Most especially, she remembered Jake Fox.

"Oh my God. Oh my God," she chanted over and over again. She had sex with Jake last night. Not once but twice, and she had enjoyed it! To make matters worse, she had begged for it like a nymphomaniac. What had come over her? How could she have let this happen with some guy she'd known on so short an acquaintance?

Charlie had to get out of here before Jake finished showering. There was no way that she'd be able to face him, not after what happened. She couldn't handle it if he walked out of the bathroom with a smug expression on his face.

He'd taken advantage of her!

No, that wasn't exactly true. She was coherent enough to remember he had tried to dissuade her—at first. She had been the persistent one. What must Jake be thinking of her? He probably believed she was some good-time girl, letting just any guy have sex with her, and without protection.

Oh shit! Who was to say where the hell that man had been before she had let him screw her? She had read articles about men and women intentionally infecting their unsuspecting partners with STDs. She didn't think Jake was that kind of person, but one could never tell.

Oh Lord. You've gone and done it this time, Charlie.

Scrambling out of bed, she rushed to don her discarded clothing. She heard the shower turn off just as she slid into her shoes. After grabbing her purse, she made a mad dash for the door.

Charlie had never been more horrified in her life. In the age of HIV and hepatitis, she let a stranger have unprotected sex with her. She would have to get herself tested immediately.

As she drove home, tears ran unheeded down her face. Last night she'd been so distraught over the anniversary of Paul's death that she had slept with a man she knew for all of one hour. There was no telling herself it was simply the alcohol that made her so uninhibited, because on a subconscious level, she had needed that physical intimacy Jake had given. She hadn't been with anyone since Paul. As a matter of fact, until last night Paul had been her only lover.

Unable to see through her haze of tears, Charlie pulled her car over to the side of the road and screamed her frustration. She couldn't stop thinking about the things she had done with Jake. Charlie doubted she'd ever forget those ice blue eyes for as long as she lived.

She blamed the alcohol. She blamed her grief. She blamed the fact that she hadn't had a man in so long. She couldn't, however, admit to herself that what happened last night was because she had wanted Jake, pure and simple.

ℬᴏᴄᴙ

Jake kept the water as icy as he could stand it, to keep his rock hard dick under control. It was a pity Charlie was still asleep. He would have liked to shower with her. Images of her dark soapy body against him while his cock slowly worked in and out of her meaty ass floated through his mind. *Get a hold of yourself, Jake.*

He stepped out of the shower whistling, feeling on top of the world. Jake thought of wrapping the towel around his waist but decided against it. Maybe he could convince Charlie to have a little workout before breakfast.

"Charlie," Jake called, stepping out of the bathroom. "I changed my flight to a later time, so now we can..." To his surprise, he found her bed empty. He surveyed every inch of his room. There was no sign of Charlie Brown.

"Fuck!" Jake cursed in frustration.

Frantically, he grabbed the phone to call the front desk attendant.

"Plaza Hotel, this is Kelly speaking. How may I help you?"

"Yes, I was wondering if there might have been a message left by a Miss Charlie Brown for Jake Fox?" he asked, trying to calm the erratic pounding of his heart.

"I would be happy to check for you, Mr. Fox. Please hold."

The few minutes he waited for the receptionist to come back on the phone was pure torture. Please let there be a message. If there weren't, he didn't know what he'd do.

"Mr. Fox?"

"Yes. Was there anything?"

"I'm sorry sir, but there were no messages. Is there anything else I can help you with?"

"No, thank you." He hung up, dejected.

His first reaction was dismay. She was gone, and with her so was the magic they had created together. Anger was his next reaction. What kind of woman could allow him to make love to her and then just disappear without a word or even a simple note? She had used him to assuage her loneliness and like a fool he had given in to her.

What kind of man was he to fall for a woman he barely knew? His father once told him, when you met that someone special you would know right away. For the first time in his life, Jake had begun to believe in that theory as well. He obviously hadn't thought clearly enough because he had wanted her so badly.

There he was fantasizing in the shower about a future with her, even contemplating asking her to move to the D.C. area to live with him. He thought about how happy his parents would be that he was finally settling down, but it had all just been a fantasy. Jake cursed his naiveté.

Charlie obviously didn't feel the same way. He would have to forget her. He tried to convince himself there were other fish in the sea, but his cock wasn't convinced and neither was he.

Damn you, Charlie.

ॐ

Three weeks later, Charlie found herself in a clinic waiting for her test results. She shifted nervously in her chair, taking a peek at her watch every minute or so. What was taking the doctor so long? How could she have been so stupid? For once in a very long time, she wasn't obsessing over Paul, but the subject prevalent in her mind wasn't very pleasant. Actually, she hadn't really given her husband much thought in the past three weeks. A wave of guilt washed over her.

Charlie replayed that night in her head several times and wondered what had compelled her to do what she had done. Jake Fox's image floated in her mind. She still couldn't believe she had begged him to make love to her. No, she had begged him to fuck her. The most unbelievable part was how much she had actually enjoyed it. He had made her body sing. She could still feel the thrust of his cock as she remembered the taste of her juices on his lips. He had touched and licked her in all the right places.

She stood up to pace, unable to sit any longer. A young girl shot her an annoyed look, but Charlie wasn't in the mood to be polite to prissy little girls. All she could think about was how a one-night stand could possibly change her life forever.

Charlie was slowly losing her mind due to thoughts of Jake Fox. She was better off forgetting Jake because she would never see him again. The last thing she needed was the complication of him in her life especially when she didn't know what it was about him that consumed her thoughts. Yes, Jake was fine as hell, but it wasn't his looks that had drawn her to him. Whatever it was, it simply would not do to dwell on it.

In the past few weeks, two huge bombshells had been dropped on her. The largest of those was her parent's decision to retire, sell their home and travel the country in an RV. Neither of them had ever ventured outside the state of North Carolina and this sudden wanderlust they had developed puzzled Charlie. They offered to take her with them, but she declined. They had been such a huge support to her for the past year that she often felt like a burden. As dearly as she loved her parents, she couldn't imagine being cooped up in a traveling house on wheels for such a long period of time.

On top of her parents deciding to pack up, her best friend Laura Tombega met some man on the Internet and decided to move to Washington, D.C., to be with him. Charlie had warned her friend about the danger of Internet predators, but Laura claimed she was following her heart. Charlie would not have been so worried if Laura wasn't the type to "follow her heart" so often. Charlie thought her friend was nuts, but Laura was a grown woman. The only thing Charlie could do was wish Laura luck and hope for the best.

With Laura deciding to leave Raleigh and her parents deciding to sell, Charlie wondered if maybe she too should move. Her support system had splintered. The house she and Paul had picked out so lovingly no longer gave her pleasure. Her job was going nowhere. Charlie's boss was a card-carrying member of the old boy's club. He promoted very few minorities and even fewer women. She'd been with her firm for five years and knew she wasn't going to get any further unless she found another job.

Charlie had lost contact with a lot of friends because she hadn't socialized much in the past year. Now, there was really

45

nothing stopping her from moving to some other place. While she was deep in thought her name was called.

"Mrs. Brown, Dr. Greene will see you now." Charlie nearly jumped when the nurse spoke to her.

She took a deep breath and followed the nurse down the long hallway of the doctor's office. This was it. She would finally find out what price, if any, she would have to pay for her stupidity.

"Hello, Charlie, how are you feeling today?" Dr. Greene asked as she entered his office.

"I'm okay, considering why I'm here."

"It's understandable, my dear. Please, have a seat."

"No. I couldn't possibly sit down. I'm too full of nervous energy."

Dr. Greene frowned, but didn't argue. She knew he realized he would be fighting a losing battle if he did.

"Okay, suit yourself. The test results just came up from the lab so I had to chart everything down. That's what took me so long."

"Please tell me everything is okay, Dr. Greene."

"You are in tip-top shape and all the STD tests came back negative. You will, of course, need to come back in six months for another HIV test, but I don't foresee a problem. The tests performed today are pretty accurate so the chance of it coming back positive a second time is slim."

Charlie breathed a huge sigh of relief at the announcement of her clean bill of health. That was that then. She could write this episode off as bad judgment and move on with her life. Something struck her as odd. The way Dr. Greene had delivered his news made her hesitate. "Dr. Greene, there's something you're not telling me. You said all my tests came back negative, so I'm fine, right? You said I was healthy," she probed.

"Yes, I said that all of your tests for STDs came back negative."

"I understand. That's what I was tested for, but you're leaving something out," Charlie insisted.

"Well, I actually wanted to leave this for last but you do remember when you came in here I told you a pregnancy test would also be taken as standard procedure."

The alarm in Charlie's head went off. For some stupid reason pregnancy had been the last thing that had occurred to her. "Please don't tell me what I think you're about to say," Charlie pleaded.

Dr. Greene sighed sympathetically. "I'm sorry to tell you this if this comes as bad news, but your pregnancy test came back positive."

"Oh my God." Charlie fainted.

Chapter Four

Three years later...

"I wanna stay wit' you, Mommy!" Charlie's daughter wailed. The vibrant child generally liked going to daycare so she could see all of her friends, but this morning, Christy was in a foul mood.

Charlie had spent the last two weeks home with her daughter, in between jobs, and she suspected that Christy had grown use to her being around more. It broke her heart to drop her baby off at daycare, but she had to provide for the two of them.

"Sweetie, don't you want to go to school and draw a nice picture for me?" Charlie tried to soothe the cranky toddler as best she could by mentioning Christy's favorite activity of drawing.

Christy stomped her little foot in frustration. "I don' wanna go! I want you, Mommy!" Christy began to cry loudly, big tears falling from her ice blue eyes.

Today was supposed to be a good day. This was the first day of Charlie's new job in a supervisory position making a lot more money.

Unfortunately, Christy didn't understand and was unwilling to cooperate. Going into "mommy mode", Charlie bent down in front of Christy to feel her forehead. "Are you feeling okay today, baby? Does your tummy or head hurt?" Charlie stroked a stray curl from her daughter's face.

"I not a baby!" Christy screamed indignantly. At the ripe age of two and a half, Christy felt it was beneath her to be called a baby; after all, according to her, she was a big girl. Charlie had told her often enough.

"Well, I guess since you're feeling okay I have to take you to daycare today."

"No!" Christy wailed.

Charlie closed her eyes and counted to ten. She had read in her parenting book that this was a good self-calming method when dealing with temper tantrums. She gathered Christy's things in one arm and her screaming child in another. Charlie endured the entire trip to daycare with Christy crying from the backseat. "They don't call them the terrible twos for nothing," Charlie muttered to herself.

Once she had dropped her daughter off, Charlie drove to her new job. It wasn't that she hated working. Truth be known, she loved what she did, but she was missing so much of Christy's life as it was. She was glad she decided to take the two weeks off between her old and new job in order to cement the already tight bond she shared with her daughter.

Charlie pulled into the parking lot of the unassuming building. As she stepped out of her car, she took a deep breath. She was still upset about the scene her daughter had caused earlier, but this job was too important to let Christy's tantrum get in the way.

She had to be focused for this new position. Charlie had found out about the job through Laura, who already worked for this company. Charlie had applied and, to her delight, she'd been offered the position. She would have more responsibility than she had ever had before and the thought, although frightening, was very exciting as well. She would be one of the supervisors in the accounting department who reported directly to the CFO.

She sighed, sliding out of her car. It was still hard to believe how far she'd actually come in three years.

When Charlie had received the shocking news of her pregnancy, she didn't quite know what to do with herself. Her first thought had been to get an abortion. What was she going to do with a baby when she didn't even know what she was going to do with her own life? She had always wanted children—but with Paul. The thought of carrying Jake Fox's child made her feel...what? Excited? No! That wasn't possible. She barely knew him. It was horrifying to be carrying a stranger's baby. Someone she would never see again. What would she tell everyone?

Charlie's parents had been bewildered and a little hurt when she broke the news to them. They had raised her to respect her body and not throw herself at any Tom, Dick or Harry without a serious commitment. Of course they had demanded to know who the father was, and how Charlie had gotten herself in such a predicament, but she'd refused to give details. Her parents, being old fashioned, were adamant that she not have an abortion or else they would never forgive her.

Although their declaration hadn't been the biggest factor in her decision to keep the baby, it was one of them. She discovered she couldn't end an innocent baby's life, one who never asked to be born. It just wasn't in her. Throughout the pregnancy, adoption had been one of her options, but when Christy was born, Charlie knew she would never let her baby go. Charlie loved her daughter from the moment she held the little bundle in her arms. She knew then she'd dedicate her life to her child.

She reached the guard's desk and showed her driver's license in lieu of work IDs carried by employees with the company.

"Newbie, huh?" he asked.

"Yep," Charlie replied. "First day."

"Let me look on my list to make sure your name is there, otherwise someone will have to let you in." He scanned his clipboard and nodded. "Yep. Here you are. Welcome aboard and good luck to ya."

Her nerves were jumping as she walked through the security door after being buzzed in. Laura had taken her on a tour earlier in the week so Charlie would know where everything was today. Since her friend was in a meeting this morning, Charlie would have to wait until later to find her and thank her for the millionth time for helping her get this job.

In addition to Charlie's giving birth, Laura was also a catalyst in prompting Charlie to make her decision to move to the D.C. Metropolitan area. Within a week of that heart-to-heart with Laura, Charlie had packed up and sold her home, much to her parent's disapproval. They didn't think it was right that she should take off with such a small child and go to a place where she had no family support. Charlie would hear none of it. It was her life and she had Christy to think about. She felt a fresh start for the both of them would be a good thing.

If someone had told her three years ago she could love someone as much as she did her daughter, especially after losing Paul, Charlie would have laughed. The child brought joy to her life every single day. Christy looked just like Charlie, down to the heart-shaped beauty mark at the corner of her little mouth. The only difference between mother and daughter was Christy's golden brown skin and pale blue eyes.

At the mere thought of her pretty little girl, she smiled. Each step she took toward her new job, her new life, made her hope with all her heart that she'd made the right decision for her and for Christy.

୨୭ଓ୧

"Fresh meat in the accounting department." Steve leaned over Jake's desk.

"Do you have to start this early in the morning? I take it you're referring to the accounting supervisor position being filled. I'm sure anyone is an improvement from the person who vacated the position. From what Brian tells me, the last person didn't get the job done," Jake said, not really paying attention to his vice-president and best friend. Steve was a perpetual skirt chaser and Jake was not in the mood to be baited right now.

"That's not what I was talking about and you know it," Steve said undeterred. "You should see this one. She's a looker. Brian didn't tell me that the lady he hired was so hot."

"He wouldn't. Brian is gay remember?"

"Well if I were a homo, this one would make me change my mind."

"Must you talk like that? And how many times have I told you not to call Brian a homo. Really Steve, you're thirty-six years old. Grow up," Jake growled.

"Take it easy, my friend. First of all, you know I like Brian. I just don't understand how he would rather stick his dick in some dude's ass when there are all those sweet pussies out there waiting to be plundered."

"And this coming from a guy who likes anal sex," Jake said rolling his eyes.

"With women. Besides, if there's not pussy to go along with a nice tight ass, where's the fun?"

"Is there ever a time when you're not thinking about pussy?" Jake shook his head, although he couldn't help secretly agreeing with his friend.

"No, and you're one to talk, Jake. You're the same age as I am and you go through women like I do underwear."

"Maybe so, but I keep my work life and my private life separate. Just be careful, Steve. Remember the last girl you dated in the office."

Steve shuddered. "I still can't believe that psycho keyed my car. How was I supposed to know the girl was unbalanced?"

"Exactly. You don't know. You'd be better off leaving the ladies from the office alone," Jake advised.

"I'd take your advice if this one wasn't so special. I'm telling you, Jake, this lady is something else. She could be the next Mrs. Suarez."

Jake rolled his eyes in exasperation. "Yeah, right. Don't you mean the next ex-Mrs. Suarez? Doesn't the fact that you already make one hefty alimony payment each month tell you something, not to mention your broken engagement?"

"Aw, come on, man. They were a couple of trial runs for the real thing. Besides, as of next month, I'll no longer have to pay alimony. Jennifer has found some other sucker to marry her. He makes me look like a pauper and, as part of the divorce settlement, the payments cease when she remarries."

"Congratulations," Jake muttered dryly, "but I wouldn't rush into another failed relationship so quickly if I were you. Look, I have tons of work to do, as I'm sure you do as well. I hardly have time to listen to you talk about your next conquest."

"Lighten up," Steve taunted. "When did you become such a tight ass, pretty boy?"

Jake hated when Steve called him pretty boy. Steve never let Jake live down the fact that he had done some modeling on the side, while he attended college for a little extra cash. Modeling had not been his cup of tea, but the money had been decent.

"Call me pretty boy again and you'll be swallowing your teeth," Jake threatened.

"Don't you at least want to know what she looks like?" Steve asked eagerly. He reminded Jake of a puppy in a pet store window competing to be purchased.

"I'm sure I'll see her around eventually." Jake shrugged, not taking his eyes from his computer.

"Fine, but when you see her, back off because this one is mine."

"I'll try to hold back the urge," Jake responded sarcastically. The office fell silent for a few minutes but Jake could feel Steve's stare. Steve wouldn't go away until he let him say his peace.

"Okay, Steve, I'll bite. Describe her to me." Jake plucked off his reading glasses, sighing with resignation. For such an intelligent guy, Steve let the little head control the big one way too much.

"Well, all I have to say is this chick is smokin' hot. She's a black lady, about average height, slim, a little small on top but her ass makes up for it. You have got to check out this woman's ass. Remember that rap video 'Baby Got Back'? Those video girls have nothing on this woman."

Jake signed. He didn't think any woman's ass could compare to Charlie's. Damn. He didn't want to think about her. He didn't want to think about how much more that night had meant to him than it had to her. After all this time thoughts of her still infiltrated his mind.

"...And her lips...very sexy..."

Charlie's lips had been very sexy, Jake thought, tuning in and out to what Steve was saying.

"...name made me laugh..."

Jake did pick up on that, and a chill ran down his spine.

"What's her name?" Jake asked more casually than he felt.

"Charlie Brown. Funny name for such a pretty lady, but what's in a name?"

"Yes, what's in a name?" Jake answered absently.

Steve leaned on the desk, waving his hand in Jake's face.

"What's the matter Jake?"

"I...I think I know her."

"Really?" Steve asked incredulously. "From where?"

"From..." Jake trailed off.

Jake had never told Steve what had happened three years ago. At the time he had been too embarrassed by the fact that he had jumped the gun in thinking there was possibly a future in store for Charlie and him. Charlie obviously didn't. Steve was a good guy, but Jake knew his friend wouldn't understand his dilemma.

What was he going to say now after all this time? That he met this woman three years ago, they had a one-night stand and then she disappeared? Or should he tell Steve that Charlie Brown had made him feel things he had never experienced with any other woman before or since he'd been with her? How could he explain to his friend that bit of information when Jake wasn't so sure of his own feelings? Charlie had never given him a chance to find out.

"From where?" Steve persisted.

"I believe I met her three years ago."

Steve pursed his lips. "Yeah, sure. You're just saying that so that you can get a piece. I know you have a thing for big asses."

Jake gritted his teeth with impatience. He didn't have time for this. "Fine. Don't believe me." Jake rubbed his now aching temples before he spoke again. "Look, I really need to concentrate on these reports. So I will talk to you later," Jake dismissed.

Steve looked lightly perturbed, but didn't press. "Sure, man. I'll drop by later with the report you requested. I also want to go over that meeting I had with the Banner group last week when you have some time."

"Sure." Jake wasn't paying attention as Steve let himself out.

Charlie Brown was probably not as uncommon a name as any, but the fact that Steve pointed out her most memorable features, Jake knew in his heart it was his Charlie. Jake thought he would never see her again. After she had disappeared he couldn't stop thinking about her so he had hired detectives in North Carolina to track her down. He had given them all the information he knew about her, but they had turned up nothing. Now she was here in the very same building. His heart raced.

Jake could still remember the taste of her, the feel of her soft chocolate skin and the way his cock had felt inside of her. He had been with several women since that encounter, trying to wipe her from his memories but to no avail. No one had felt the way she had in his arms.

Did she have a lover? Was she finally over her husband? Would she remember him? From the sound of it, Charlie was as sexy as he remembered. She may have used him three years ago, but this time things would be different. Finally the time had come to find out exactly what his feelings for her were. One thing hadn't changed in the past three years. He still wanted her.

Chapter Five

"So, Char, how's your first day going at MBF?" Laura asked, taking a sip of her iced tea. The two women had decided to have lunch at a local Italian restaurant close to their office building.

Charlie sat back and looked at her friend over her glass of diet cola. She owed her so much.

Charlie and Laura had been best friends since middle school. Her friend was of Filipino and Irish descent, petite and compact, and one of the most stunning women Charlie had ever seen. From an early age, the boys followed Laura wherever she led. The woman was never short on dates. Although tiny, Laura made up for her small stature with her loud, outspoken ways. Charlie was the more sedate of the two. Where Laura was high strung, Charlie was laid back. Despite their differences in personality, the two women got along very well, each willing to lay down their life for the other.

Charlie returned her glass to the table after finishing off the glass of cola.

"It's great. I can't believe how nice everyone is. Brian is awesome. He's very helpful and friendly and definitely not the micromanaging type, like my last boss. I can honestly say that I won't mind working for him. I don't think I've ever worked for a company with such a diverse cast of workers. I feel like I've always belonged here. Brian has spent most of the morning showing me the ropes."

"Yes, he's a nice guy. He's not stuck on himself because he's the CFO. You know how guys in high-ranking positions can be. I knew you would like it here." Laura smiled affectionately, reaching across the table to squeeze Charlie's hand. "The moment that position opened up, I knew you would be a perfect fit."

"Thanks for looking out for me, girl. It's almost too good to be true. I wonder what happened to my predecessor? When I asked Brian, he kind of rolled his eyes, but he didn't answer."

"Well, I'm not really allowed to discuss HR issues because they're confidential but between you and me, I think she wanted more than Brian was willing to give her," Laura confided.

"Really? I got the impression that Brian is..." Charlie broke off.

"That Brian's gay? Bingo. It's no big secret, but I guess she didn't know. Brian is such a hottie, but you know what they say?"

"No, what do they say?"

Laura sighed, shaking her head. "You can be so dense sometimes when it comes to men. They say all the really hot ones are either taken or gay."

"Oh." Charlie laughed. She didn't care about her boss's sexual orientation. That was his business. "Girl, I don't know how you work in HR. You can't keep a secret to save your life."

"I'm very good at what I do." Laura sniffed indignantly. "I gave you the unofficial reason for your predecessor leaving, not the official one."

"I see." Charlie didn't see the difference between the two but she knew when to keep her mouth shut.

"So how is my little goddaughter?" Laura asked.

"She's great. Can you believe she'll be three at the end of the year? Christy's growing up so fast. She's been asking about you, by the way. She wants to know when you'll come visit her again."

"I'll visit soon. I promise. I've been seeing this guy and he's wonderful." Charlie rolled her eyes. It was always a new guy with Laura. She had packed up and moved to D.C. to be with some Internet guy only to have that fall through the cracks after five months, which was actually a record for Laura. Now Laura was with some new guy apparently as wonderful as she had claimed the other guys to be. Bouncing from relationship to relationship was not Charlie's thing, but she knew Laura had her own issues to work out. She only hoped her friend would be careful.

After what Charlie had shared with Paul, Charlie was content to be alone. No man had ever made her feel the way Paul had, except maybe for...

Shut up, Charlie!

She swore she would stop thinking about Jake Fox. She had convinced herself their brief encounter had meant nothing. Charlie had never told anyone about him, not even Laura. She just wanted to forget, but it was so hard, especially when she saw his eyes every day in their child.

"Hello?" Laura waved her hand in Charlie's face to get her attention.

"Oh, I'm sorry. What did you say?" Charlie shook her head a little to dust off the daydream.

"Where were you just now?" Laura asked.

"I guess my mind kind of wandered. I'm sorry Laura. I was just thinking about Christy." It wasn't exactly a lie, but there was no way she was going to tell Laura what she was really thinking about.

Laura was instantly concerned. "What's wrong? Is she okay?"

"She's fine but she threw a tantrum this morning and it's just not like her."

"Well, I guess that's to be expected with a toddler right?" Laura shrugged.

"I guess, but it breaks my heart when she's upset like that. She's such a good kid. Terrible twos or not, she doesn't generally throw tantrums like she did this morning." Charlie sighed, thinking about her normally happy-go-lucky daughter.

"She is an angel, I have to agree, but she is still young. Don't stress yourself out so much. You're doing a great job with her."

"I try." Charlie shrugged.

"Your trying is much better than my mom's own half-assed attempts at parenting. I know how much you love that little girl. Don't let it get you down, okay?"

"Thank you, hon. I really needed that pep talk. I'll make it up to her tonight by making her favorite dish, spaghetti and meatballs. How is it that you always know the right things to say?"

Laura flipped her long, dark hair over her shoulder and winked. "What can I say? I'm just damned good."

"And modest." Charlie lifted a brow. "Speaking of your mom, have you heard from her lately?"

Laura grimaced. "Why must you bring her up? We were having a nice conversation."

"Actually, you were the one who brought it up, but from the look you gave me, I take it things aren't going so well? I thought you'd resolved to let the past stay in the past."

"You know the hell that man put me through and she did nothing about it. Why should I cut her any slack when I never received any from them? Why did it take so long for her to suddenly remember I'm her daughter, too?"

Charlie sighed knowing her friend's pain would never heal if she didn't learn to let go. "I know, sweetie. I think it was rotten how they treated you, but she's trying to make amends now."

Laura rolled her eyes. "Sometimes it's too little, too late for the 'I'm sorrys'. And you know what? I can give a rat's ass. She's made her choices and now I wish she'd respect me in mine. I've found a parent who loves me unconditionally. Maryanne is more of a mother to me than she could hope to be."

"I'm sorry you feel this way."

"You—Oh dear Lord." Laura broke off.

"What?" Charlie asked, puzzled at Laura's expression.

"It's Steve Suarez. He's the VP and the head of marketing."

"I can tell by the tone of your voice you don't particularly care for him. He's cute," Charlie observed, looking over to see a tall Latino male who made Antonio Banderas look quite average.

"Yes, he seems to think so." Laura sounded annoyed for some reason. Charlie didn't pursue the subject, although her curiosity was piqued by Laura's obvious dislike of the gentleman.

"If you think Steve is hot, you should see the owner of the company, now he's a knock-out. The man used to be a model for Christ's sake," Laura turned her attention back to Charlie.

"Really?"

"Yes. I saw his picture in a magazine once, but he looks much better in person."

"Hmmm."

"He's not just a pretty face, though. He's really smart. He started this company when he was twenty-two, and he still designs a lot of the software this company sells. You'll flip when you meet him."

Charlie rolled her eyes. "I'm sure he's all you say he is, but I'm here to work Laura, not scope out hot men."

Laura's grin widened. "Yeah, but there's a lot of hot guys around here."

"Well, by your own theory, they should be either taken or gay," Charlie teased.

"Oh, don't be such a pain in the ass." Laura stuck her tongue out playfully. "Anyway, what's wrong with getting a little action if you can?"

"Girl, you are too much. Besides, you know I'm not interested in any action, let alone with someone from the office." Charlie shook her head. She didn't know how Laura's mind could stay occupied on men ninety-nine percent of the time.

"Good afternoon, ladies." A suave voice came from the side of their table. Charlie and Laura looked up to see Steve Suarez standing over them.

"Hi, Steve," Laura said between clenched teeth. Anyone with eyes could tell Laura wasn't happy to see him.

Steve looked down at Charlie with a predatory gleam in his eyes. "Laura, aren't you going to introduce us?" He asked Laura, but he was looking at Charlie.

"This is Charlotte Brown. She's in accounting. Char, this is Steve. He's head of marketing," Laura introduced with obvious reluctance.

"Hello, Charlotte. I saw you this morning and wondered who the lovely new face belonged to."

Oh brother. This guy was a smooth operator.

"Charlie, please." She shook his hand, bestowing the kind of smile she would have given anyone, but he seemed encouraged by it.

"Well, Charlie, I hope you enjoy working for MBF. Perhaps I can welcome you properly by taking you out to lunch sometime." He smiled revealing large white teeth. He reminded her of a shark zeroed in on a rather tasty morsel.

"I do like MBF. Hopefully, I'll be in the full swing of things in a couple of weeks," Charlie answered, smoothly ignoring his lunch invitation.

Steve looked as if he wanted to press the issue, but thought better of it. Laura thought Charlie was dense where men were concerned, but Charlie knew a bullshit artist when she saw one.

"Well, ladies, I would love to join you two for lunch but I see my lunch date coming through the door."

"Well, I guess it's a good thing we didn't invite you to sit down with us then," Laura snapped.

Steve had the good grace to blush. "Laura, it's always such a pleasure talking to you," he said caustically, making a lie of his words. He turned back to Charlie. "I hope to see you around very soon, Charlie." He smiled at her before joining a petulant-looking blonde.

"Laura, that was so rude," Charlie scolded. As annoying as the guy had been, she still had to work in the same building with him and didn't want to make any enemies on her first day, or at all for that matter.

"So what? That man is a menace." Laura gnashed her teeth together.

"What's going on between you two? You could cut the tension with a knife," Charlie observed.

"Let's not go there."

That was Laura's answer for anything she didn't want to talk about and pursuing the issue would only earn Charlie an earful.

"Okay."

"Stay away from him. He's trouble," Laura warned.

"He seems nice enough."

"Sure he is. He's a very nice guy if you're looking for a quick roll in the hay." The vehemence in Laura's voice indicated there was much more to the story than she was letting on.

"I guess it's a good thing that I'm not looking for a roll in the hay then," Charlie assured.

"That's good to know." A brief silence fell across the table before Laura spoke again. "Char, I know you don't like to talk about it, but you can't live the life of a nun forever. You're much too attractive to bury your head in the sand just because you're scared to love again. There are some very nice men out there and Christy needs a father."

Here we go again, Charlie groaned inwardly. "For someone who doesn't like having her idiosyncrasies delved into, you sure like trying to figure mine out. I won't get myself involved with someone just for the sake of my daughter, who, by the way, is happy with the way things are." Charlie couldn't help being defensive about this subject. It was bad enough she never heard the end of it from her parents, she didn't need a lecture from Laura either.

"She's happy now, but when she gets older, she'll ask questions."

"Please don't start. I got an earful from Mom last night. When she wasn't satisfied with my responses, she put Daddy on the phone to wear me down. Frankly, I find this topic exhausting."

"I'm just trying to give you something to think about. I know you don't like talking about it, but is there any chance of you contacting her father?"

"Absolutely not!" Charlie hissed. "I've already told you he's out of the picture."

ഇൗൽ

Jake hadn't been able to concentrate all day thinking about Charlie being so close to him. What a wild coincidence that the Charlie from three years ago would end up working at his company. If this wasn't a sign, then he didn't know what was.

As soon as Steve left his office that morning, Jake's phone rang. It was an important client who kept him on the phone for over an hour. By the time he got off, he had to rush into another meeting. When that was concluded, he went straight to the accounting department only to find out Charlie was at lunch. Brian informed him that when Charlie got back she would be in orientation for the remainder of the day. Jake felt a bit dejected.

The minute Steve had revealed that Charlie Brown was an employee at MBF, his heart raced with excitement at the thought of seeing her again, but as the day wore on, anxiety hit him. What if she wasn't as eager to see him again as he was to see her? He thought he had gotten over the fact that she had left him after their explosive encounter, but with the reappearance of her in his life, he knew that wasn't true.

Jake had done some asking around about Charlie and found out Laura Tombega in Human Resources had recommended Charlie for the job. He learned from Brian that she had quite an impressive resume, and she originally hailed from Raleigh, North Carolina.

Instead of getting any work done, Jake sat behind his computer for the rest of the day trying to make sense of a program he was designing. He could barely concentrate because his thoughts kept drifting back to Charlie Brown. By four-thirty he gave up all pretense of working and decided to throw in the towel for the day. There was always tomorrow.

Jake waved to his personal assistant as he headed out the door. Jennifer was still sitting at her desk, pecking away at her keyboard. "You're leaving early today," she observed, not bothering to look up from her typing.

"Yes. It's one of the benefits of being the boss. Besides, I can't seem to get my head straight today."

"We all have those days and no one deserves time off more than you do. You haven't taken any sick or vacation days in a very long time." Jennifer had been with the company since it was started. She had children Jake's age and treated him like her son instead of her employer. He didn't mind, though. Jennifer was one of the sweetest ladies he knew, but he would never cross her if his life depended on it. She could be as fierce as any mama bear protecting her cubs. Sometimes she could be a managing busybody, but she was invaluable to him, and he wouldn't trade her for the world.

"Please don't start that again, Jen. You know I don't have time for a day off. Kiss the grandkids for me," he said, remembering she babysat her daughter's children every Monday night. Jake rushed out the office to avoid any more inquiries from Jennifer.

"Jake, you ought to slow down." Jennifer's voice trailed behind him.

"Goodnight, Mr. Fox," the security guard called to Jake as he was leaving the building.

"Have a good one, Gary," Jake called back as he walked toward the door to leave. Before he could fully turn toward the door, someone catapulted into his back, knocking his briefcase out of his hand and nearly plowing over him in the process.

"Oh my God. I'm so sorry," a panicked voice said from behind him.

Jake, who was not easily riled, would have laughed this off in any other circumstances, but he was already extremely tense because of his frustrating day. He turned to snap at his assailant.

"Watch where you're going next—" He broke off abruptly. There before him bending down to pick up his briefcase was the woman who had occupied his thoughts all day, not to mention the past three years of his life.

"I'm really sorry. I was in a hurry because I have to pick up my daughter from daycare and I wasn't watching where..." When she stood up to face him, she froze. "...Watching where I was going," she finished automatically.

"You remember me." Noting the recognition in her eyes, he was pleased by that knowledge. Charlie was obviously shocked to see him.

She was just as beautiful as he remembered. She wore her hair in a short, sophisticated do now, but pretty much looked the same. Her lips were slightly parted and her eyes wide with surprise. It took an enormous amount of self-control not to grab her and kiss her like he had wanted to for so long.

Charlie shook her head, almost as if she were coming out of catatonic shock. "What are you doing here?" Her voice was no more than a whispered squeak.

He smirked at her wickedly.

"I own this company." His eyes probed hers for a reaction.

"Oh dear God," she whispered.

Chapter Six

Charlie's jaw dropped as she stared at Jake Fox as if he were an apparition.

"Is that a problem?" he asked with one sexy eyebrow cocked. He took her elbow, pulling her aside from the door. Charlie was speechless. She never thought she'd see him again, yet here he was as plain as day, and he was her boss. "Cat got your tongue?"

Charlie finally spoke. "No. I'm just surprised to see you."

"Obviously. As I am you, but it's a pleasant surprise, Charlie. I've been looking for you. Why the hell did you run off the way you did? You have no idea what torture you've put me through these past three years." His voice was gruff with emotion.

Charlie heard the anguish in his voice and her stomach flipped. Why did she feel the need to throw herself in this man's arms? Thoughts of her daughter flashed through her mind. "I have to go," she stated, and would have walked away from him if he hadn't grabbed her arm.

"Where do you think you're going? You owe me an explanation."

"What explanation do you think I owe you?" she asked defiantly.

Jake's face grew red from apparent temper at her flippant words. "You can ask me that after what we shared?"

Charlie felt the blood drain from her face. This wasn't supposed to happen. She couldn't allow herself to give in to this man. "What we shared was just one of those things, Jake. My God, haven't you ever heard of a one-night stand? We're both adults and these things happen, besides, I was missing my husband and you made a fairly adequate substitute," she said, knowing it was something that would crush any male ego. He would at least let her go then.

Jake stepped back as if he had been slapped. His jaw tightened as he grinded his teeth. "I see." At the look in his eyes, Charlie almost wished she hadn't said what she did. "Despite what you say this conversation is far from over."

"It is over, Jake. Accept it."

"I won't accept anything from you except your total surrender."

She gasped. "Stop talking like that."

"Go pick up your daughter, Charlie—your daughter? Funny. You didn't mention a kid when we were together."

"Because it was none of your business," she said storming off. By the time she reached her car, she didn't think she would make it home. What was she going to do? There was no way she could continue working for this company. What if Jake found out about Christy and tried to take her away? Worst yet, how was she going to combat her feelings for him when he was in such close proximity.

When she finally made it to Christy's daycare, the two-year-old was back to her jovial self.

"I drawed you a picture, Mommy." Christy proudly displayed her latest work of art when Charlie walked into the daycare center.

"It's beautiful, darling. We can put in on the refrigerator when we get home."

"Super!"

Super was Christy's new word, and it always amused Charlie to hear her daughter use it, but she was so distracted she barely paid attention to anything her daughter said as Charlie strapped her into her car seat and drove home.

"Mommy!" Christy yelled to get her attention.

Charlie shook her head, trying to get rid of thoughts of Jake. "Yes, sweetie?"

"Can I have a ice cweam?"

"Maybe after dinner."

"Okay." Christy seemed to accept this.

Charlie went on autopilot the minute she got home. She cooked dinner, letting Christy assist her with rolling the meatballs. After Christy was fed and bathed, Charlie read her daughter a story before putting her to bed.

She breathed a sigh of relief when the toddler nodded off to sleep. Charlie was a bundle of nerves as she contemplated what she should do next. After pacing her living room floor for at least an hour, she decided to give Laura a call. She had never told Laura who Christy's father was and she knew her friend would flip when she finally did and Charlie was right.

"Jake Fox! Are you fucking kidding me?" Laura screamed through the phone after Charlie broke the news to her.

"I wish I were kidding, but I never thought I would see him again which is why I never went into details with you." Charlie was very close to tears.

"Oh my God, girl. Still waters sure run deep. If you're going to have a drunken one-night stand, it might as well be with a hottie like Jake Fox."

"Laura, this is no joking matter. I can't work there anymore. What if he finds out about Christy?"

There was silence on the other end of the line before Laura responded. "Charlie, are you high? Not only do you want to give up this very high-paying job, but you also want to keep Christy a secret from her father? It's one thing when you didn't think you would ever see him again, but it's an entirely different issue now that you know how to contact your daughter's father. That's pretty low, Char," Laura reprimanded.

"But what if he tries to take her away from me? He's obviously in a better financial position than I am."

"He'd be crazy to try. Any fool can see what a great mother you are. You were born for all that motherhood shit. Now calm down. It would be in your best interest as well as Christy's to tell him about her. With his money, Christy could have the best of everything."

"I don't want anything from him. I've given Christy everything she ever needed!" Charlie said fiercely.

"I know you have, but like I said before, what are you going to say when she starts asking questions? What I know about my father I found out myself and let me tell you, I've always resented my mother for that. I don't want Christy to grow up feeling that way toward you." She broke off for a moment. Charlie knew Laura's own upbringing was still a sore point. "Is there another reason why you don't want to tell him? Jake's a pretty nice guy. I can't possibly see him doing anything that would hurt you or Christy." What Laura said sounded reasonable enough, but Charlie wasn't in the mood to be rational.

"I understand what you're saying, but I just can't take the chance of losing her."

"Is it the prospect of losing your daughter or allowing Jake into your life that bothers you so much?"

Charlie paused. She didn't want to let her friend know she was getting too close to the truth. "What do you mean?"

Laura sighed. "You know what I mean, Char. You haven't dated since Paul died. You've become commitment phobic. Are you scared you may have feelings for Jake?"

"No! Absolutely not! How could I after a one-night stand three years ago?"

"The lady doth protest too much, methinks."

"Cute, Laura, real cute. Look, I don't have time for this. I'll see you at work tomorrow."

"You're being pigheaded and you know it. Stop thinking about yourself for a moment and think about that beautiful little girl of yours. You can't up and quit your job like this. Promise me that you'll at least stay on at MBF until you find another job comparable to what you have now. You know how I feel about you telling Jake the truth about Christy, and that is your decision, but giving up your job like that in the blink of an eye would be beyond selfish."

Damn Laura for being right. Charlie sighed to herself. "Okay."

"Promise me!" Laura demanded.

"I promise."

"Good. Now go get some sleep. When you wake up your mind will be much clearer, and you'll have a better idea what you want to do.

"Okay. Thanks for listening, girl."

"That's what I'm here for. Night, sweetie."

"Goodnight, Laura." Charlie hung up the phone.

Laura's words still reverberated through Charlie's mind as she spent a sleepless night in bed. What did she feel for Jake? She couldn't possibly have feelings for him based on one night of lovemaking. Or could she?

ဆၢ

Three months. It had been the longest three months of Jake's life. Three months of Charlie avoiding him and with each day that passed, he wanted her more. Jake couldn't eat, sleep or breathe without thoughts of her passing through his mind. He still couldn't put his finger on why he put himself through the constant torture of pursuing a woman who made it obvious she wasn't interested in him.

The first day she had run into him that instant chemistry was there again. Was he fooling himself into believing there was something there when there really wasn't? Or could it be his ego guiding him? The fact that she had taken off after their lovemaking was a blow to his male vanity, but something deep within told him there was more to it.

He wanted her in his life, and in his bed, but each time they saw each other around the building, she would either turn around and go the other way, or flash by him so quickly he didn't get a chance to speak to her.

When she couldn't avoid him she ignored him. Because he wanted her so badly, it galled him when she pretended they had never met. He tried to be gallant by giving her some time, but that didn't seem to work. Jake threw himself into his work, but even that didn't help. He began to date different women to ease his suffering and even slept with a couple of them, but he ended up more miserable than before because none of those women were Charlie.

Now, as he sat here on his living room couch, downing vodka like it was water, he wondered what his next move should be or if he should bother to make a move at all, when the doorbell rang.

Damn. He hoped it wasn't his sister, who never thought anything of just dropping by unannounced with her herd of boys in tow. When he opened the door, he realized to his annoyance he would rather have put up with his sister than his visitor now. Cynthia Dupree was one of the women he had dated in the last few months, but Jake had never conveyed to her he was interested in a permanent relationship. Cynthia, however, was a woman convinced of her own charms and didn't take a hint, which is why he had been avoiding her calls lately.

Jake wasn't in the mood to be hospitable. "What are you doing here, Cynthia?"

She gave him a toothy grin, flipping a lock of blonde hair over her shoulder. "I was visiting friends in the neighborhood, and I took the chance you'd be home. Aren't you glad to see me?" She spoke in the little baby voice that annoyed the hell out of him.

"Umm, sure. I was having a chill-out night. You know, just relaxing—by myself," he finished pointedly.

"Well, it's a good thing I came then, so now I can keep you company." She pushed past him to enter his house.

"Come on in, Cynthia," Jake said sarcastically.

Cynthia laughed. "You're so funny, Jake. I won't keep you long, though."

God, I hope not. The woman had the hide of a rhino.

His inbred manners prompted Jake to offer her a drink.

"What are you drinking, darling? I don't know if I can handle anything really strong. When I get tipsy, I get very...amorous," she hinted.

"I'm having straight vodka. Shall I make one for you?"

"If you could mix it with cranberry, that would be great."

Jake took a deep breath before going to his bar to make her a drink. When he returned to his living room, Cynthia was sprawled on the couch; her miniskirt had ridden up so high that it barely covered her vagina. She lay on the couch in a way that gave Jake a good look down the inside of her blouse.

"Here's your drink." Jake handed it to her, choosing to sit in the armchair across from the couch.

She pouted. "Won't you come and sit with me?"

"I don't think so, Cyn. How about finishing your drink?"

"You're not trying to rush me off, are you?" she asked coyly, twirling a strand of her hair with her fingers. He knew she was trying to entice him, but it wasn't working.

Cynthia began to babble, taking a long time to finish the vodka and cranberry he had offered her. Jake was too distracted with thoughts of Charlie to even half listen to what the blonde had to say. It wasn't long before Cynthia got bold and walked over to his armchair and plopped into his lap.

When Jake attempted to push her off, she rubbed her surgically enhanced body against him, and against his better judgment, he gave in to her not so subtle seduction. Hell, if he couldn't have the woman he wanted, why couldn't he take what was being so freely offered to him? He was a man after all.

Putting his drink aside, he dragged her upstairs to his bedroom, where they both undressed and fell on the bed.

Jake rolled the condom over his burgeoning shaft before sliding it into the folds of Cynthia's wet and ready cunt. No foreplay was necessary. He simply needed to ease the ache created by Charlie. Perhaps by fucking Cynthia, he could drive out the demons riding him. Fortunately, Cynthia was moist and ready for him. His cock slid easily into her channel without a problem. He pushed until his balls rested against her bottom.

Cynthia ran her fingers through the dark mat of his chest hair, while looking at him with her fuck-me eyes. Jake could always count on her for being wild in the sack. He lifted her hips as he thrust in and out of her, not bothering to take his time. He didn't want to be gentle with her, didn't even want this to be anything like what he'd experienced with Charlie.

"Faster, Jake! Fuck me faster!" Cynthia demanded.

He slammed roughly into her to show her who was in control.

Cynthia squealed with pleasure. "Mmm, no one's cock feels as good as yours, Jake." She took matters into her own hands and bucked wildly against him, increasing the pace. Her muscles tightened around his rod and Jake thought that he would lose it right then and there.

She wrapped her legs around his waist and met him thrust for thrust. Her nails dug into his flesh. They fucked at a frenzied pace. Her silicone-filled breasts bobbed up and down and their bodies grew slick with sweat from their exertion.

"Oh shit! I'm going to come!" Cynthia screamed, but Jake ignored the sound of her voice. He continued to fuck her as if he were possessed. After a time, she laid beneath him, writhing and moaning. Cynthia came two more times before he grunted loudly, signaling that he had finished.

Jake collapsed on her in an exhausted heap. When he caught his breath, he rolled over to his back to put some space between the two of them. Cynthia rolled over as well to wrap her arms around his waist. The last thing Jake wanted at that moment was to cuddle. "That was wonderful, Jake. You've never been so ferocious before, but I loved it," she purred.

Jake absently kissed the top of her head and lay back on his pillow before closing his eyes. He didn't feel like talking. He actually wished she would leave, but it seemed she had other ideas by the way she held him so tightly. Jake opened his eyes to look down at her. Her eyes were closed as if she were about to fall asleep. Knowing Cynthia, it was probably an act. He was no fool. She wanted him to ask her to spend the night, but Jake wasn't feeling particularly chivalrous tonight. "Cynthia, I am getting rather sleepy," Jake said, trying to drop a hint.

"Hmmm," she murmured softly, cuddling even closer to him.

Jake tried a more direct approach. "I think it's time for you to leave."

As he suspected she hadn't really been sleeping because she shot up with lightning speed. "I'm being dismissed? Are you dismissing me as if I'm some dime-store whore?" she demanded through narrowed blue eyes. His eyes narrowed right back.

Jake knew he should have been more blunt with her when they broke things off a few weeks back, but he didn't want to hurt her feelings. Agreeing to remain friends with her had been a concession he made when she had cried and pleaded with him. She became his fuck buddy. Jake was aware Cynthia wanted nothing more than to start things up again, which was why he knew he would now need to sever all ties with her completely.

If he hadn't been thinking with his dick, he would have told her to get lost, but he had needed to assuage the ache aroused within him by a certain exotic beauty. He felt like slime for using Cynthia so shamelessly, but he'd been upfront with her at the beginning of their relationship.

"You told me you were only coming over for a brief visit, and I do remember telling you I wanted to be alone tonight."

"So you just fuck me and send me on my way?" She placed her hands on her hips

"It seems you're suffering from a selective memory, Cynthia. You were the one who threw yourself at me and I only took what you so freely offered," he pointed out.

"Why are you being such an asshole? How could you just fuck me like that and tell me to leave?"

"You knew the deal, besides, you weren't invited so I hope you will see yourself out." He knew he was a being a jerk, but it was time she got the message loud and clear. There would be no more nightly romps between the two of them. While he fucked her, all he could think about was Charlie. He knew no one else would satisfy him now that she was within his grasp.

"You're a miserable bastard." Cynthia got off the bed in a huff to get dressed. "You'll be sorry, Jake. Nobody treats me like this and gets away with it," she threatened.

"I never meant to hurt you, Cynthia, but I wish you would have taken my words at face value when I said there could never be anything long-term between you and me." Jake sighed tiredly. He closed his eyes to block out her angry red face.

"Fuck you, Jake Fox!" she screeched as she stalked indignantly out of the room. He felt like an asshole but what could he do? It would hurt her far more if he had strung her along.

After getting rid of Cynthia, Jake knew there was only one way he would be able to exorcise Charlie Brown from his system, or at least find out what his feeling for her actually were. He would have to become more aggressive in his pursuit and no one would stand in his way. Not even Charlie.

හ)(ෙ

Monday came too quickly for Charlie after a restless weekend. She didn't think she had a decent night's rest in the past three months. Thoughts of Jake Fox haunted her every night when she lay in bed.

Maybe Jake wouldn't want anything to do with his daughter but she couldn't be sure, so she decided she would continue to keep Christy a secret. Since Laura had convinced her to keep her job until she found another one, Charlie had been searching in earnest. So far, Charlie had had no luck there.

It was a shame, because she liked her job. The only two problems she had with the company were Jake and Steve. Steve. She was beginning to agree with Laura. The man was a menace. Steve Suarez thought he was God's gift to women and it was embarrassing how he constantly asked her out.

Charlie hated being the center of office gossip, but with the persistent Don Juan constantly finding reasons to show up in her department Charlie had to set him straight on several occasions. He had extremely thick skin, unfortunately. Short of telling him to go to hell, she simply started ignoring him. As annoying as Steve was, Jake was another story altogether.

Charlie rarely saw Jake, but when she did, she turned the other way. Being so close to him wrecked havoc on her nerves. Her mind raced to the incident when they'd shared an elevator last week.

Just as the doors were closing, a strong, sinewy hand reached out to stop their progress.

Charlie gasped to see Jake step inside. He, however, didn't seem very surprised. She moved to the far corner of the elevator, attempting to move as far away from him as she could. The wolfish grin he gave her sent Charlie's pulse racing.

"Good afternoon, Charlie."

She nodded in acknowledgement, not trusting herself to speak.

"I haven't had a chance to ask how you like the job."

She looked frantically at the numbers over the door. Why was this friggin' thing so slow? "I like it a lot, thank you."

"I'm glad to hear it. Brian says you've quickly become an invaluable asset to the finance department." His eyes looked as if they were undressing her.

Charlie couldn't hold back the shiver which shot through her. "Please don't," she groaned involuntarily."

He lifted his brow in question. "Don't what, Charlie?"

"Look at me that way."

"How am I looking at you?"

She took a deep breath, her hands balling into fists at her side. "You know how."

"If I did I wouldn't be asking."

"Please don't insult my intelligence. You're looking at me like you see right through my clothing."

"Ah. It's not my intention to make you uncomfortable, Charlie." The elevator stopped one floor above her destination and Jake moved to leave, but not before one parting shot. "Oh, and while I don't have the ability to see through your clothes, I don't need it, because I already know what you look like underneath them." Then he left her to stew. She realized then it was growing more dangerous to be in the same workplace as Jake. Something had to give.

He was obviously still smarting over her comment about using him as a substitute. Charlie wished she hadn't said it because it was a pretty rotten thing to say, but she had to let him know their one-night stand had been just that. Not that it probably mattered to him anyway, she had heard through the grapevine that Jake wasn't hurting from lack of female attention. Now why did that bother her so much?

Charlie was going over some numbers with Brian, when he asked her to deliver a proposal for him upstairs.

"No problem. Who do I need to drop it off to?"

"Jake."

Charlie stiffened.

"Is there a problem?"

"Umm, no. Not at all. I...well, I was just a bit surprised because you usually make this particular delivery yourself."

"Yes, but Jake asked for you specifically."

"Why?" The word was out of her mouth before she realized how it must have sounded. "I mean, I'm just a low person on the totem pole. It surprises me that he even bothers with the peons." The lie didn't sound convincing even to her own ears.

"Every position in this company is valuable. He probably wants to talk to the person whose praises I've been singing lately. You're a real jewel, Charlie. I don't know how we managed without you." Brian grinned at her.

"Me?" she asked in amazement. What the hell was Jake up to? She didn't doubt Brian was pleased with her work, because she worked damn hard, but it made her uneasy that Jake would ask for her specifically.

"Yes, you. He always takes an interest in our shining stars, and since you're one of them, he wants to meet you. Go on, he won't bite," Brian prodded.

How could she tell Brian that Jake's interest had nothing to do with the work she was doing, and she was indeed certain

Jake Fox did bite? She couldn't very well tell him no. "Okay. I'll take it up," she said reluctantly.

Chapter Seven

Charlie headed upstairs to the executive suites. She was glad to be wearing her black power suit today. It usually gave her confidence, and right now she could use as much of it as she could get.

Damn you, Jake Fox. Why do you persist on making things harder than they have to be?

When she reached the president's suite, Charlie took a deep breath before entering, trying to calm her jittery nerves.

"May I help you?" asked a curious older woman, sitting at the desk in front of Jake's office. She was obviously his personal assistant. The woman had a kindly enough face, which made Charlie relax. Nothing bad could possibly happen with her around, right?

"I need to drop off this report from Brian Shaw. He asked me to deliver it here."

"Oh yes, Charlie Brown. Jake is expecting you. I'm Jennifer Collins, by the way. It's nice to finally meet you. I've heard so many wonderful things about you." She smiled warmly at Charlie.

"They're all lies, I tell you," Charlie teased, feeling totally at ease with Jennifer.

"I highly doubt that, my dear."

Charlie wondered from whom Jennifer had heard all these "wonderful things" about her. "What should I do about this report? Should I just go in or can I just leave this here with you?" Charlie asked hopefully.

"Hold on, let me check first." Jennifer buzzed the intercom.

"Yes?" Jake's sensual voice came over the speaker.

"Charlie Brown is here," Jennifer announced.

There was a slight pause, and Charlie could have sworn she heard him taking a deep breath. "Okay. Send her in."

"You may go in now, Charlie...umm...that's a rather, famous name." Jennifer blushed. "I'm sorry, that was rather rude of me."

Charlie laughed. "No worries. I get that quite a bit. Charlie is short for Charlotte actually. I was teased a lot when I was growing up, but in an ironic twist of fate, the man I ended up marrying also had the last name of Brown. I think I'll be cursed with this moniker for the rest of my life."

Jennifer laughed at Charlie's self-deprecating tirade. "Oh dear, how awful for you, but I think Charlie suits you very well." Jennifer assured, wiping a tear of laugher from her eye. "Did you say you were married? I understood you were single." Jennifer turned slightly red. "There I go again. I didn't mean to pry."

Charlie shrugged. "It's okay. I'm a widow."

"I'm sorry, dear. You know how office gossip is."

She wasn't sure she liked the idea of being fodder for office gossips, but what could she do about it? "Yes, I know, but don't worry about it." Charlie smiled to show there was no harm done.

"Is she still here, Jen?" Jake poked his head out of his office.

"She's right here, Jake," Jennifer answered.

Jake swiveled his head to look at the object of his inquiry. "Charlie, please step in to my office." He beckoned her to him.

Charlie looked at Jennifer for reassurance, but Jennifer was already busy pecking away on her keyboard. Once in the office Jake closed the door behind him. To Charlie's dismay, he locked the door.

Her throat went dry at his nearness. She didn't remember him being quite so sexy and smelling so good. She gulped nervously.

"Is that the report you're holding?" he asked.

Charlie could only nod.

"Good." He took it from her seemingly boneless fingers. "Have a seat." Jake gestured to the huge black leather couch in the corner of his office. Charlie stood in awe for a moment. Jake's office was nearly the size of her living room.

"If it's all the same to you, I'd prefer to stand."

"Please sit. I won't bite." He gave her a lopsided grin that nearly made her knees give out. "Unless you want me to."

She had to stay strong and not let him get under her skin. "I came to drop off the report and I have. Now, if you don't mind, Mr. Fox, I have a lot of work waiting for me at my desk." She turned to leave, but Jake was quicker.

"Oh, but I do mind. I mind very much." He placed his palms against the door on either side of her head.

"Please move," she said through clenched teeth, her body tightening with awareness. She could feel his body heat. Good Lord, had the temperature just increased in here?

"No. You owe me something else, Charlie."

"What are you talking about? I don't owe you anything," she protested, turning her head to the side so as not to get mesmerized by his hypnotic gaze.

"Oh, but you do."

Before she could protest further, he grabbed her forearms, pulled her against him and lowered his head. Jake's hot, hungry mouth moved over hers relentlessly. Too stunned to struggle, Charlie leaned weakly against his chest.

To her chagrin, her body trembled in response to his forceful kiss. He cupped her face, his thumb lightly stroking her cheek. Her lips parted instinctively allowing his tongue access. Charlie's body went up in flames when his other hand held and squeezed her bottom, kneading it. He caressed her rear as if to reacquaint himself with the contours of her body.

Her panties grew moist as his hands began to roam all over. Against her better judgment, she wrapped her arms around his neck, listening to her body instead of her head. How could something that felt so good, be wrong? It was as if those three years had melted away, and things had always been this way between them.

She pressed her body more aggressively against him. The head of his throbbing erection rubbed against her thigh. Charlie was lost in the moment. She didn't know how she got there, but she found herself on the couch with Jake on top of her, kissing her with the hunger of a man who had been denied for years. Three years to be exact.

Jake opened her jacket and unbuttoned her blouse. In the back of her mind, Charlie knew exactly where they were and what they were doing, but she couldn't have stopped him had her life depended on it. Her small breasts were alert and ready for his mouth. Each taut peak ached to be sucked and loved. Jake obliged. He flicked one nipple with his tongue, sending waves of pure delight tingling up her spine. When Jake captured the tight bud with his teeth, she moaned.

Charlie grasped Jake's hair to keep his head against her chest. Jake seemed to be in no hurry, nibbling, sucking and licking each of Charlie's breasts. He slowly ran his tongue over the highly taut mounds. She shivered under the rough caress of his tongue. For the life of her she couldn't remember what she'd come to his office for in the first place.

"You're so beautiful," he murmured, kissing the valley between her breasts. He nipped her flesh, his body moving down the length of her until he was eye level with her belly button. Charlie had the sexiest navel he had ever seen. Everything was sexy about this woman. He tongued the indented flesh, which made her shiver in reaction. His tongue imitated the action of a cock thrusting in and out of a pussy.

"Oh, Jake," Charlie moaned softly, rolling her head back and forth.

For three long years he'd waited for this moment: Charlie underneath him, wanting him and loving everything he did to her. His need had only been heightened the last three months with being so close to her and unable to do anything about it. But she was here now. Jake unbuttoned Charlie's pants as he continued to place kisses on her belly. He explored the sweet taste of her that he had not forgotten. She was just as delectable as he remembered. The softness of her under his lips made his dick throb.

Jake nearly lost control when he got a whiff of her treasure. The intoxicating smell of her pussy made his cock so hard he was sure the seams of his pants would burst. "Do you want this, Charlie? Do you burn for me like I do for you?" he whispered against her silky skin.

Charlie moaned loudly in response, seeming oblivious to everything except how he made her feel at that moment. It excited him to know he could elicit such a response from her.

Only when Jake freed Charlie of her panties did he unbuckle his pants. He wanted to make this last, but he knew it would be quick because he wanted her so damn badly. He had to fuck her now. His cock was barely free from his pants before he thrust deeply into her wet, waiting pussy. Her warm tunnel was moist and welcoming. Jake felt as if he were home at last. Wrapping his arms around her, he buried his face against her neck. She was tight. Her vaginal muscles squeezed his cock so lovingly, sucking him deeper within her welcoming sex.

"I've waited a long time for this," he groaned against her skin.

Charlie whimpered her pleasure as he thrust deeply into her. The sliding motion of his cock filling Charlie's wet channel produced a savage passion within the pit of his belly. Her pussy was maddeningly addicting. Jake doubted he could ever get tired of it, or Charlie for that matter.

"Mmm, Jake. You feel so good," she moaned.

Charlie clung to him tightly, her arms around his neck and her legs around his waist. Jake's mouth crashed down on hers once again. He thrust his tongue into the cavern of her mouth, exploring the sweet recesses and savoring her delightful taste. Charlie's tongue shot out to meet Jake's, kissing him back with a hunger to match his.

Jake lifted his head to look deep in her eyes as he continued to thrust. He looked down at her. The sexy way she was nibbling her bottom lip was threatening to push him to the edge. "I don't know how I lived without this sweet pussy, baby, but I don't intend to deny myself ever again, nor will I allow you to."

With one last powerful shove, he blasted his seed deep within her hot cunt, shuddering against her uncontrollably. He let out a loud throaty groan. They lay motionless for several minutes clinging to each other and breathing deeply. This was Jake's release of sexual frustration that had been built up over the last three years. Now that he had another taste of her, he wanted more.

Charlie lay in stunned silence, not believing what had just happened. What the hell had just come over her? It was a good thing she was on the pill...otherwise... She shivered at the thought. She'd just had unprotected sex with Jake yet again. This man must have put some kind of spell on her. Why else would she respond to him so readily or do something so irresponsible like having sex in the office? His last declaration worried her most of all. *I don't intend to deny myself ever again, nor will I allow you to.* Jake had to be nuts if he thought he'd get a repeat performance.

She tried to wiggle from beneath him. "Get off of me. I have to go."

"Please stay. We won't be disturbed. No one gets by Jennifer without the threat of death," he joked, tightening his arms around her. His eyes devoured her face as if he couldn't get enough of the sight of her.

Charlie's heart flipped. When he looked at her like that, she found it hard to refuse him anything, but refuse him she must. She couldn't afford to get involved with anyone, especially with Jake.

She pushed against his chest in an attempt to free herself. Jake held her tighter still. "Let me go, Jake," Charlie ordered.

Jake flinched as if he had been smacked. A look of confusion crossed his handsome face as he loosened his grip, enabling her to slide out of his arms. He sat up abruptly.

"There's no rush, Charlie."

"There is a rush. This shouldn't have happened."

"What the hell are you talking about? Of course this should have happened. It was inevitable it would happen. From the moment we saw each other again, it was there. You felt it too, so don't lie to yourself about this being a mistake, sweetheart." He rolled away from her and stood up. Jake then pulled her against the length of his taut body. His cock was hard once more. Charlie's pussy contracted with longing for him. Her nipples hardened. She silently cursed her traitorous body. It didn't seem to know when to quit.

"Don't try to lie to me again, because your body will tell me the truth every time. You can't use the excuse of your dead husband this time can you?" he accused before crushing her lips with his.

They were interrupted by a loud knock on the door. "Jake, Steve is outside waiting for you and he's insisting that he sees you," Jennifer called through the intercom.

"Tell him to go away," Jake growled. Charlie used Jake's distracted state to twist out of his arms and get dressed in a hurry.

"This will not happen again," she hissed as she buttoned up her blouse. She smoothed out the wrinkles in her clothes and patted her hair back into place in hopes she at least looked presentable again.

Jake didn't respond. He merely grunted while he adjusted his own clothing. In his rush to possess her, he hadn't even undressed.

"For once, Steve, you are going to pay for this," he muttered under his breath, but Charlie could still hear him. She was thankful Steve had shown up.

Jake watched as Charlie finished adjusting her clothing. "Damn, my make-up is probably a mess"

"You look beautiful as always, but when you get a chance, you may want to repair your lipstick."

She glared at him. "And you may want to wipe it off your lips."

Jake picked up a tissue from his desk and rubbed the lipstick off his lips. "Better?"

Charlie nodded and made a move to leave, but Jake halted her by grabbing her wrist.

"Regardless of what you say, this is far from over." His ice blue eyes glittered with determination and Charlie found herself shivering under his intense stare. How was she supposed to respond to that?

Charlie turned to flee when he let go of her wrist. She went flying out the door as if the devil himself was at her heels. Steve came strolling into Jake's office, and he didn't look happy. Whatever his problem was, Jake was not in the mood.

"What was so important it couldn't wait?" Jake asked, taking a seat behind his desk.

"I came by a half hour ago looking for you, but Jennifer told me you were in a meeting going over the monthly figures."

"And?" Jake shrugged.

"And you told me to let you know when the Garrison deal came through. You were insistent that I interrupt you when I received the news," Steve reminded him.

"And so I did," Jake conceded. "How did it go?"

A stormy expression crossed Steve's face. "What the hell was she doing in here?" Steve demanded.

Jake decided to play dumb. Regardless of what had just happened, it was none of Steve's business. "Charlie?"

"Who the hell do you think I'm talking about?" Steve, his face getting redder with his apparent anger, demanded.

"She came in here to drop off a report, is that okay with you?" Jake asked sarcastically, in no mood to have this conversation.

"Do me a favor and don't insult my intelligence. I saw how Charlie looked when she tore out of here. What the hell happened?"

"Steve, I don't think you're in a position to demand anything right now. Either you want to tell me how the Garrison deal went or you can come back later. I have far too many things to do with my time than to play twenty questions." Jake realized he was coming off a bit heavy-handed, but he'd be damned if he told Steve about anything that just happened. It was strictly between him and Charlie.

"I know something happened in here, Jake. For one thing, you always go over the financials with Brian and not his subordinates."

"There's a first time for everything, Steve. What's your point?"

"Why did she go tearing out of your office? What did you do to her?"

"What makes you think I did something to her?"

"Don't be a jackass. I told you how I felt about her. She's mine!" Steve exploded.

"For God's sake, she's a woman, not a thing. And I should think the decision belongs solely to her. The whole office knows how you've been sniffing around Charlie, and they also know that she doesn't want anything to do with you," Jake pointed out cruelly. "Didn't I tell you Charlie and I had met before?"

Steve ground his teeth together, his eyes shooting green daggers at Jake. If looks could kill, Jake knew he'd be dead on the spot. "Yes, you did, but we both know you made that up. If you knew her so well then why haven't you mentioned her before? If I had met someone like her I sure as hell would have told you. How could you, Jake?"

"How could I what?"

"I smell sex in this office, you son of a bitch. I thought we were friends. You knew how I felt about her." Steve accused.

Jake refused to feel guilty about what had just happened between him and Charlie. He wasn't going to cater to Steve's fragile ego, especially where Charlie was concerned.

"Did I really? You fall in and out of love with women so fast, what's she to you? You're not upset because you actually like her, your ego is bruised because she turned you down."

"How the hell should you know how I feel?"

Jake raked his fingers through his hair. "Be honest with yourself, Steve, had she went out with you when first asked, you would probably have lost interest by now."

Steve averted his gaze, and Jake knew he'd hit the nail on the head. "How the hell will I know now? You never gave me a chance to find out how I felt."

Jake shrugged. "I think you already know, you're just being stubborn."

"You don't know everything, Jake." Steve glared at him before turning on his heel and slamming the door behind him. Reasoning with Steve when he was in one of his moods would have been pointless. Steve had a tendency to blow his top before gathering all the facts. His friend was right in that Jake didn't know everything, but one thing he was certain of, he and Charlie Brown belonged together.

Chapter Eight

A week had passed since that incident in Jake's office and Charlie still couldn't get him out of her mind. Just thinking about it was slowly driving her insane. Charlie's nerves were so frazzled she felt as if she would snap at any moment. Now was not the time for anyone to get on her bad side. She'd just come out of a meeting she had barely paid any attention to, and to top things off, her head was throbbing.

While Brian had been outlining the quarterly goals for their department, Charlie found herself in the middle of a daydream, remembering every graphic detail of that fateful day. She remembered the way he had kissed her, the way his tongue had trailed its way over her skin, tasting it, and the feel of his cock inside of her. The very thought of those hard, thick nine and a half inches made her tingle between her legs. And had she been alone in her room, she would have massaged her clit to relieve some of the ache built up inside of her.

Everywhere she had looked she saw Jake, or at least she imagined she did.

Charlie couldn't believe how easily she'd surrendered to him. It was as if she'd become a slave to her hormones. When she had lost Paul over four years ago, she vowed she would never let herself to love anyone the way she'd loved him. No other man would be allowed to pierce her heart that way again, and that's the way she wanted it.

She had loved Paul with such intensity that the pain of losing him was emotionally crippling. Although the pain had lessened, in her heart Charlie knew that she would always love her handsome big-hearted husband, but now it was a closed chapter in her life. Charlie was too much of a coward to put herself through that again. Loving someone didn't always guarantee they'd be around.

The way Jake made her feel scared her. She couldn't let him into her life and if that meant keeping his daughter a secret, then so be it. Granted, she had needs, but it wasn't something her vibrator couldn't handle. It was too bad, though, because her pussy tingled at the mere mention of Jake's name. It certainly didn't help matters that she saw him so often. He made more trips to her department in the past week than he had the entire time she had worked for MBF.

Not only that, he always managed to brush up against her. Charlie swore the man was doing it on purpose in order to mess with her head. Jake also seemed to know how disconcerting his presence was to her. If the job didn't pay so well, she would have been out the door. She still looked through the classifieds in earnest, but nothing was comparable to what she had at the moment.

She walked back to her desk from the meeting still deep in thought. When she sat down, the phone rang.

"MBF accounting department, this is Charlie speaking."

"Charlie, Jake here."

She nearly dropped the receiver. He had never called her desk before. What did he want?

"Yes? Can I help you?" she asked, silently congratulating herself on the coolness of her tone. She refused to let him know how flustered his call had made her.

"I know this is late notice, but I was wondering if you had plans on Saturday."

Charlie paused. He had to be joking, she thought. "Umm, why do you ask?"

"Let's not play games, Charlie. You know I want to see you."

"Do I? That's not the impression I've been given. As I recall, you seem more interested in getting me into the sack." She pulled no punches.

There was a pause before Jake spoke again. He let out a long sigh. "I won't lie to you and say I don't want that delectable body of yours again, but I would like to see you. Socially, I mean. We can do a little sightseeing around the city for the day, and then have dinner. Or we'll do whatever you want. I'm game. This isn't just me trying to get you back into bed, because if sex was all I wanted, we wouldn't be having this conversation."

For a brief moment, Charlie wanted to say yes, but she quickly dispelled any notions in that direction. "No, I don't think that would be a good idea."

"Why not?" he demanded. "I think we would have a good time together. Give us a chance, Charlie. All I'm asking for is one date."

"Jake, you're my employer. I don't think it would be a good idea for us to fraternize outside the office." Charlie pointed out.

"But you'll let me fuck you inside of it?"

Charlie gasped, robbed of words.

"I'm sorry. That was uncalled for. I just find this situation a little frustrating. Surely you know how I feel about you."

"Actually, I don't," she said, finding her voice once more, "and frankly, I really don't care. Like I said, I work for your company and I don't think it's a good idea."

"Don't give me that crap. I find you attractive and I know you feel the same—"

"That's awfully presumptuous of you to tell me how I feel," she interrupted, not liking where this was headed. Why did he have to be so damn persistent? With Steve, it wasn't difficult to turn him down at all, but Jake made her think twice and Charlie hated second-guessing herself.

"But we both know it's the truth, otherwise you wouldn't react the way you do when you're in my arms."

He was right, but she wouldn't let him know it. "I'm beginning to find this conversation very distasteful. I hope my job isn't hanging in the balance based on my response," she said coldly.

"I'm not that kind of boss and that cheap shot was uncalled for. I wasn't asking you out as your employer, but as a man to a woman." A long sigh followed. "It wasn't my intention to start an argument with you. I just don't like being accused of conducting business that way. I didn't realize you had such a low opinion of me, Charlie. What did I do to deserve it?" She could hear the hurt in his voice.

It was now Charlie's turn to apologize. Accusing him of unsavory business practices had been below the belt. "I'm sorry, too. I know you're not like that, Jake."

"Look, I'll guarantee your going out with me will not jeopardize your job one way or another. I'm not petty."

"I don't mix business with pleasure," she said primly.

"News flash, doll face, you already have and you liked it. We both did. Charlie, please reconsider. I would really like to spend some time with you."

"Can't you understand that I don't want to go out with you?" Charlie asked.

"Why? If it's a problem with getting a babysitter for your daughter, we can work something out," he offered in a conciliatory tone.

At the mention of her daughter, Charlie panicked. "What do you know about my daughter?"

He paused for a moment. "Nothing except for what you mentioned. I gathered that she's still pretty young since you were only married for a short period of time. You daughter is around three or four right?"

Charlie let out a soft sigh of relief. Jake obviously believed Christy was Paul's daughter. "Yes, that's right."

"What's her name?" he asked curiously.

"Why do you want to know?" she asked, a little more harshly than she intended.

"Just curious. I didn't realize it was such a big secret." He paused before changing the subject. "Getting back to what I originally called you about, will you at least think about it? There's something between us that can't be denied."

"It's called sex, Jake. And it was a mistake. It won't, I mean, it can't happen again," she said vehemently.

"A mistake? Call it what you want but it wasn't a mistake and it will happen again. You may be willing to cut your nose off to spite your face but I'm not. If it helps you sleep better at night, you can pretend I'm your dead husband, but deep down, you'll know the truth," he ground out.

Charlie sat in stunned silence for a moment. She couldn't believe that Jake had the nerve to say that to her. "You didn't know my husband, so I will thank you not to mention him again. This conversation is over so please don't call me again, unless it's business related." She hung up the phone with a decisive click.

Jake stared at the receiver. She had hung up on him and he couldn't blame her. What in the world had possessed him to say such a foul thing to her? He hadn't meant to upset her, but she frustrated him to no end with the way she ran hot and then cold on him.

Charlie was obviously still hung up on her husband, but he knew his comment was way out of line. He would apologize when he saw her next, but damn it, why did she continue to deny the chemistry they had together? No other woman had disturbed his equilibrium at such a level and he wondered why he even bothered.

Why bother when there were so many willing women out there who practically threw themselves at him? Cynthia, for instance, still called him. Those calls were not welcome, but at least someone wanted him.

Charlie was even coming between him and his long-standing friendship with Steve. Steve, who wasn't slow on the uptake, knew exactly what had happened in Jake's office last week. In Steve's mind, Jake had committed the ultimate sin of going after someone he wanted for himself.

Never mind Steve had done it to Jake many times over the years, but Jake wasn't as competitive when it came to women as Steve was. And never mind Charlie hadn't shown the slightest interest in Steve, but Steve's ego was bruised nonetheless. Jake had succeeded where Steve had failed, and for a man like Steve, who had never had to work particularly hard for female attention, that was unforgivable.

Jake knew in time that his friend would get over it, but in the meantime, he'd had to endure the cold shoulder for a little while. Maybe he should have tried harder to explain his involvement with Charlie when the subject had come up, but something had stopped him. How could he lay prior claim to a woman who had left him after a one-night stand with no explanation?

Jake's phone rang, breaking into his thoughts. It was his private line, and since no one but Steve and his family had the number, he figured it was one of his family members.

'This is Jake," he answered a little tersely.

"Of course it is, dear, who else would be answering your private line?" Moira Fox laughed.

"Hi, Mom. To what do I owe the pleasure of this call?"

"I'm just making sure you're coming to dinner tonight," she answered breezily.

Jake rolled his eyes heavenward, glad his mom couldn't see his face. His mother was probably one of the sweetest ladies anyone would have the good fortune to meet, but she had the unfortunate tendency to nag sometimes.

"Yes, Mom, I'm still coming. You've already called yesterday and the day before about my coming over and nothing has changed, Mommy Dearest."

"Jake, you know I hate when you call me that. Surely you don't think of me that way."

"No, I don't. Joan Crawford was not as relentless as you are," he said dryly.

"Humph. I swear, Jacob Andrew Fox, you have the most twisted sense of humor," she scolded lightly, but he could still hear the laughter in her voice. He and his mother shared the same sense of humor.

"I learned from the best. So what's so great about tonight of all nights? I have dinner with you guys every week."

"I know but your brother and sister canceled. The twins have colds so Carl is helping Bridget out at home, and Helen twisted her ankle."

"That's too bad. Is it anything serious?"

"No. It's not so bad, just a light sprain. That's how it goes when you're dealing with a bunch of rambunctious boys. I can't tell you how many times I injured myself chasing after you, Helen and Carl when you were kids. I guess I'm finally getting my payback. I'm a bit disappointed though, I was looking forward to seeing my grandkids tonight." Moira sighed wistfully.

Oh God, here it comes. Jake, braced himself. Since Jake hit thirty, his mother never failed to bring up his single state in conversation. They could be talking about something as mundane as the weather and Moira would manage to twist it around to marriage and babies.

"It would be so nice to have more grandkids, particularly a sweet little boy or girl with your eyes. You have your father's eyes. Imagine those eyes in a little baby. You were such an adorable baby, Jake. The twins have my eyes, and Helen's boys take after their father." She let out a long, pained sigh, laying it on thick.

Jake shook his head in exasperation. "Mom, I know where you're going with this, but you're barking up the wrong tree."

"Is it so wrong for me to want to see you happy and settled down with some children of your own? Look at how happy Helen and Carl are with their families. Forty isn't that far off for you, Jake. No one deserves to kick loose as much as you do, honey, especially after you've worked so hard to build your business, but I think it's time for you to stop sowing those wild oats of yours and give your father and I some more grandchildren," Moira lectured

"Gee, Mom, and I thought the idea was for me to be happy, not for you and Dad to have more grandchildren. Isn't five enough?" Jake asked, getting a bit irritated. It was hard to be angry with his mother, but she had called when he was already in a bad mood.

"Yes, we have five grandchildren, but none of them are yours," Moira pointed out.

She sounded hurt and Jake felt like the biggest asshole on Earth. Lately, he seemed to be rubbing everyone the wrong way. "Mom, I'm sorry. I'm just a little stressed."

Silence.

"Mom, are you there?"

"Yes, I'm here. I'm sorry too. Sometimes I forget you're a grown man capable of making your own decisions, but you're still my baby," she said fiercely.

"I know, Mom." Not knowing what compelled him to do it, he said, "I've met someone."

"Really?" The happiness in her voice was enough to bowl him over through the phone. "Will you bring her to dinner with you? I would be happy to make room for one more."

He would have laughed at how quickly she snapped back to her cheerful self had he not been so depressed. "No. It hasn't gotten that far yet," he said dejectedly.

"Is everything okay, son?"

"She doesn't feel the same," he said hoarsely, his voice full of emotion.

"Who is she? What woman wouldn't want you? I don't think I like the sound of her," Moira huffed indignantly.

"Take it easy, Mom," Jake laughed at his sweet-as-pie mother turning into a fierce lioness. "Remember, you were the one who taught me anything not worth fighting for wasn't worth having."

"I know, but really, Jake, I can't see how anyone could turn you down. I remember when you were a teenager and all the young ladies would call asking for you. It drove your father and me nuts. You were voted nicest smile, eyes and hair in your senior class. Is this woman blind?"

He wished she hadn't reminded him. Those superlatives had been embarrassing enough in high school, and to this day, his brother and sister still teased him about it. "Mom, that was years ago, and looks aren't everything."

"I know but I don't ever recall you having problems with a lady before."

"You can't always get want you want, I suppose," he said, his throat tightening.

"Well, I guess all I can say then is good luck."

"Thank you. Can I bring something for dinner tonight?" He changed the subject.

"No, we have it covered."

"Okay, Mom, I'll see you guys tonight. I love you."

೮೦೦೪

Later that night Jake lay in bed trying to sleep. It was good spending time with his parents. His mom had cooked his favorite dish of spaghetti and meatballs. He was actually glad Carl and Helen hadn't shown up with their families. It wasn't that he didn't adore them and his nieces and nephews, but at times he felt a little out of place.

Lately, he had started to feel envious of them all. He wanted what his parents and his siblings had. He wanted it all, companionship, love, and a family to fill his big empty house. The problem was he had found that one person to share his life with and she ran the other way whenever he was near.

For the past three years, he wondered what it was about Charlie he simply couldn't forget, but when he held her in his arms again, he knew. He was in love with Charlie Brown. His father was right. When you found that special someone, you knew right away.

Chapter Nine

Saturday morning the doorbell rang insistently.

Charlie grumbled with irritation. She had really been looking forward to sleeping in. Her daughter shared her loved for sleeping in as well, so Charlie was a little peeved that she had to get up so early. Glancing at her nightstand, she noticed it was only seven thirty in the morning. She grumbled all the way down the hallway.

Standing at the door were her parents.

"Mom! Dad! What are you doing here?" Charlie asked dumbly.

"We came to visit. Are you going to let us in or what?" Delores asked.

Charlie stepped aside to let them in. Her father engulfed her in a bear hug. "What are you still doing in bed so late in the morning?"

"Dad, it's not even eight o'clock yet. Not many people are up this early on a Saturday morning." She exchanged hugs with her mother next.

"Where's my grandbaby?" Keith looked around as if expecting to see his granddaughter right away. He had a teddy bear in his hand. Charlie groaned. Whenever her parents were around, they spoiled Christy like crazy.

"She's sleeping," Charlie said in a whisper so they would get the hint.

"Well, go wake her up. We can't wait to see her," her mother insisted. Charlie sighed. This was going to be a long weekend. She almost wished she hadn't answered the door.

"Let me get you guys some coffee. Christy should be up in another hour or so." They both looked a little disappointed, but didn't argue. She should have known they'd do as they pleased anyway, because when Charlie came back from the kitchen with coffee in hand, Christy was in the living room swinging around her new toy.

"Mom, Dad, why did you wake her?" Charlie asked irritably.

"Stop fussing, girl. We don't get to see our grandchild that often," her father chided gently, looking proudly at Christy.

He had a point. Charlie knew she was being grouchy because she had been woken up early. Her parents adored Christy and she couldn't begrudge them that. Christy enjoyed the attention that her grandparents lavished on her.

"Look, Mommy. Look at Teddy." Christy ran to her mother in order to show off her new toy.

Charlie inspected the big fuzzy brown bear. "Wow, he's something else. What are you going to call him?"

"Teddy. I already said that," She explained to her mom as if she were the adult and Charlie, the toddler. Christy took her bear back and ran back to her grandparents. The kid was way ahead of her time.

"So how long are you guys staying?" Charlie asked.

"Well, we were hoping to stay for a few days and then we're heading to Williamsburg. It's so nice there around this time of year," Delores said, tickling her giggling granddaughter.

"Oh. How long is a few days?" Charlie persisted. She loved her parents but she dreaded the lectures she was in store for this weekend.

₧₧

Lecture number one came later that afternoon while Christy was napping. Charlie and her parents were sitting in the backyard enjoying a glass of ice tea after an exhausting day in the park. Running after a two-year-old was exhausting for Charlie, so she could only imagine how her parents were feeling.

"Charlie girl," her father began, affection evident in his voice. "I think you're doing a fine job with Christy." Keith wiped the sweat from his dark forehead before taking another sip of his tea.

Charlie could almost sense what was coming. She folded her hands in her lap, waiting in tense anticipation for what he'd say next. "But?"

"But your mother and I have been thinking. A child needs a father and you don't seem to be making much of an effort to provide Christy with one. Aren't you seeing anyone yet? I mean, you're a beautiful young lady, and you're young. I see no reason why you shouldn't remarry, and maybe give Christy a little brother or sister. Your mother's and my one regret was that we could only have one child. There's no reason why you shouldn't have any more. You're only thirty-three."

Charlie sighed heavily. Being from the old school, her parents never really approved of her bringing up a child on her own, especially since she refused to disclose the name of Christy's father. She knew they loved Christy as much as any grandparent could, which is why they felt justified in thinking

Charlie should do right by her daughter. Doing right by Christy meant marrying again to provide her with a father.

"Dad, we've been through this before. I've been married before and I don't feel I should have to get married again because I have a child."

"Charlie, you're being selfish. You don't have just yourself to think about anymore. When I see you struggling on your own needlessly, it breaks my heart," Delores piped in.

"Mom—"

"Don't you 'mom' me. You have an adorable little girl who deserves a daddy. Since you won't tell us who the father is, the least you can do is settle down and get married."

"Don't you think I'm doing a good enough job with her? Yes, there are things I'd like to give her that I'm financially unable to, but we do okay. If anything, I think I'm doing better than average. I own my own home, have a car, a good job and Christy wants for nothing. Sometimes I have to make some sacrifices for my daughter, but she's worth it This is the twenty-first century. Believe me, Mom and Dad, there are lots of single women raising children on their own and doing a great job of it."

"And that is exactly what's wrong with the world today. I've never been able to figure out what kind of man can impregnate a woman and not take responsibility for his child and the kind of woman who—" Her father broke off.

"What were you about to say, Dad?" Charlie challenged. "Were you going to say, what kind of woman would get herself in that kind of trouble? Were you implying I'm a loose woman?"

Keith looked away, his lips pinched together mutinously. "Now don't t-take that tone of voice with me, young lady," he stammered.

Charlie wiped away a stray tear. Sometimes dealing with her parents was emotionally exhausting. "I'm sorry, Daddy, but it really hurts when the two of you are constantly throwing my one mistake in my face. I know you mean well, but I'm doing the best I can for my daughter."

"No one is faulting how you raise Christy. Anyone can tell that you're doing an amazing job," Delores wisely intervened. "And we don't mean to make you feel bad. We just care about you, Charlie.

"Then why can't the job I'm doing with her be enough? Look, I know you guys mean well, but Christy is fine. She's probably one of the most well-adjusted kids you're likely to meet," Charlie reasoned.

"We know she's a good kid, but you deserve some help. Tangible things aside, you can give her a mother's love, but just because she's a girl, it doesn't mean she doesn't need a strong male figure in her life." Delores said quietly.

"She has Daddy."

Her father shook his head. "And how often do we come around?"

Charlie stood, knowing this conversation would go for another hour if she didn't end it now. "I'm going to go check on Christy. I hope we can drop this subject when I get back."

No more was said about it for the rest of the afternoon, but Charlie knew that the subject was not closed.

৪৩

Lecture number two came later that night after dinner. They had all gone out for seafood at a restaurant on the Wharf in D.C. After going out for ice cream, the four of them went back to Charlie's house.

They were sitting around the living room chatting easily and watching television. Christy was curled up fast asleep in her grandpa's lap and Keith was snoring soundly. It didn't escape her notice how Christy seemed to favor her grandfather's attention when he was around. Could what her parents said have some validity? Was it possible, Christy already realized she didn't have a father and wanted male attention? She was a bright child, and it certainly gave Charlie something to think about.

Charlie was happy to get through dinner without her parents once mentioning men, but she should have known her peace wouldn't last.

"Honey, did you notice that fine-looking young man staring at you during dinner. He looked like a young Nat King Cole." Her mother sighed, a dreamy expression on her face.

"No, Mom. I guess I wasn't paying attention. I was too busy chasing my child around the table." Charlie sensed impending doom.

"How could you have missed him, dear, all the young ladies were looking his way."

"I was enjoying your company too much to pay attention," Charlie answered with barely contained temper.

"You're a very attractive woman, baby, any man would be happy to take you, even if you do have a child," her mother pressed on.

"Mom, we've been through this already so there's no point in going over it again. I don't want a man, so please stop pointing out every single man you see." Charlie wanted to throw something, but this was her mother.

"That's not true. Why do you always exaggerate? I don't point out every single guy to you." Delores rolled her eyes.

"You pointed out a one-eyed fisherman to me and he didn't have a tooth in his mouth," Charlie argued.

"So? He seemed like a nice enough man. I didn't realize you were so superficial when it comes to looks." Her mother shrugged.

"I'm not, but I think there has to be a degree of attraction between two people. Even if I did settle down, the man doesn't have to be drop dead gorgeous or handsome, just someone who doesn't make me cringe when I look at him. That man was old enough to be my grandfather," Charlie said, on the verge of screaming.

"Fine. How about that nice boy playing the piano."

Charlie had no clue who her mother referred to, but bit out, "Not my type."

"Then what is your type? Are you into white men now?" Delores probed.

Charlie froze. "Why do you ask that?"

"Well, it's obvious to us Christy isn't completely black. I don't know many blue-eyed black people with her texture hair. I know our people come in all different shades from milky white to onyx, but I'm not stupid." Surprisingly, neither one of her parents had brought up Christy's race before and Charlie had never volunteered the information.

"Why have you never said anything about it before?"

"Because she's our grandbaby, and we love her no matter what."

"If it didn't matter before, what difference does it make now? Christy is my daughter whether the person who fathered her is white, Chinese or Puerto Rican," Charlie defended.

"It doesn't make any difference at all. You know your father and I didn't raise you to discriminate. I was just making an observation. Charlie, why won't you tell us who Christy's father is? It's just not right that you should be raising her on your own while he gets off scot-free."

"It's the way I want it, Mom. I'm sorry it hurts you guys, but I just can't talk about it."

"We only want you to be happy."

"I know but please accept that this is the way things are going to be."

₧₨

By Monday Charlie was ready to commit murder. She was at her boiling point. Far from letting the subject of her single status drop, Charlie's parents brought it up at every single lull in conversation.

Her parents dropped her off that morning in her car, deciding to stay a little longer and do some sightseeing around the city. Charlie loaned them her Passat since it was more convenient to navigate the city in her smaller vehicle than their cumbersome RV.

Charlie let Christy stay with her grandparents for the day, knowing her daughter would enjoy spending time with her grandma and grandpa. She kissed them all and waved goodbye, feeling as if a weight had been momentarily lifted off her shoulders. At least at work she would have a temporary reprieve from her parents. She was glad to see the back of them when they drove off with the promise of picking her up at five sharp.

When she made it to her desk, she gasped. A huge bouquet of roses and calla lilies sat on display. Who would send her such an ostentatious arrangement? Charlie heart clenched as possibilities ran through her mind. Her suspicions were confirmed when she read the card.

Thinking of you and hoping you'll change your mind and give a desperate guy a chance. Jake.

Charlie's first reaction was wonder. Why would Jake send her flowers as if he were courting her, especially when she had already made it clear she wasn't interested? Her next reaction was anger. How could he? How dare he presume she'd appreciate his offering?

Charlie had a notion to throw the flowers in the trash can and she probably would have if a coworker had not chosen that precise moment to appear. *Oh Lord, here comes Sandy the Mouth.*

Sandy was justifiably called "The Mouth" around the office because gossip spread like a forest fire whenever she was around. If you told Sandy a secret, it wouldn't be one for long.

"Hi, Charlie. That's a nice arrangement you have there. Who sent it to you?" Sandy asked without preamble, batting her eyelashes innocently.

"No one special," Charlie answered nonchalantly. Of all the people who saw this arrangement, why did it have to be this nosey heffa?

"Hmm, seems like a pretty expensive arrangement for it to just be from no one special," Sandy pressed, casually bending over to take a whiff of the floral scent.

"What can I say?" Charlie shrugged, wishing the bothersome woman would go away or jump off a cliff. At the moment, Charlie preferred the cliff. Sandy reached over to pick up the card but Charlie beat her to it, snatching it up before the busybody could get a peek. "That's private, if you don't mind." Charlie smiled insincerely. This woman had balls the size of grapefruits.

Sandy pursed her lips, her eyes narrowing slightly. "What's the big secret? I mean, if it's from a friend like you say it is, I'd show it off to everyone in the office. If I got an arrangement like this I would tell the world."

"I'm sure you would," Charlie said, not bothering to hide the sarcasm dripping from her voice.

Sandy had thick skin. Charlie wouldn't get rid of her that easy. "You're hiding something. Are they from Steve?"

"What? Why would you think that?" If Sandy didn't leave within the next minute Charlie was going to lose her temper.

"Well, everyone knows how he's been asking you out."

Charlie used the same technique she used with Christy and silently counted to ten. Why didn't this blasted woman just go away? "Sandy, I don't know why you have such an insatiable need to gossip but it's not cool. If you can't take a hint, I'll have to be blunt. This is none of your business. If I didn't answer the question the first time you asked, what makes you think I would answer it the second or third time?"

Sandy recoiled as if she'd been slapped. "Well, you don't have to get so nasty about it. I was only trying to be friendly." Sandy sniffed, sounding offended.

Charlie wasn't fooled for one second. Sandy could probably make a career as an actress if she set her mind to it. Realizing she'd have to make something up to get the pest off her back, Charlie said the first thing that popped into her mind. "It's a secret admirer, Sandy. Let's leave it at that, shall we? As a matter of fact, since you're so interested in these flowers take them." Charlie picked up the bouquet and stuffed them in Sandy's hands.

"You're giving these away? You're crazy." For once Sandy seemed to be at a loss for words.

"Maybe so, but if you don't mind, I have a lot of work to do. Take them and enjoy." Charlie handed them over with her blessing.

Sandy walked away with the flowers, a confused look on her face.

Charlie sat down at her desk hoping she wasn't in for any more surprises today.

໐ງ

Jake decided to throw in the towel for the day around five. He normally didn't leave so early, but he wanted to catch his nephew's little league game. Jennifer was packing up as well as he stepped out of his office. "Let's walk down together." He waited for her at the door.

"I can't believe you're leaving this early with the rest of us worker bees, Jake," Jennifer teased.

"Yeah, I guess I am. Helen has been on me about attending more of my nephews' events, so I'm going to a little league game tonight."

"That sounds like fun."

They chatted easily as they took the elevator downstairs. When they made it to the lobby, Jake saw an older black man sitting in one of the couches with a little girl on his lap.

"Isn't she the most darling little thing?" Jennifer observed.

"Mommy!" The little girl shrieked with delight, wiggling out of the man's lap. Jake watched the child run across the lobby to the woman she called mommy. When Jake saw who she belonged to his heart sunk to his feet.

Frozen to the spot, Jake watched as Charlie scooped up her daughter and gave her a big hug and a kiss. The little girl hugged Charlie back as if she didn't want to let go.

"Dad, I thought you guys were going to wait outside for me." Charlie approached the man who stood up from the couch.

Jennifer looked at her boss with concern. "Jake, what's the matter? You've gone as white as a sheet." She tugged at his arm, but he couldn't stop staring at the scene in front of him.

Charlie was holding her daughter. She must have sensed his intense stare because she turned toward him, noticing him standing there for the first time. She nearly dropped the toddler. Their eyes locked. Blood pounded in his ears as his anger slowly began to rise. The girl in Charlie's arms didn't look four, and she had his eyes!

Chapter Ten

"Jake, what's wrong?" Jennifer looked from Charlie and then to Jake.

He didn't answer right away, unable to tear his eyes away from the little girl who had his eyes. It felt as if someone had punched him in the stomach. Hard.

"Jake, what is it?" Jennifer persisted.

"Jen, I'll see you in the morning. I forgot something in my office, so you go head without me."

Jennifer opened her mouth as if on the verge of saying something, but then thought better of it.

"Goodnight," Jake said more firmly this time.

"Okay, then, I'll see you in the morning, Jake." Jake nodded curtly as Jennifer left the building.

Jake watched as the man approached Charlie and the young girl. Charlie quickly thrust the little girl into the man's arms.

"Come on, Charlie girl, we're ready to go. What's the hold up? Your mother is waiting outside for us. We were hoping to get something to eat on the way home," Jake heard him say. So the man was her father. It didn't matter to Jake because he wasn't going to let her leave without having his say.

Jake walked the short distance, quickly closing the gap between them. His eyes were intent on the wiggling child who was trying to reach for her mother. Charlie looked at him like a deer caught in headlights. She should be scared of him Jake thought, because at this moment he wanted to wring her pretty little neck.

"Hi, I'm Jake Fox. How do you do, sir?" he asked smoothly, holding out his hand. Charlie's father shifted Christy in his arms and took Jake's hand, seeming uneasy.

"I need to borrow Charlie for a minute if you don't mind. I promise I won't keep her though. I couldn't help but overhear you guys are going out to dinner afterwards so I'll have her back to you in a jiffy."

Charlie's father looked confused as to why Jake was introducing himself.

Jake was on the verge of elaborating, when Charlie intervened.

"Dad, this is my boss. Jake this is my father Keith Brown," she introduced hastily.

"Oh. Nice to meet you, Jake." Keith smiled briefly before turning to his daughter. "Don't be too long, Charlie. I'll take the baby, and we'll wait for you outside in the car."

"I not a baby," the little girl said with indignation, glaring at her grandfather.

"Bye-bye, Mommy. Bye-bye, man." She waved to Charlie and Jake as her grandfather carried her away.

"Uh, she calls every male 'man'. It's her new thing," Charlie began nervously, but Jake was too choked with emotion to register exactly what she said. Jake's heart caught in his throat. He watched his daughter leave the building.

Holy shit, I have a daughter.

When they were gone, Jake turned to Charlie and grabbed her elbow forcefully. She didn't protest as he propelled her to the first empty office they came upon.

He pulled her inside and slammed the door behind them. Charlie jumped at the loud thud. She looked scared, but Jake didn't care. The way he was feeling at the moment, she should have been scared. To think, after all this time she had been with MBF, she had kept his daughter from him. He was not in the mood to feel charitable toward her sensibilities right now.

Jake was seething—no, he was pissed! Looking at Charlie with contempt, he was torn between strangling her and shaking her until her teeth rattled. He stood absolutely still, not trusting himself to move or speak, because he had never felt such a strong surge of rage in his life. Never had he understood how someone could so easily commit murder—until now.

He watched Charlie as she wrung her hands in front of her, shifting her weight from one leg to the next. The forlorn expression on her face left him cold. Good, she deserved to suffer some after what she'd done. How could she do this to him? Any number of times she could have told him about their daughter, but she didn't bother. Did she hate him that much?

Charlie was finally the one to break the silence. "Jake, I can imagine how you must feel," she began.

Jake narrowed his eyes, clenching his jaw. "Do you really, Charlie? I don't think so. I don't think you have any idea how I feel."

She gulped. "Fair enough, but will you at least hear me out?"

"Let's not get into what's fair and what isn't, because you would lose this argument in a heartbeat," he retorted.

Charlie took a deep breath before speaking. "The thing is, I didn't think I would ever see you again, which is why I never said anything in the beginning. The fact that you're my boss made things a little awkward."

"Really? Imagine how awkward things are about to get for you."

"Please don't look at me like that."

His nostrils flared. "How am I looking at you, Charlie? Would I happen to look like a man who's been kept in the dark about his own child? She is mine, isn't she?"

Charlie nodded. At least she didn't try to lie about it, not that she could anyway. In his heart of hearts, Jake knew the child was his the moment he set eyes on her.

"You must have had a good laugh behind my back." What a fool she'd played him for.

"Jake, it wasn't like that. Look, I won't ask you for any money, so please don't think she'll become a financial burden to you and I promise I won't say anything to anyone about her. I'll resign and no one will be the wiser for it." She paused giving him a pleading look, but he wasn't about to let her off the hook.

"I don't think there was anyone else in the lobby other than Jennifer who saw her so no one has to know. I didn't know my Dad would bring her inside. You see my parents are visiting me and—"

"Shut up. Just shut the hell up," he finally said. "Charlie, you've made me feel a number of things these past few months, but I never thought hate would be one of them. What kind of woman are you to keep me from my child? How dare you think I would want to keep my daughter a secret? Is it because you think I'd be ashamed of her skin color?" When Charlie didn't answer, he yelled. "Answer me, goddamn it!"

Charlie said a hasty no but Jake didn't believe her.

"So not only do you think I wish to be a deadbeat dad, you think I'm racist to boot?"

"I never said that, Jake. I know you're not those things. I just wanted you to know she's taken care of and you don't have to be a part of her life if you don't want to," Charlie protested.

"Charlie, you're treading on a very thin ice at the moment." Jake took a deep breath to calm himself. "What's my daughter's name?" he demanded.

"You don't have to sound so proprietary about her," Charlie muttered defensively.

"If I were you, I wouldn't play games, now tell me her name!"

"Christy. Christy Elizabeth Brown."

"Her birthday?"

"December 12th."

"Exactly nine months from that night." He calculated in his head.

He knew the answer before he asked, but had to hear it from her lips. "What did you put for the father's name on her birth certificate?"

"Unknown," she said so softly he had to strain to hear.

Jake abruptly turned away from Charlie, hating the very sight of her at this moment. "You labeled our daughter a bastard," he accused.

"Jake, I didn't think I'd ever see you again. It was a one-night thing and I thought...well, I didn't think..." He could hear the tears in her voice, but no sympathy came. Let her feel miserable. She deserved it after the stunt she'd pulled.

"That's right, you didn't think. You've been with this company for some months, not weeks, months, and yet you couldn't have told me in that amount of time?" Tears of fury and hurt sprung to his eyes.

"I'm sorry, Jake. In retrospect, I probably should have said something, but I didn't consider your feelings in the matter. It was selfish to keep Christy a secret," she began hesitantly.

"I don't want to hear it. There's absolutely nothing you can say at this moment to justify what you did, but I guess I should thank you, though." He turned back, feeling his temper slowly reining in. At Charlie's puzzled expression, Jake smiled humorlessly. "From the looks of things, you've taken good care of her, and for that I thank you. She's seems like a sweet little girl. It's too bad her mother is a cold bitch," he hissed at her.

Charlie gasped. "I know you're upset, Jake, but I'm not going to stand here and be called nasty names." Tears ran down her eyes as she turned to leave, but Jake was too quick for her.

He grabbed her and turned her back around to face him. "After what you did, nasty names are the least you deserve. How could you, Charlie?" He was still trying to make sense of it all. How could someone he thought he loved do something so underhanded?

Charlie closed her eyes as if trying to block out his anger and hurt. "I'm sorry, Jake." She sounded contrite, but he wasn't ready to hear her apology.

"You keep saying you're sorry but your apology comes too little, too late. I'll be in touch with you, and I *will* have access to my daughter. If you try to keep her from me, then you'll know the true meaning of sorry. Now get out of my sight!" he barked at her.

Charlie scrambled out of the room like a scared mouse. When she closed the door behind her, Jake punched a hole in the wall.

After Charlie went scurrying out of the office, Jake screamed his frustration. He rubbed his sore fist. All this time, Charlie had been deceiving him. Jake thought about all the times he'd seen her at work and that time in his office when they made love. She had plenty of opportunities to tell him.

To keep their child a secret was the lowest thing to do in his eyes. Jake ran through the events in his head wondering what he may have done to make her not want to tell him, and he couldn't think of a thing.

When he composed himself enough to leave the building, Jake found himself driving. He drove for what seemed like hours in the rush hour traffic, eventually winding up in Baltimore. Then he turned back and drove to his parents' house.

His mom answered the door with a look of delight on her face. "Jake! What a wonderful surprise. Helen is here, too. She's a little miffed at you for missing the little league game you promised to attend."

Jake wasn't in the mood to deal with his sister's histrionics. "Something more important came up. Where's Dad?"

"He's at a friend's house. You know Monday nights are his poker nights."

"Oh yeah, I forgot about that."

His mother frowned, concern in her hazel eyes. "Okay, spit it out, young man. Your eyes are bloodshot and you're looking less than your immaculately dressed self. What's the matter?" Moira asked, leading him to the kitchen table to sit down.

The minute Helen saw him, she started in on him. "Jake, I hope you know your nephew was really disappointed when you didn't show up. You shouldn't make promises you can't keep."

"And how do you do, too, Helen?" Jake's voice dripped with sarcasm.

Helen glared. "If you had to stay late at the office or whatever it was you had to do, you should have extended me the courtesy of a call."

"Helen, for once can you keep quiet?"

His sister gasped and opened her mouth to speak when their mother raised her hand. "Enough. Helen, go make some tea. Can't you see your brother is upset about something?"

Jake waited until his sister left the table, finding it hard to get the words out. He still couldn't believe what had happened. He wished Helen wasn't here looking on. She was such a busybody, but he figured that she'd find out eventually. "Mom, remember when I told you I had met someone special?" Jake began.

"Yes, I remember. What happened, sweetheart?" His mother asked with caution.

"You're distraught over a woman?" Helen interjected with a laugh. "Jake, I have to say you had it coming. The way you go through women is a sin," Helen finished, not bothering to hide the righteous indignation in her voice.

"This doesn't concern you, Helen!" Jake yelled, feeling the need to do something juvenile, like throwing something at her.

"Hey, I'm only pointing out—"

"I came to talk to Mom, not you, so will you shut your trap?" he roared.

"Kids, please!" Moira scolded. "You both need to calm down, and Helen, you keep your two cents to yourself or go home. Your brother is obviously upset," she lectured to both of her children.

Jake and Helen glared at each other.

"I'm sorry, Hel, I just...it hasn't been my day."

"I'm sorry, too, Jake," Helen apologized. "You really do look like you've had a rotten day."

"Please continue, Jake," his mother prompted.

"She's been working at MBF for some months now, but it wasn't the first time I met her. We actually met over three years ago. I think I was infatuated with her from the very beginning, kind of like how Dad was with you. She's a widow, and her husband died a year previous to the night we met." He broke off, finding it difficult to continue. Different emotions warred through him and he wasn't sure how to handle them all. Moira patted her son's hand in reassurance.

"One thing led to another and...we made love." Jake blushed. He may have been a grown man, but there were still things he felt uncomfortable taking about in front of his mother.

"After one night? Eww," Helen interrupted again. Moira shot Helen an icy glare. "Sorry," Helen muttered, having the good grace to blush as she rejoined them at the table. She pushed a cup of tea in Jake's direction.

"Yes, it was after one night. I won't pretend it was the first time I've slept with a woman of such a short acquaintance, but with her, it was special. The morning after she was gone. I felt so sure about our instant connection that I hired private investigators to find her, but they never did."

"Three years ago?" His mother furrowed her brows. "I remember you went through a period when you didn't want to be around the family around that time. Did this woman have anything to do with it?"

"You could say that. I tried to get on with my life, but imagine my surprise when she turned up at MBF. It was like I was getting a second chance with Charlie," Jake said with conviction.

"Charlie?" his mother asked, her eyes gleaming with curiosity.

"Charlie is her name." Jake sighed before continuing. "In the beginning, she acted as if she didn't want anything to do with me. It was tearing me apart, but I just couldn't let go. I know there was something between us even if she wouldn't admit it, and then..."

"Then what?" Helen prompted.

"Something happened that made me think she wasn't as adverse to me as she had led on." He wasn't about to explain the passionate interlude he and Charlie shared in his office to his mother and sister.

"You didn't sleep together again, did you?" Helen asked with her usual bluntness.

"Helen, if you interrupt one more time, I'm going to choke you," Jake threatened.

His sister rolled her eyes. "Take it easy. Sheesh."

"Anyway, I began to think with time, she would give me a chance, so you can imagine my shock as I'm about to leave the office today and I come face-to-face with a little girl who has my eyes, and wouldn't you know it, she's the exact age a child would be if she was conceived around the time Charlie and I were together."

Moira gasped. "Are you meaning to tell me, you fathered a child you had no knowledge of? I...I have another grandchild I'm just finding out about? This woman kept it from you?"

Jake nodded, finding the words difficult to say. His mother and Helen sat with their mouths wide open at Jake's shocking revelation. "I'm sure you can imagine how I felt when all along I'd been thinking about how great it was to have finally found someone I could spend my life but she's been playing me for a fool," Jake concluded huskily. He blinked away unshed tears.

"That bitch!" Helen piped in yet again. "How dare she do this to you! Who the hell does this slut think she is?"

"Helen! Watch your mouth, young lady," Moira scolded.

"She's not a slut." Jake groaned, a deep misery setting in. If that were the case, he wouldn't have to beg for her time at every opportunity. Despite what she'd done, he couldn't allow his sister to talk about Charlie that way.

Helen heard none of it however. Once she got on a roll, it was hard to steer her away from it. "But, Mom, this woman keeps her child a secret from Jake and I'm the bad guy? Look at your son for Christ's sake. Can't you see how much he's hurting? How can you sit there so calmly? Isn't finding out that you have a grandchild you knew nothing about enough to make you angry at what this bitch did?"

"Helen, the mother in me wants to rip this Charlie person's heart out, but you don't get to be my age without learning a thing or two," Moira answered softly. It was obvious she was still processing this situation herself. "Things aren't always so black-and-white, dear. Now, I really appreciate you coming for a visit tonight, but I think Jake and I need to have a little mother-son chat. Alone." She smiled at her daughter, but her tone made it clear she wouldn't take any back talk.

Helen didn't look pleased with being dismissed, but she shrugged it off. "You haven't heard the last of me on this subject. If I ever meet this Charlie woman, I'm going to give her a piece of my mind." She kissed her mom goodbye and gave Jake a big hug before leaving.

When Helen was gone, Moira pulled her chair closer to Jake's.

His mother wrapped her arms around him and cradled him against her bosom much like she did when he was a child. He held on to her tightly, comforted by her warmth. He could almost imagine he was a child again and Mommy would make things all better, but he knew that the only person who could make this all better was him.

Jake, overwhelmed with the recent emotions raging through him, shuddered against his mother's body and let the tears silently fall. He hadn't cried since he was eight years old and broke his leg sliding into home during a little league game. He cried for the lost years with his daughter and for how thoroughly Charlie had duped him—so strong was his hurt.

After a long silence, he looked up at his mother, seeking her guidance. "Mom, what should I do?"

"Sweetie, it tears my heart in two to see you like this, and I would like to say I have a clear solution for you but I don't. Only you hold the answers. You'll need to choose your own path, but I know you'll make the right decision whatever that may be. I'll be honest with you and say I'm certainly not pleased with this young lady's deception, but I am happy to know I have another granddaughter."

"Mom, you should see her. She's absolutely gorgeous," Jake reflected, remembering every single detail of his daughter's face.

"Well, I'm certainly eager to meet her, and I'm sure your father will feel the same way. I would like to meet Christy and Charlie. I'll talk it over with your father, and perhaps we can set up a dinner this weekend. I'll call you in the morning to let you know."

"She may turn my dinner invitation down."

"Don't be such a defeatist. You can charm the bees from the flowers. Invite her and I'll handle the rest. Now my question to you is this, Jake, has this changed your feelings for Charlie?" Moira asked.

Jake took a minute to think. Charlie had been wrong for what she had done, but he couldn't imagine life without her.

"No, my feelings for her haven't changed."

ℰᎧℛ

The next day Charlie called out sick. She simply couldn't face Jake. He had been so angry and if she were being fair, she would have to say he was justified in his anger. Her father had questioned her about the incident in the lobby the moment she got back to the car. Keith Brown was no one's fool and she suspected he knew it wasn't a coincidence his granddaughter had Jake Fox's eyes.

Charlie refused to talk about it, however. The conversation still weighed heavily on her mind.

"Who was that man, Charlotte?" Keith asked later that night when Christy was in bed. Charlie knew by his mannerism that her father had been holding his question in until that moment. She was in for it. Neither one of her parents ever called her Charlotte unless she was in trouble. It had the affect of making her feel like she was a child again.

"He's my boss, Dad, like I said."

"Don't get smart with me, girl. I may not be the smartest man, but I do have eyes in my head. It's time you came clean," Keith insisted.

Charlie rolled her eyes. Why did people always ask questions to things they already knew the answer to? "Jake is my boss," Charlie answered stubbornly.

Delores intervened. "Your father told me about what happened in the office. Are you going to sit there and lie to our faces? We've raised you better than that, young lady."

"Okay, Jake is Christy's father. Is that what you wanted to hear? When I started working for MBF, I didn't know Jake was the owner, nor did I think I'd see him again so he didn't know about Christy until today," Charlie confessed.

"Do you mean to tell me, you've been hiding her from him all along?" Delores sounded astonished.

Charlie groaned inwardly. "It's a little more complicated than that."

"From where I'm sitting, it doesn't seem that complicated," her father contradicted. "Judging from the way that boy was looking at the baby, he was pretty shocked. How in the world did it happen? You've always refused to tell us how you became pregnant with Christy, but by God, you're going to tell us now!" He finished with his voice raised several decibels.

"Dad, do I have to remind you that Christy is sleeping? It's been over three years now. The hows and whys Christy is here are no longer important, what is important is that she is here. Why delve into something you guys know I don't want to go into?"

"Because we care, Charlie. You were obviously upset when you came out of your office building today," Delores answered.

"If you cared, you'd drop the subject and trust me to handle this as I see fit," Charlie argued.

"We've trusted that you would eventually tell us what happened. We also trusted that you would do the right thing by Christy and settle down again, but I see our trust has been misplaced." Keith shot her a look of disapproval.

After the emotional roller coaster Charlie had been on, she snapped. "Okay, do you really want to know? I had a one-night stand with a stranger, on what should have been my anniversary with Paul. I panicked the next morning and ran away, thinking I would never see him again, but surprise, surprise, I learn he's my new boss three years later. I didn't tell him about Christy because I was scared of losing her. Now you know. Are you happy? Can you guys get off my back now?"

The minute the words were out she regretted it. She had never talked to her parents like this before. She'd been raised better than that. Even though they were beating a dead horse, she knew they had meant well. The hurt expressions on their face cut her to the quick.

"I'm sorry," Charlie apologized. It seemed as if she had been doing a lot of apologizing lately. An awkward silence followed. Keith and Delores looked at one another and then at Charlie, making her feel lower than she already felt. They murmured something about getting on the road early the next day.

ဆဩ

Charlie's parents expressed they no longer felt welcome in her home because of her outburst. They decided to head out the next morning even against Charlie's protests. She woke up early to make them breakfast. She was sorry they were leaving in these circumstances, but it couldn't be helped. When she saw them off, she kissed and hugged them like normal, but there was still some tension and restraint between them.

Charlie dropped Christy off at the daycare as usual when her parents left, needing some time to herself. She spent most of the morning driving around but going nowhere. She couldn't help remembering Jake's angry words. Charlie wished she had listened to Laura and told Jake about Christy, at least then she wouldn't have caused him so much pain.

The look of hurt in his eyes ripped at her heart. She sincerely wished she had been upfront with Jake from the beginning, instead of hoarding her secret selfishly to herself.

She went over the reasons as to why she had decided to keep Christy a secret until it finally dawned on her.

Charlie wanted Jake.

She wanted him more than she had wanted anyone in a very long time and it scared the hell out of her, but that only brought on a new set of problems. If she allowed herself to give herself over to him completely, Charlie could be opening herself up to heartache. She'd been down that road before and didn't think she could deal with it again.

Still, it didn't keep the carnal thoughts at bay. The things he'd done to her body gave her many sleepless nights. She would wake up with her body damp with sweat after dreaming about his delicious cock damp with her pussy juices. Even thinking about it now made her pussy contract. She was finally able to admit to herself it had been more than just grief that had allowed Jake to make love to her that night over three years ago.

She had been fiercely attracted to him, and she still was. Now that she could see the situation more clearly for what it was, she wondered how she'd deal with him where Christy was concerned.

After driving around for a few hours, Charlie came home to find a black BMW in her driveway. The moment she pulled up, Jake climbed out of the vehicle. Charlie slowly got out of her car, bracing herself for another verbal assault.

"You didn't show up for work today, so I looked your address up in your file. May I come in?" he asked politely. Jake stuffed his hands in his pockets, a look of uncertainty on his face.

Charlie was taken aback by his manner. This was a totally different man from the angry avenger of the day before. He seemed more humble today.

"Sure." She led him into her house. "Shouldn't you be at work?" she asked.

"Shouldn't you?" he countered.

"Touché. How did you know I would be home?"

"I didn't, but I was prepared to wait it out. I had to talk to you, Charlie."

He looked around him when he walked inside. "You have a nice place."

"Thank you. Would you like something to drink?"

"No, thank you." Jake picked up a photograph of Christy. It was the one of her standing beside a large number two, a wide smile on her angelic face. Charlie's heart skipped a beat at the longing look in his eyes. "Where's Christy now?"

"I dropped her off at the daycare center. I...I needed some time to myself," she said clumsily, not knowing exactly how she should act around Jake now.

"She's very beautiful. She looks like you," he said quietly still looking at the photograph.

"She has your eyes," Charlie remarked.

"Yes, I noticed. I told my parents about her last night, by the way. They're anxious to meet you both. They would like it if you could come to dinner with Christy on Saturday."

It was a simple enough request and Charlie could hardly refuse. She had a lot of time to think about it, and Christy had a right to know her father and her other family.

"Do they know we're black?" she asked hesitantly. She knew Jake didn't care about skin color, but she wasn't so sure about his parents. Charlie wasn't so naïve as to think everyone would just accept them so willingly.

Jake gave her a funny look before replying. "Yes, they know. When you meet my family, you'll realize that race isn't important to them. Believe me, they're probably the most unbiased two people you're likely to meet." There was a brief moment of silence.

"Jake, I'm really sorry. I thought a lot about what you said and you were right. It was wrong of me to keep Christy from you. I was just scared of losing her." And of my lust for you, she added to herself.

"Why would you think you would lose her?" he asked gently as he approached her.

"Because I thought maybe you would think that you could do a better job at raising her. You're in a better financial position than I am."

He cupped her face, tilting her head up so she could meet his eyes. "I think you've done a great job. It's obvious you love her and she loves you. I wouldn't dream of taking her away from you, but I do want an active role in her life. And that means spending time with her and helping you out financially. I'm missed out on so much of her life and I don't intend to miss out on any more."

When Charlie opened her mouth to protest, Jake brushed his thumb across her lips to silence her. "I have plenty of money. The least I could do is help you and my daughter out. You shouldn't have to bear the responsibility alone. There's another reason I came."

"And what reason is that?" she asked, mesmerized by his beautiful light eyes.

"To apologize."

"You have nothing to apologize for." She shook her head. "I'm the one who kept Christy a secret from you. It was a rotten thing of me to do."

"It was, but I do owe you an apology. I was such an asshole yesterday. I shouldn't have ripped into you the way I did.

137

Instead of unleashing my temper, I should have walked away so I could calm down. Then I would have been able to discuss the situation with you like a rational adult."

"Please don't, Jake. You were justified in your anger. What I did was..."

"Yes, it was pretty rotten. I was angry that you would keep my daughter's existence from me, but the truth is...I felt betrayed. I thought there was a bond between the two of us."

Charlie pulled away from him, unable to handle the ramifications of what he was saying. She turned her back to him, unable to meet his eyes. "I don't know what you're talking about," she denied.

Jake stepped behind her and grasped her shoulders. "You do. The times we've been together, we set the world on fire. It's more than just sex between us and you know it."

"No," she whispered even though she knew it was a lie.

"Yes." He dipped his head to kiss her neck.

"This isn't what I came here for, but whenever you're around, I can't keep my hands off of you." His soft whisper was like a gentle caress against her skin. Charlie couldn't hold back her shiver.

He lowered his hands to fondle her breasts, squeezing them gently in his palms. Charlie found herself arching back against him, almost as if her body had a mind of its own. Jake gyrated his hips, rubbing his erect penis against her ass. She molded her bottom against his hardness.

He lowered one hand and unbuttoned her jeans. One arm gripped her waist tight, holding her against him as he ran his tongue over the delicate curve of her ear. A flood of heat rushed between her legs. This man had cast a spell on her. Why else did she burst into flames with a simple touch? Jake slid his other hand inside her panties, finding her hot little button.

Charlie let out a low moan. Her knees would have given out on her if Jake hadn't been holding her upright. He rolled her swollen bundle of nerves between his thumb and forefinger. "Do you like that?" His breath fanned her cheek.

"Yes," she answered, trying to catch her breath. "You know I do."

His fingers released her aching clit before sliding into her moist hole.

"Oh God, Jake," she groaned as she rode his hand. He finger fucked her until a gush of warm liquid flowed from her damp channel. Jake removed his hand and turned her around before covering her lips with his. They were hard, hungry and savage. Charlie melted as his tongue slid between her lips. Jake was such a great kisser.

He quickly undressed her, but when she attempted to do the same to him, he stopped her. "Let me do this, Jake," she begged.

"No. If you touch me, I think I'll lose control."

Charlie laughed. "And you haven't already?"

"You haven't seen anything yet." He made short order of removing his clothes before pulling her to the floor. His body fell on top of hers, and Charlie welcomed his warmth, reveling in the feel of his hardness. Jake's hair-roughened chest rubbing her sensitive skin created a delicious friction like nothing else. Pulses of delight sped through her body.

They kissed and caressed each other's bodies. Not one inch of flesh was left unexplored by either of them. Charlie, feeling bold, rolled on top of Jake and began to plant kisses all over his chest and stomach.

She shimmed down his hard frame until she reached his stiff shaft. Charlie grasped his cock in her hand and licked the head in circular motions. It felt like smooth velvet. The salty, musky taste of him was intoxicating.

Jake moaned when she opened her lips over his length. His cock was so thick and hard. She took him into her mouth inch by delicious inch, the taste of him delighting her senses. Jake held each side of her head and thrust his cock in and out of her hungry mouth. She sucked greedily, her head bobbing along his length.

"Your mouth feels wonderful. Almost as wonderful as your pussy, baby," he praised with a husky quality to his tone.

He fucked her mouth with slow and steady thrusts, while Charlie squeezed and fondled his balls. Jake was drowning in a sea of lust. Everywhere she touched him set his pulses racing. His sac tightened. Jake knew he was close to spewing his seed down her thirsty throat. He pulled out of her mouth before he came.

"No, Jake, I want more," Charlie protested making a move to grab his cock.

"No way. You've teased me enough, woman. I want some pussy."

"But I want to do this. Please let me. Please," she pleaded, staring at him with lust-glazed eyes. When her tongue slid in one slow movement over full lips he nearly gave in to her, but when Charlie dipped her head toward his cock again, he halted her. Jake was now in control. He flipped Charlie over on her stomach and positioned her until she was on her knees, showing her who was in charge. He rubbed his cock against the tight globes of her ass and slid it across her damp slit.

"Jake, please don't tease me. Put it inside of me."

"How bad do you want it?" he teased.

Charlie pushed against him, forcing his hand. She must have known he wouldn't be able to hold out for very long, but in the meantime, Jake wanted to see how far he could push her. He guided his cock head between her labia without fully pressing inside of her.

"I need it bad. Please, Jake, now!" She bucked her hips against him, her impatience for him evident.

Jake could no longer hold back. He slammed into her wet cunt like a man possessed. Charlie screamed with pleasure. She felt so tight, so exquisite. In his heart, Jake knew this was the woman made especially for him.

He gripped her hips as he fucked her with a vigor like nothing he'd ever experienced. Only this woman could make him lose control like this. It was her pussy alone that felt so right around his cock. The mind-numbing sensation of fucking Charlie Brown was like no other.

"Oh, Jake! Fuck me harder. Ram that big, beautiful cock of yours inside me, lover," she begged.

Jake needed no further prompting. He slammed into her hot pussy. "Oh, hell yeah!" he grunted. She felt so damn good. The steady rhythm of his pounding made his balls to slap against her pussy and heightened the sensation of his desire, causing waves of pleasure to run up his spine.

Jake was highly turned on by watching his long white cock slide in and out of her dark body. She was his chocolate angel and she tasted just as sweet. Jake pounded into Charlie over and over again, until she began to scream and convulse underneath him. Her legs buckled under her and she collapsed flat on the floor. Jake followed her, still pumping with furious strokes. He stiffened, feeling the sudden rush of his passion flowing through his body. "Oh God, Charlie, I'm going to come!"

he shouted with one final thrust; he shot his seed inside of her. He heard her satisfied moan and knew he'd pleased her.

He eased his still hard cock out of her and turned her over on her back. Charlie's eyes widened in surprise when he inserted himself back into her. "You're insatiable, Jake."

"Only for you, Charlie, only for you," he groaned. "It's your fault, you know," he said, moving inside or her.

"My fault?" she asked.

"If your pussy wasn't so good and fuckable, I would be able to control myself," he accused.

Charlie laughed, but then her laughter turned to moans of pleasure. He wanted this time to be tender, to show how he felt about her. He became alarmed as tears filled her beautiful brown eyes. "Charlie, what's wrong?" He stopped in mid-stroke.

Charlie wrapped her arms around him. "Nothing, Jake. It's just that...you're a wonderful lover. Please don't stop."

Jake would have sworn that she wanted to say more, but he didn't press the issue. All that mattered now was pleasing her.

Jake held Charlie tight, kissing and petting her body, letting her do the same to him as he made love to her again.

When they were both sated, they lay on the floor entwined in each other's arms. He wanted this moment to last forever, but the floor wasn't where he wanted to hold Charlie.

Jake picked Charlie up in his arms and carried her to the bedroom.

ℰᏅ

Charlie woke to the ringing of the telephone. She automatically reached for it even though her mind was still clouded from sleep.

"Ms. Brown, this is Sherri Farmer from the Ponderosa Day Care Center."

Oh my God. I forgot Christy!

At her abrupt movement, Jake stirred beside her.

"It's past six o'clock and we are trying to close. Will you be here to pick up your child anytime soon?" Sherri's voice dripped with sarcasm.

"Yes, I'll be there in twenty minutes. I'm terribly sorry about this."

"Okay. We'll expect you then, but please be aware that there is a late charge of twenty-five dollars for every fifteen minutes you're late," Sherri said, sounding miffed at being held up before she hung up on Charlie.

Charlie scrambled out of bed. She couldn't believe she had forgotten to pick up Christy. Jake watched from the bed, resting on one elbow. "What's the rush? Come back to bed." He said, giving her his best come-hither smile. If she didn't have to rush to the daycare center, she just may have been tempted.

"I forgot to pick up Christy. The daycare center closes at six and it's six now!" She threw on a pair of jeans and a T-shirt.

Jake scrambled out of bed. "I'll come with you." Charlie would have protested but the determined look in his eyes told her arguing would be futile.

Chapter Eleven

During the ride over to the daycare center, Jake made it clear he wanted to be properly introduced to his daughter right away. Charlie protested, not knowing how Christy would react but Jake was adamant. Would her daughter accept Jake? She did have a fascination of men of late, but that could mean any number of things.

"I think we should hold off telling her until she gets used to you," she began, trying to reason with Jake.

"No. I'm not going to argue about this, Charlie. I want her to know exactly who I am. The sooner she knows, the easier it will be for her to accept."

She saw merit in his point, but still, she had her concerns. "But Jake—"

"Charlie, I think it would confuse her if she got to know me as someone else, only to later find out I'm her father. It's not fair to her or me."

He had a point. She had no choice but to agree.

When she pulled into the parking lot and parked, Charlie turned to Jake before getting out of the car. "Stay here, Jake. I'll be a few minutes. I have a feeling words may be exchanged with Miss Farmer."

She assumed Jake would stay put since he didn't argue.

"You left me," Christy accused with tears in her eyes when Charlie walked into the daycare. Christy's hands were on her little hips and her lower lip poked out. She glared at her mother with censure in her eyes. Her child was not easily angered, but Charlie knew she was in trouble. Guilt washed through her. She knew how sensitive her daughter was about being the last kid picked up and Charlie had always been careful to pick her up in a timely manner. This was yet another reason why allowing Jake into her life wasn't a good idea. He made her forget her responsibilities.

Charlie lifted her recalcitrant child into her arms and gave her a quick hug. "I'm sorry, sweetheart, I lost track of time, but I'll never let it happen again. Will you forgive me?"

Christy didn't look like she was ready to forgive so soon. "Bad Mommy," the child chastised.

"I know, sweetie, Mommy has been very bad."

Charlie could see Christy's anger wavering and decided to go in for the kill. "We can stop for ice cream on the way home. Would you like that?"

At the mention of ice cream, Christy's eyes lit up. "Ice cweam? Okay, I forgive you. Can I get cho'lat?"

"Sure." Charlie laughed. Christy was a tough negotiator.

"I should hope this wouldn't happen again, Ms. Brown. You are forty-five minutes late and, as I already pointed out on the phone, a late fee will be accessed," Sherri Farmer said, interrupting the mother-daughter moment. Charlie could never figure out how someone wound as tight as Sherri Farmer could end up running a daycare full of boisterous toddlers. Had the Ponderosa Day Care Center not come so highly recommended and her daughter hadn't made so many friends, Charlie would have taken Christy elsewhere.

"I understand. I'll write you a check." She gave Ms. Farmer a strained smile, not appreciating the woman's tone. "Christy, go get your things from your cubby." Charlie put her daughter down to dig in her purse for her checkbook.

"Okay, Mommy." Christy ran off to collect her belongings. Charlie wanted to point out that she'd never been late in picking up her daughter before, but she didn't feel like getting into a battle with this woman because she was likely to lose her temper. Besides, Jake was waiting outside for them.

"Is there a problem?" Jake asked, stepping forward. Charlie shook her head in disbelief. She didn't hear him enter the daycare center, but she should have known that he wouldn't listen by staying put.

"W-who are you?" Miss Farmer stammered when Jake approached them. Her tongue was practically falling out of her mouth at the sight of such a hunk.

"Jake Fox. I'm Christy's father." He held out his hand and gave the daycare provider a lopsided smile. It was the same smile that made Charlie's heart go pitter-patter. Why did he have to be so damn fine, Charlie wondered. Ms. Farmer blushed before shaking the offered hand. It was obvious the woman was smitten. "Now about that fee?" He extracted his wallet from his pocket.

"Well, I think we can let it slide this time. Christy is such a delight to have here at the Ponderosa and it was no problem at all," Sherri simpered, batting her eyelashes.

"Uh, do you have something in your eyes? You may want to go to the eyewash station over there." Charlie couldn't keep the sarcasm from her voice if she wanted to.

Ms. Farmer turned an unbecoming shade of red and shot Charlie a hostile look before turning back to Jake. Her smile returned. "Don't worry at all, Mr. Fox, that fee is no big deal at all. We were having so much fun while we were waiting for you, I barely noticed the time." Charlie rolled her eyes again. What a hypocrite. If Jake hadn't stepped forward, Charlie was well aware she would have been charged the late fee.

"Please call me Jake."

"Okay," the woman gushed. Charlie wanted to hurl. "And you must call me Sherri. Should you need my assistance for anything, please don't hesitate to call."

Jake's grin widened. The bastard. "I'll remember that."

Charlie scooped Christy up when she returned and headed outside. Jake seemed to be handling the dragon lady just fine. Did he have to be so charming to her? Charlie groaned. She couldn't be jealous. No way, no how. She was ticked about Ms. Farmer's readiness to break the rules for Jake and not for her. Yes, that had to be it. Wasn't it?

Jake caught up to them just as Charlie made it to the car. Christy stared at Jake and he stared back. The little girl was the first to speak. "Who are you, man?"

Charlie's heart skipped a beat. This was the moment of truth. Charlie and Jake exchanged glances and Charlie nodded. Jake turned his attention back to Christy.

"I'm your daddy," Jake said solemnly. His eyes filled with tears and Charlie couldn't help but be touched by Jake's look of uncertainty. A flicker of shame passed through her as she thought of her duplicity.

Christy's mouth formed a perfect O as she took in this bit of news. She cocked her little head to the side and looked at Jake for several moments. Christy turned to her mother. "I have a daddy, like Suzy?" she asked her mother.

Tears were threatening to spill from Charlie's eyes and she could only nod. "Suzy is her best friend this month," she explained to Jake.

147

Charlie hadn't realized Christy was aware of not having a father around. Sure her daughter was an intelligent child, but there were certain things Charlie took for granted. "Yes, sweetie. You have a daddy, right here," Charlie croaked, her voice full of emotion.

To Charlie's surprise, Christy held out her arms to her father. Jake sought eye contact with Charlie as if to gain approval. Charlie smiled and nodded in acquiescence.

Jake lifted his daughter into his arms for the first time and he squeezed her tight. Charlie could see the instant love in Jake's eyes, and she knew he and Christy belonged together.

"I can't breathe, Daddy," Christy protested, squirming within his tight grip.

Jake looked at Charlie with a big smile on his face. Christy had called him Daddy with such ease, almost as if they'd always been together.

Jake turned back to Christy looking sheepish. "I'm sorry, baby."

"I not a baby!" Christy huffed with exasperation.

"But you're my baby," Jake countered. Charlie should have warned Jake about Christy's aversion of being called a baby but the scene playing out amused her.

"No. I a big girl. Silly, Daddy." Christy laughed as if she'd just told the funniest joke. It was the most beautiful sound.

Charlie knew then Christy held Jake's heart in the palm of her little hand.

ℐщ

Jake stayed for dinner that night. He insisted on helping Charlie with Christy's bath and putting her to bed. It was obvious he fascinated Christy, just as she did him. Her eyes filled with wonder at his every move. When Jake and Charlie put her to bed for the night, Christy looked at Jake and smiled. "I glad I have a daddy."

Almost too choked with emotion to speak, Jake stroked his sleepy daughter's cheek. "I'm glad I have a daughter," he said, leaning over to kiss her forehead and refusing to leave her bedside until she'd fallen asleep. He took that time to study her features. She was perfect, from the top of her head filled with dark shiny curls to the tips of her tiny toes. His daughter. As he watched her, he vowed to protect and love her forever. Just as he intended to do with her mother.

"You're very good with her." Charlie said when Jake came out of Christy's bedroom. He appreciated Charlie giving him some time alone with their daughter.

"It's very easy to be good to her. She's a sweet girl." Jake fell in love with his daughter the moment he laid eyes on her. The fact that Christy looked so much like Charlie, Jake could only love her more. "She speaks well for a two-year-old. I don't think my youngest nephew spoke until he was three, and even now he has a bit of a speech impediment."

"She's extremely bright, but I started teaching her things right off the bat. I did the baby Einstein thing, flash cards, the whole nine yards. The only programs she's allowed to watch are on PBS. She loves *Sesame Street* and *unfortunately* Barney. That big purple monstrosity creeps me out."

"No Disney Channel or Nickelodeon? I know my nieces and nephews watch those channels religiously."

"No. Those shows are a little too old for her right now. I know I'm probably one of those overzealous parents, but I just want her to give her a head start. Besides, she likes to learn and she's very mature for her age."

"She's two going on thirty." Jake laughed.

"Don't say that," Charlie groaned. "I don't want my little girl to grow up so fast. As much as I love Christy, I'm already dreading her teenage years."

"I bet. That kid is going to be beating the guys off with a stick." Jake sighed, remembering what he was like as a teenage boy. He had a feeling that he would be in for a lot of gray hairs.

"Please don't remind me, Jake." Charlie laughed. "I've already thought about it. As a matter of fact, just before I started working at MBF, Christy got into a little trouble for punching a little boy on the nose. He was trying to kiss her apparently and wouldn't take no for an answer."

"Really? That's my girl." Jake grinned, imagining his tiny daughter belting some kid.

"I don't encourage violence, Jake, but it was kind of funny. I felt so bad because I had to lecture to her on why we shouldn't hit, all the while I was laughing on the inside." Charlie smiled in recollection. "Christy's really a good girl. She hardly ever gives me trouble and she always has a smile on her face. She has lots of friends at daycare and everyone who meets her tells me how well behaved she is." Charlie babbled.

He realized she was putting him off, but the time had come to get down to business. "Charlie, we need to talk." He took her hand and led her to the couch.

"What about?" she asked, a wary expression on her face.

"Well for one thing, we need to figure out how we're going to work out visitation arrangements."

"Oh. Okay."

Jake waited until Charlie made herself comfortable then took a seat on the couch next to her before he continued. "Obviously I would like to see her as much as possible, but I'll respect your wishes as well. I was thinking of having her every other weekend, holidays, and maybe a whole week once a month."

"But the weekends are when the two of us do things together and our holidays are special," Charlie protested. "Maybe you can have her one weekend a month and every other holiday?" she offered.

This wasn't going to be as easy as he thought.

"Be reasonable, Charlie, you've had her all to yourself up until now. She's nearly three and I've missed so much of her life, like her first steps, her first tooth and her first words. I don't want to miss anything else," he pointed out, hoping Charlie's sense of fairness would kick in.

"I really think we should start off with one weekend a month and then we'll see."

"What?" Jake jumped to his feet.

Charlie flinched.

"Just until she gets used to you," she amended in haste.

"At that rate she'll never get use to me."

Charlie looked down on at her feet. "I think my offer is fair, Jake."

"Fair to whom?" he demanded. What was Charlie playing at? Considering what had happened to them earlier that day, he thought that she would be more cooperative. He took a deep breath. *Calm down Jake, we can still work this out amicably.*

"Jake, keep your voice down or else you'll wake Christy up," Charlie shushed.

"Look, Charlie, I know you're probably worried I'll encroach on your time with Christy, but I just want to share in her life. Please see this from my point of view. I only found out yesterday that I have a daughter, but crazy as it may sound, I love her.

When she opened her arms to me earlier today, I didn't want to let her go. Charlie, I'd like to spend some time with her and I know we can work something out to both our satisfactions."

Charlie was silent for a moment before she spoke. "Jake, it takes two to compromise. Okay, we'll do every other weekend but we'll split the holidays. I think that's somewhere in the middle of what we both want."

Jake would have liked more, but he knew the deal was fair. If he had his way, he would have his daughter all the time along with her mother. "You have a deal. Can I have her next weekend? I promised my nieces I would take them to the zoo and they won't let me forget it. I think Christy would enjoy it."

Charlie paused.

"Charlie?"

"I'm sorry if it seems like I'm hedging, but it will be my first time away from her for more than the time at work. I'm so used to fixing her breakfast, putting her to bed and reading her a story."

"I may be a novice at those things, but I'll do my best. You do trust me with her, don't you?"

She nodded. "I trusted you with her the minute I saw you two together. I guess I'm just being an overprotective mom. Okay, you can have her next weekend, but I suggest you childproof your house. Christy is in her inquisitive phase. Sometimes she likes to take things apart to see how they work."

"I got it covered. My mother can help me with that stuff. Don't worry. I'm sure Christy will have a great time at the zoo."

"I think she'll really like it too. I'm sure she'll be thrilled to spend time with her new cousins," she agreed.

"Charlie?"

"Yes?"

"What about us?" Jake couldn't help asking.

Her eyes darted away from his. "What about us?"

"You know exactly what I mean. Where does this leave us?"

"Other than the fact that we have a daughter together, Jake, there is no us," Charlie denied.

"How can you say that after the way we made love earlier?" He glanced at her, wanting to pull her in his arms and prove once and for all they belonged together.

"We didn't make love. We fucked." Charlie was blunt in her assessment.

Jake's hackles were raised. It may have been fucking to her, but he had made love. "So is fucking all there is between us?" he challenged.

"No. There's nothing between us." She got up to pace the floor.

"You're starting to sound like a broken record, Charlie. You keep saying there is no us, but you melt in my arms each time.

"Not anymore," she protested.

Jake was behind her in an instant. He grabbed her shoulders and forcibly turned her around to face him.

"You're a liar, Charlie Brown." Jake pulled her body against his hardness. "I can feel your body responding to mine already. Your nipples are hard. They're poking through your shirt, waiting for my touch."

She opened her mouth to protest and then immediately closed it. He knew she didn't have a leg to stand on and so did she. Already Jack was rock hard and he needed her.

Bad.

He rubbed his stiffness against her thigh, desperate to be inside of her again. She pushed against his chest, but Jake's arms tightened around her. "Don't deny me, Charlie, especially when you know we both want this." Jake lowered his head.

He crushed her rose-petal-soft lips beneath his. His hunger for her knew no bounds. Charlie tried to twist her head away, but Jake cupped the back of her head, keeping it immobile.

She muttered something against his lips, but Jake was too aroused to hear what she said. His tongue shot out, demanding entry into her sweet mouth. With a sigh, Charlie leaned against his body, surrendering to the wave of passion created by their mutual desire. Jake took his time exploring her body, touching her breasts, her ass and her thighs. He loved the way she trembled within his arms.

Jake unzipped her jeans and slid his fingers between her legs, pushing past the silky fabric of her panties in order to touch her throbbing pussy. He was eager to feel her damp heat.

He slipped his middle finger between the moist folds. "Mmm, just how I like you—wet and ready for me."

Charlie wiggled, making his finger go deeper inside her hot sheath. She moaned. "Oh God, Jake! That feels so good. You always know how to touch me in all the right places."

Jake smiled, pleased he could give her so much pleasure. Her juices wet his hand as he continued to finger her. "Do you like this, sweetheart?" he whispered against her ear.

"You know I do," came her breathy reply.

With great reluctance, he removed his hand. He rubbed his dew-slicked fingers over her bottom lip. "Lick it. Taste how delicious you are."

Charlie obeyed, capturing her essence with her tongue. His cock twitched when he saw her seductive motion. The heat in the room must have gone up a hundred degrees, because he was on fire.

Jake then slid his fingers between her lips. "Suck them," he commanded in a whisper.

Charlie sucked the fingers into her mouth, her eyes never breaking contact with his. Jake realized he couldn't wait any longer. He had to have her now! Pulling his fingers away, he lifted Charlie off her feet and carried her the short distance to the couch.

Jake removed Charlie's clothes in a hurry, pressing hungry kisses against each inch of skin he exposed. He squeezed her breasts, but his mind was on her other prize. The heady scent beckoned him.

He dove into her waiting pussy and stabbed her slick channel with his tongue. Charlie squirmed beneath his mouth, grabbing his hair to pull his face closer to her. "Oh, Jake! Yes, just like that." Her moans were like music to his ears. He stroked her swollen labia, making Charlie sigh with delight. The taste of her didn't abate his hunger. The more he had, the more he wanted. She'd made him a glutton and he didn't care. Jake sucked on her clit voraciously, milking her pussy of its nectar.

As he brought her close to her peak, he looked up suddenly. "Do you want me, Charlie? Do you want this?" he asked, taking a broad lick on her exposed pussy as he maintained eye contact with her. Charlie nodded. "Say it. Tell me that you want me," he commanded.

"I want you," she whispered.

"Say my name. Say 'I want you, Jake,'" he ordered, sliding two fingers between her damp folds. When Charlie hesitated, he jammed in and out of her, harder and faster. "Say it!" he demanded again.

"I want you, Jake!" she complied.

Jake removed his wet fingers from Charlie's warm tunnel and licked them clean.

"Delicious."

When she looked at him, her were lips slightly parted and her eyes blazed with desire. It had been his intention to walk away. In his mind it would have proven once and for all how much she really wanted him, but he should have known it would backfire. Jake could no more walk away from her than he could cut off his air supply. With a groan, he stood up and tore his clothes away, not caring if he popped buttons or ripped material. He had to have her now.

He took a seat on the couch and pulled her on his lap, his cock pressing against her luscious rear. Cupping her face, he caught her mouth in a seeking kiss. This time Charlie's tongue darted out to meet his, initiating a seductive dance. Jake fondled her taut nipples, rolling the hard pebbles between his forefinger and thumb.

Charlie dug her fingers into his hair, deepening the kiss. She tasted sweet, tangy and wild. It drove Jake crazy how she gave herself so fully. The need to be one with her became more than he can bear. Ripping his mouth away from hers, he gasped for breath. "Straddle me, Charlie. Take me inside of you."

She wasted no time doing just that, throwing a slender thigh over his.

"That's it, honey, take my cock in your hand and guide it into you...that's it. Easy."

When Charlie stuffed him inside her soaking wet cunt, Jake groaned with pleasure, throwing his head against the couch, his eyes rolling in the back of his head. No matter how many times or ways they made love, she always managed to make Jake feel a burning lust that threatened to set them both aflame.

Jake gripped her hips, his fingers digging in to her flesh. Charlie wrapped her arms around him, bouncing up and down on his cock. Each time he was fully inside of her he hit her G-spot. Rational thought flew out the window whenever this man was involved. All she could think of was how good he felt. The responses he elicited from her were mind shattering.

With Paul, the loving had been wonderful, but different. It was gentle and sweet. With Jake, however, it was animalistic and raw, but no less satisfying. Jake brought her down on his cock, harder and faster, his hips bucking against her. She tightened her vaginal muscles around his member, sucking him deeper into her tunnel.

Hot flames of lust licked up her spine, creating a throbbing pressure in her body. "Jake, I'm going to come," she panted.

"Don't hold back, Charlie. Don't ever hold anything back from me."

Wrapping her arms around him, she buried her face against his neck. An explosion blasted within her when she reached her peak. Jake continued to thrust into her pussy, unrelenting. She writhed and shuddered against him, too weak to do anything but hold on.

"There's no denying this chemistry between us. You can try to fool yourself all you want, but your body knows who it belongs to." With a grunt, he pounded into her, before sending a stream of come into her pussy.

Jake's hands fell then, his breathing ragged.

Charlie lay against him, trying to make sense of what just happened. Dammit, she'd done it again. What the hell was wrong with her that she couldn't resist him? The token protest she'd given him at the beginning of their lovemaking had been a joke. Jake was a very dangerous man indeed. Charlie realized she had to nip this thing in the bud right now or he'd take what happened for granted.

When she tried to pull away from him, he grasped her waist. "Where's the fire?"

"Jake, please let me go. We shouldn't have done this."

"Charlie, you're starting to sound like a broken record. Why do you keep fighting so hard when you know this is how we always end up?"

"Let me go. Right now, Jake. Sometimes Christy gets up and asks for a drink of water." Actually, once Christy was down for the night, she slept like the dead, but Jake wouldn't know that.

At the mention of their daughter, Jake released her, a sullen drop to his sensual lips. "Why didn't you say something?"

Charlie wiggled off his lap and retrieved her clothes. "You never gave me a chance. You were too busy manhandling me."

"Don't give me that shit. You know damn well you wanted me, too."

"Could you just stop it? Why do you insist on pursing this so-called thing between us? Okay, I admit, you're attractive. Actually, you're fine as hell, but you know what, I don't need the complication of an *us* in my life. I can't shirk my responsibilities for something purely physical.

Jake stood up, grabbing his own clothing and putting them back on. His blue gaze bore into her with an intensity that made her shiver. "It's more than physical, Charlie, and you know it. I don't know what your deal is, but it's time you faced reality. What we have is special and I won't let you pretend anymore," he warned.

"What exactly do we have other than sex, Jake? Can't you see I don't want to get involved with you? Or with anyone for that matter," she said stubbornly. "I have no choice concerning Christy, but I do have a say in how I want to run my life, and I can't have you in it."

"Why, Charlie?"

"Because...I...I just don't want to." She looked away from his probing stare. Why must he persist? Charlie wished he'd just leave well enough alone. She didn't think she had the strength to love anyone the way she had Paul, and the sooner she made him see it, the better. But how?

Jake looked at her for a long moment before speaking. "You may not want there to be anything between us, but there is. Look, I'm not going to stand here and argue with you about something we both know is true. Tomorrow morning I'm flying out of town for business. I'll be back on Saturday in time to pick you and Christy up to take to my parents. I'll be here about six." He grabbed her forearm and pulled her against him, then dropped a swift kiss on her lips. Jake stepped back not giving her a chance to protest.

"I wish you wouldn't kiss me without my permission."

"Oh, but I had it. Every time you look at me, the way your lips tremble and body quivers, it's like an open invitation to do whatever I please to you. Why else do you go up in flames when you're in my arms?"

Why did she indeed? "Goodnight, Jake." Arguing with him was futile.

"I'll see you Saturday," he said, stopping at the threshold.

She nodded, walking him to the door, all while keeping her distance. When he was gone, she flopped onto the recliner with a loud sigh.

Charlie sat there for a long time before moving. Jake had made a fool of her, by exploiting her weaknesses where he was concerned, but she only had herself to blame. He was right about her. She wanted him like mad. If she were being honest with herself, not even Paul had brought her body to the frenzy that Jake did.

Paul had been an excellent lover, considerate and giving, but for some reason, her traitorous body clamored for Jake's. She wished he didn't have such a strong hold over her, but he did. Then it came to her. Why keep fighting it when she knew she'd never win? Perhaps if she took charge of the situation, she'd be able to keep her emotions under control. That was it! She'd call the shots from now on.

It was just sex, right? Just because she wanted him physically didn't mean they had to get involved further than the bedroom. *Okay, Mr. Fox, you want my body? Then you can have it, but that's all you can have.*

Chapter Twelve

Charlie had just finished cleaning her house when the doorbell rang. Her heart did a flip-flop when she opened the door to find a casually dressed Jake. She had only ever seen him in business suits so far, but tonight he wore a pair of jeans that clung to his lean hips and tight buns, and indecently outlined the large bulge between his legs. Dark tufts of hair peeked out from the vee of his black crew neck shirt, which served to enhance the masculinity of his sinewy torso. Charlie's mouth watered.

Jake carried an armful of toys. He gave her a sheepish grin when Charlie raised an eyebrow at his gifts. "I couldn't help myself. Where is she, by the way?"

"She's in her playroom, putting the finishing touches on your present."

"A present for me?"

Charlie didn't have a chance to answer him.

"Daddy!" Christy screeched, running to Jake. Christy had talked non-stop about him the entire week. Jake's face lit up when he saw his daughter. He put his armload down in a hurry and lifted the little girl in his arms and twirled her around. Christy giggled, enjoying her father's attention. When Jake stopped spinning her, he gave the child a big hug and kiss.

"How's Daddy's big girl today?"

"Super! Daddy, I drawed you a picture," Christy had been eager to show off her drawing since she'd created it.

"You did? Can I see it?" he asked.

"Sure. Put me down," she ordered and then ran to her room once she was on her feet again.

"She amazes me every time I see her," Jake said.

"She's an amazing kid," Charlie agreed.

"I suppose her drawing is the present you referred to."

"It's not just any present. She doesn't draw pictures for just anyone. I appreciate you inviting us to your parents' for dinner tonight. Christy has been looking forward to this visit all week. She couldn't stop talking about you," Charlie explained. "Thanks for calling every night while you were away. Christy enjoyed talking to you. She's at the stage where she loves talking on the phone."

"No problem. I missed her." He smiled.

"I never realized that she knew she didn't have a father, but I guess most of the kids at daycare talk about their fathers and Christy is so smart...I just never thought...I mean, she never mentioned it. I should have known." She made a clumsy attempt at explaining her predicament.

"Don't worry about it, Charlie. It's the past. I'm here now, so we won't talk about it again."

"But—"

Jake placed a finger over her lips.

"We won't talk about it again," he repeated.

"Daddy, look at my picture." Christy returned, tugging on Jake's pant leg to gain his attention.

Jake took her drawing and scrutinized it as if he were a die-hard art critic. Charlie appreciated that Jake was making such a big deal over the picture although she knew it was just a bunch of squiggles on a piece of paper. She could tell Christy was thrilled.

"It's beautiful, sweetheart. Can I keep it?"

"Sure. I drawed it for you." Christy rolled her eyes.

Jake chuckled, making eye contact with Charlie. "I was right. She's definitely a thirty-year-old trapped in a two-year-old's body.

Charlie smiled at the picture father and daughter made. "Don't I know it," she replied.

He turned his gaze back to Christy, smiling indulgently at her. "You look pretty today, sweetie. Did you pick out your outfit yourself?"

"Mommy did, but I helped." Christy seemed quite proud of herself.

She looked adorable in a mini jean skirt and a pink T-shirt. Her two curly pigtails were tied with little pink ribbons. Charlie was usually very diligent about how Christy looked when she left the house, but she was extra careful dressing her child tonight. The last thing she wanted was for Jake's family to find fault in anything concerning Christy.

"I brought something for you, too, sweetie," Jake said to the two-year-old.

Christy's eyes widened at all the gifts before her. Jake had brought several stuffed animals and a doll.

"If she didn't love you before, she'll love you forever now. She already has so many toys, though," Charlie pointed out.

"Not from her father. Look at this one." Jake handed Charlie a doll with *café au lait* skin and blue eyes like Christy's.

"I didn't realize they made dolls like this." Charlie examined the obviously expensive toy. The quality of the toy shouted money.

"They have a shop in San Diego, that's where I was, by the way, that specializes in making dolls. You can have them customized to your specification."

"You must have spent a lot of money."

"That's inconsequential where my daughter is concerned."

He sounded so proprietary already. Charlie knew it was wrong, but she felt a slight twinge of jealousy at Jake's lack of concern for finances. She bit it back, not wanting to be petty. "She'll really like this doll. You're going to spoil her with all this stuff." Charlie sighed.

He shrugged. "So what? I have two and a half years of gift giving to make up for." At the mention of Jake's two year absence from their daughter's life, Charlie clammed up.

Jake squeezed her hand. "It wasn't meant as a criticism, Charlie. I passed the toyshop and I wanted to buy her something. By the time I finished, I had a shopping cart full of things. As a matter of fact there are more toys at my place, but I thought I'd keep them there, for when she visits me."

"I know you didn't mean to criticize, Jake. Here, give her the doll." She handed the toy back to him.

Just as Charlie predicted, Christy was enthralled by the doll that "looked like her".

"So are you ready to go?"

"Yes. Let me go get our jackets." Charlie headed to the coat closet.

Jake turned to Christy "Alright, kiddo, we have to get going." Jake affectionately tugged on one of Christy's pigtails.

"Okay," Christy agreed. "Can I take my toys?" she asked Jake.

"Maybe not all of them. I think just one will be okay. Which one do you want to take?" he asked.

"Can I take my doll?"

"You sure can. How about putting your jacket on?" Jake said, taking Christy's jacket from Charlie's hand.

Charlie watched on the sidelines, annoyed at how Christy had deferred to Jake instead of her.

Little traitor.

⅚∟

Charlie didn't know what to expect when she met the Foxes. All week she fretted about what they would be like, wondering what they'd think of her. Would they be snobby? Would they look at her with disdain because of what she had done to Jake? Would they be uncomfortable about the fact their son had had an affair with some strange black woman? Jake had already assured her his parents didn't care about race, but she still had her doubts.

Charlie trembled, a wave of nervousness spreading through her body. Oh, why did she agree to this dinner? She just knew they would hate her. Her heart beat faster as they pulled up to a large modernized farmhouse in the suburb of Fairfax. The house was surrounded by a rose garden. By the look of the well-kept garden, Charlie could tell the people who lived here took pride in their home

Before they walked through the door, Jake, with Christy in one arm, looked over to Charlie and smiled. "Don't worry, Charlie. My family will love you." He gave her a tender look, taking her hand in his, and Charlie relaxed a bit, knowing she had Jake's support. At times like this, she wished that she wasn't such a coward. She wished she could let go and love him.

A short, pleasantly plump woman with a huge smile greeted them at the door. "Come in. Welcome. Jake, we were wondering what was keeping you."

"Hi, Mom. I was going to call, but I forgot to charge my cell phone, so the battery is pretty much kaput," he explained, leaning down to kiss her cheek. "Mom, I'd like you to meet Charlie Brown, and this is Christy. Charlie, this is my mom Moira Fox."

Jake's mother seemed quite friendly. If she felt any animosity toward Charlie, she hid it well. "It's very nice to meet you, Charlie. Jake has said so many wonderful things about you. I expected you to be pretty, but his description didn't do you justice."

Charlie shot Jake a curious look. He gave her a sheepish grin.

"Thank you for having us." Charlie smiled hoping her nervousness didn't show.

"It's my pleasure, dear."

Charlie felt immediately at ease in this woman's presence. If the rest of the family were as nice, the night would go smooth.

Moira turned to her attention to Christy. "Hi, sweetie, you must be Christy."

"Who are you, lady?" Christy blinked at the stranger.

"I'm Nana." Moira gave Christy a warm smile.

"This is my mother, honey."

Christy took a moment to process this. "Like Mommy's Mommy?"

"Yep," Jake said.

"Grandma?" Christy asked.

"Yes, but you can call me Nana. Just like your cousins," Moira said.

"Okay. Hi, Nana. Wanna see my doll?" Christy practically shoved her toy in Moira's face.

Moira laughed. "Oh, Jake, she is a delight. And she's just as cute as a button." Her warm hazel eyes welled up for a second. Charlie watched the exchange still holding Jake's hand, relieved Jake's mother seemed to accept her granddaughter so readily.

Moira was examining the doll under Christy's watchful eyes. "Daddy gived it to me," Christy explained with an air of importance.

"She's a cutie. What's her name?" Moira asked.

"I haven't sided yet, but I'll let you know," Christy said, taking her doll back.

"And she's only two?" Moira asked of Christy's extensive vocabulary.

"Amazing isn't it?" Jake grinned like the proud father he was.

"Well, I'm not that surprised. You were putting full sentences together around Christy's age." A tear spilled from Moira's eye. "Oh, dear me. Now I'm crying like an old fool." She sniffed.

Christy leaned over to touch Moira's cheek. "Don't cry, Nana. You can hold her some more." Christy handed her doll back to Moira.

This only made Moira tear up more. She took Christy from Jake and gave her granddaughter a quick hug. By the end of the exchange, all three adults were misty eyed. "I gotta tinkle," Christy announced, interrupting the moment with her immediate need.

"Uh-oh, we have to get her to a bathroom fast. She's recently potty trained, so she doesn't tell you she has to go until it's almost too late. Where's the bathroom?" Charlie asked.

"I'll take her." Jake took Christy out of his mother's arms.

"Good idea. Then take her into the living room. Carl and Helen are here with their families. Charlie and I can get to know each other."

"You didn't say anyone else would be here." Jake furrowed his brow.

"Well, they could hardly stay away after they heard the news. Everyone is anxious to meet Charlie and Christy."

"I gotta tinkle," Christy said, with more impatience this time.

"Get her to the bathroom quick, Jake," Charlie said nervously. Oh dear Lord, this is exactly what she didn't need, Christy to piss all over these people's floor.

Jake turned to Charlie looking as though he didn't want to leave her alone with his mother so soon after their arrival. Charlie nodded, letting him know she would be okay. Jake hesitated before he rushed off with Christy in tow. Charlie crossed her fingers in hopes they would make it to the restroom on time.

When they were gone, Charlie stood alone in the hallway with Jake's mother. Charlie shifted on her feet. What must this woman be thinking? Shrewd hazel eyes accessed Charlie for a moment before Moira spoke. "I'm so pleased that you could join us tonight. I'm glad to finally meet you and Christy. My other two granddaughters will be pleased to have another girl in the family."

Charlie looked at Jake's mother in surprise. She'd been so sure Jake's mom would let her have it the minute Jake walked out of the hallway. "Thank you again for having us, Mrs. Fox."

Charlie was humbled by the warm greeting but still waited for the ball to drop. There had to be a catch somewhere.

"Don't you give me that Mrs. Fox crap. I'm Moira, and when you meet my husband, he's Bill," Moira scolded.

"Thank you."

"Christy is a lovely child. She seems very comfortable with strangers," Moira observed.

"Yes, she normally likes everyone. I don't know if it's a good or bad thing, especially with so many nuts out there who would snatch a child without a thought. Part of me wants her to keep her innocence, while another part of me wants her to understand there are bad people out there. She's so good-natured and sweet, I don't think she would grasp the concept right away." Charlie tried her best to explain the situation and hoped the other woman wouldn't hold a grudge.

"Well, I don't know about that. Jake was the same way when he was a child, but I wouldn't worry too much. I can already tell how smart she is. I think she'll know a bad guy when she sees one." Moira reassured. "I sometimes think children, especially the younger ones, understand and see far more than we as adults do."

At the mention of Jake's name, Charlie tensed. "Moira, I don't know what Jake told you about our situation, but I'm sorry," Charlie said remorsefully, feeling the need to unburden her guilt.

The older woman gave her a funny smile. "Sorry for what, dear?"

"Didn't he tell you?" Charlie was baffled.

"Well, he did tell me he didn't know about Christy until recently and he had met you a few years back, but I also know there are two sides to every story."

So Jake had told his mother. Why wasn't she angry? "You mean you're not mad at me?"

"Why should I be? You've given me a beautiful granddaughter. I despaired of Jake ever settling down and having children. I can't exactly say I approve of what you did, but in time, when you're ready to tell me your side of the story, I will be happy to listen."

"But Jake and I aren't together in the way you may think," Charlie blurted out.

Moira gave her conspiratorial wink. "If you say so, dear. I just wanted to put your mind at ease before you met the rest of the brood. You're very welcome here and we're glad to have you. I hope we can see Christy with some regularity."

Charlie was humbled by this woman's kindness and she felt at ease with Moira Fox.

"Now let's go meet the rest of the family." Moira took Charlie's hand and lead her to the living room.

Charlie entered the living room to see a set of twins fawning over her daughter with delight and a few adults hovering over her. Christy seemed to be on cloud nine from all the attention she was receiving. Charlie was relieved to see Jake had made it to the bathroom on time with Christy.

Jake was talking to a man who could only be his father; they were so close in looks. They might have been twins if the older man wasn't grayer. Father and son were roughly the same height and build and shared the same startling eye color. Jake stood when Charlie and his mother walked in the room. He smiled at Charlie, taking her arm. "Charlie, I would like you to meet the rest of my family. This is my father Bill." Jake indicated the man who Charlie had already guessed was his father.

Bill Fox gave her a big smile, leaning over to give her a kiss on the cheek, and Charlie immediately knew where Jake had gotten his charm. "It's very nice to finally meet you. Thank you for bringing Christy to us. She is an angel."

"Thank you." She smiled back, liking Jake's father right off the bat.

Jake steered Charlie around. "This is my brother Carl. He's the jokester of the family, or at least he thinks so."

Charlie giggled as she shook hands with Carl. He took after his mother in looks but was still a very well put together man. "You'll soon learn Jake is a terrible liar. He's just jealous because I'm the favorite." Carl winked at her.

"Oh, Carl, you're going to scare the poor woman off." A redhead walked over to them. She wore a friendly expression on her face, looking at Charlie with curiosity.

"This woman is Saint Bridget. She's a saint for being married to my brother for so long," Jake explained to Charlie.

"Nice to meet you, hon, and those two carrot tops over there, fawning over your little darling are our daughters Kara and Kammy. They were thrilled to learn there was another girl in the family." Bridget pointed to the twins playing with Christy.

"You need to meet a few more people." Jake took Charlie's hand, leading her to the other side of the room where a blonde woman sat in a chair, giving her a cool stare. Charlie felt a little uncomfortable under the woman's direct gaze. "This is my sister Helen. Her bark is far worse than her bite. Her husband is downstairs with their little holy terrors playing video games."

The blonde didn't look amused. "Very cute, Jake. How do you do, Charlie?"

Charlie didn't feel any warmth in Helen's greeting, but everyone else seemed nice, so maybe she was imagining it.

"It's nice to meet you." Charlie smiled at Helen, who didn't return it. Just then a tall, dark black man entered the room, followed by four loud little boys who were clearly biracial. A smile crossed Helen's face then.

"That's Helen's husband, Jason, and their sons Jason Jr., Mark, Dylan and Caleb," Jake said to Charlie as he drew closer. She gave Jake a look. This must have been what he meant when he'd said race didn't matter to his family.

Jason had a broad, welcoming grin on his face, when he and Charlie shook hands.

Jake's family was a joy. Being an only child, Charlie often wished for siblings. From what she could tell, Jake was very close to Carl and Helen. They all teased each other mercilessly like a bunch of kids, but anyone could see the mutual love and respect they all shared for each other.

Charlie liked every single member of the Fox family. Bill Fox, the patriarch, had a laid-back charm that put Charlie at ease. She liked the way he would wink or smile at Moira every now and then throughout the course of the night. It warmed her heart to see the elder Foxes still obviously in love.

At dinner she learned Carl was indeed the jokester of the family. He had the whole table cracking up throughout the entire meal. Jake's sister, Helen, was the kind of person to "tell it like it is", yet anyone could see her heart was as big as her mouth. Helen was the type who was fiercely loyal to her family and friends.

Even the kids were great. Christy was especially thrilled at all her newfound cousins. The nine-year-old twins had taken to Christy and she to them. The boys were rambunctious as four-, five-, six- and seven-year-olds would be, but basically, they were good kids. The evening was turning out better than she thought it would.

৪৩

As the night progressed, Charlie saw sides of Jake that she hadn't realized he possessed. He was the caring son, the playful brother, and the protector. Jake was never far away from her or Christy the entire evening, making sure everything went smoothly for them. Charlie could feel a tug on her heartstrings each time she made eye contact with him during the course of dinner. She found herself enjoying her visit so much that when it was time to get going, she felt a little sad.

When the families were standing around talking and getting ready to leave, Charlie stood apart from them all and observed the camaraderie. She leaned against the wall and watched them with envy.

This family represented all she had wished for with Paul. The love shown by the husbands in attendance to their wives was touching. Charlie had that special bond with someone once. She missed that feeling of being loved and cherished more than she cared to admit. Charlie smiled wistfully, thinking about how her life with Paul could have been.

She and Paul would have a couple of children together by now. Paul had been good with children. He had been a volunteer at a local boys and girls club. The kids he had mentored loved him. Knowing what a generous and kind-hearted man he had been, she knew Paul wouldn't begrudge her relationship with Christy.

She was confused about how she felt about Jake. On the one hand, Jake brought her to heights of rapture she only thought existed in romance books. Charlie had already decided they would become lovers if he brought up the subject again, but could she allow him to become more? On the other hand,

Jake seemed to want more than she was willing to give. She was so confused. The one thing she did know for sure was she couldn't put herself through the hurt of loving someone deeply again, only to lose them.

Jake Fox posed a big threat. Every so often he would sneak into her thoughts and she would banish his image from her mind. There was no way she could allow him to creep into her heart, which she feared he was already doing more and more each day. It was already bad enough she conceded to her physical needs, but to allow herself to feel more just couldn't happen.

"A penny for your thoughts." Jake approached her with a smile on his face.

"I was just thinking about my husband." Charlie said the first thing that popped in her mind, and not wanting him to know he was the center of her thoughts.

Charlie looked away from his suddenly pale face.

"I see." In one abrupt motion he turned and left Charlie alone once more. Charlie watched his retreating figure. She had the sudden urge to call him back, but thought better of it.

"Charlie, I'm glad to finally get a chance to talk to you without everyone else crowding around." Charlie looked around to see Jake's sister approach. Helen wasn't smiling.

"Hi." Charlie felt wary all of a sudden. She didn't think she had the emotional strength to deal with whatever Helen wanted to get off her chest. During dinner, Charlie had thought she caught Helen glaring at her a couple of times, but the other woman would immediately look away. Now Charlie knew she hadn't imagined the hostility.

"It was nice you could come join us for dinner tonight. Christy is a little angel." There was no warmth in the other woman's eyes.

Charlie went on the defensive.

"Yes, I got pretty lucky with Christy," Charlie answered cautiously.

"Jake obviously adores her," Helen pointed out.

"Yes, and Christy adores Jake. Helen, I get this feeling Jake and Christy's feelings for each other isn't what you want to talk about."

Helen looked as if she were biting her tongue. "I understand you've worked for Jake's company for several months now, yet he's just found out about his daughter's existence?" Helen asked caustically.

Charlie sighed. *Here we go.* She knew she'd been in the wrong for what she'd done, but Charlie didn't appreciate Helen's tone. "Yes, that's correct."

"How could you do that to him? Everyone else might be skirting around the issue as if everything is fine and dandy, but I'm not. I was here when he came to Mom, practically in tears. What kind of woman are you to do something so rotten? How could you keep Christy from him?" Helen demanded through narrowed eyes.

"I'm sure nothing I could say at this moment will satisfy you, but I had my reasons. Reasons that are none of your business," Charlie replied with a calm she didn't feel. She didn't want to stand here arguing with Helen in front of Jake's family, but she wouldn't be cowed by her either.

Helen's face turned scarlet at Charlie's reply. She was obviously a woman who was used to getting her way. "It is my business when you mess with my family. Jake is my brother, and I love him. After what you've done, you have a lot of nerve to show your face around here." Helen tossed her blonde hair back in an angry gesture.

Helen looked as if she wanted to slap Charlie silly. Charlie silently counted to ten before she spoke. "I don't want to argue with you, Helen. I know what I did was wrong, but like I said, I don't want to get into those reasons. And the only person I owe an explanation to is Jake. Besides, my reasons shouldn't be important to you. The important issue here is Christy and Jake. They adore each other, and I won't stand in the way of their relationship."

Helen's eyes were still narrowed, but her words lost a lot of their bite when she next spoke. "And what about you and Jake?"

"What about us? He's my daughter's father." Charlie shrugged.

"I see," Helen said slowly. "Don't jerk my brother around or you'll have me to deal with," Helen threatened before turning around, leaving Charlie standing on the wall watching her angry figure retreat.

What had Helen been implying about her and Jake? Although the evening had started off great, she was relieved when Jake returned with her coat. She didn't avoid eye contact with Helen as everyone said their goodbyes.

On the way home, Christy slept in her car seat, wiped out from the night's events. Jake wasn't in a talkative mood. In fact, every attempt Charlie made at conversation Jake either ignored or answered with one syllable retorts. Charlie finally gave up and they drove the rest of the way home in silence.

When they arrived at her house, Jake carried a still sleeping Christy inside. They both put their daughter to bed. After they left Christy's room, Charlie turned to him. "Jake, I had a nice time tonight. I liked your family." She omitted her confrontation with Helen.

"They liked you, too. Well, I guess I'd better be heading out. I'll see you on Monday. By the way, I'll have a support check for you." He was so formal.

Charlie was stunned by Jake's coldness. What had happened tonight that made him do a one-eighty turn from his happy contentedness earlier?

She made one last effort to bring Jake to a friendlier disposition.

"Would you like to stay for coffee?" Her mouth said stay for coffee, but her eyes said stay for more.

Jake paused, but only for a second. "No, thanks. I'm actually kind of tired. Goodnight, Charlie."

"Oh...goodnight, Jake."

Why did it bother her so much to see him go?

Chapter Thirteen

The minute she got out of bed, Charlie knew it was going to be a bad day. Christy was extra sluggish and fussy. It took longer than usual for her car to start, and she broke a heel, all before eight o' clock in the morning. By the time she got into the office, she felt an impending sense of doom.

She was about to go into her cubicle when she saw Sandy approaching. Oh dear God. The woman was a plague. This is not how I wanted to start the day, Charlie thought warily, but she pinned a smile on her face. The best defense was a good offense.

"Good morning, Sandy, how are you today?" She didn't want to hear the answer, but did the polite thing and waited for a response nonetheless.

"Oh, I'm good. I had a wonderful weekend. I stayed with some friends at their beach house. It was gorgeous. My friends have the hugest house on the Jersey Shore I've ever seen. I sat by the beach, soaked in the sun and drank mimosas," Sandy bragged.

"How nice for you." Charlie didn't give a damn, but figured those were the appropriate words to say. "Well, I have to get to work now, I hope you have a good Monday." Charlie took a seat at her desk.

Sandy followed. "What did you do this weekend?"

Didn't this woman have work to do? Charlie couldn't remember ever seeing Sandy doing any work, but she did see her quite often running her mouth. "My weekend was nice, thank you for asking." Charlie didn't care to elaborate. She knew any grain of information she gave to "The Mouth" would be the topic of conversation by noon.

Sandy's eyes narrowed. Charlie pretended she didn't notice Sandy's venomous look. She refused to play games with this woman, especially one so annoying. Charlie was familiar with her type, a gossipmonger who needed to constantly be in the know, when most things weren't her business.

Since Charlie began working at MBF, she was aware Sandy had been making inquiries about her, trying to dig up some dirt. She didn't know what it was the woman got out of gossiping, but it was grating. "Charlie, I know they call me 'The Mouth' behind my back, but you can trust me. I wouldn't dream of telling your little secret." Sandy gave her a smile that didn't quite reach her blue eyes.

The other woman was obviously fishing. Charlie had been very careful to keep her private life and work life separate. "And what secret might that be, Sandy?"

The woman pouted in obvious frustration at her failed attempt to get information. "Anything you might want to get off your chest. I'm a good listener."

"It's not your listening skills I question, but your lack of discretion. Look, don't you have some work to do, Sandy? Because if you don't, I do." Charlie gave her the stare down hoping it would embarrass Sandy enough to go away, but she should have known better. The Mouth didn't know the meaning of the word shame.

"I'm just trying to be friendly. There's no need to play the ice queen with me."

Charlie's fingers itched to slap the bitch into next week. Instead of giving in to her urges, she ignored the pesky woman, but Sandy did not seem to want to go away.

"So, Charlie, did you figure out who your secret admirer was?" An assessing gleam twinkled in her eyes.

Charlie paused. "No. I haven't." The moment the words left her mouth she realized they'd come out too fast, making her seem guilty.

A sly smile spread across Sandy's face. "Hmm, how odd. You would think you'd have found out by now. This person must be an awful loser," Sandy mused.

The only loser around here is you, Charlie wanted to say, but instead she shrugged, showing a nonchalance she didn't feel. "Perhaps he's shy, I don't know, and really it's not something that's keeping me up at night. I really have to get some work done and I suggest you do the same." Charlie's patience faded.

Sandy didn't look happy. "Okay, I will talk to you later. Maybe the next time we talk, you'll have found something out." Sandy's smile didn't quite reach her eyes.

"Maybe. See you later."

Charlie was glad to see that creature go. One day, Sandy would get her comeuppance and Charlie was positive a lot of people would cheer because of it.

"Is everything okay, Charlie?" Brian approached her.

"Yes, everything is cool. I guess I just have the Monday morning blues," she said.

"That's understandable. Was Sandy giving you problems? I've told her a thousand times not to hang out in my department."

"She doesn't bother me. I guess it just amazes me she still has a job. Since I've been here, all I've seen her do is hang out in other people's cubes and gossip," Charlie observed.

"She's cousins with the head of the admin." She could hear the disgust in his voice. "Personally, I would like nothing more than to see the back of her, but you know how things are."

She didn't actually, but then again, this wasn't her company to run, she only worked for it. "Relative or not, if she's not getting the job done, why do they keep her on?"

"Habit, I guess. It's hard to fire people nowadays without the threat of a wrongful dismissal suit, and she would definitely be the type to file one."

"I guess." Wanting to change the subject from that horrid woman, she asked, "Did you need to see me for something?"

"Yes. I just wanted remind you that I'm going away tomorrow on that business trip. Is there anything you needed to go over today?"

"Not really, I have everything pretty much under control."

"Okay, but if you need me for something, come by my office. And chin up, the day can only get better, right?" he said with a smile. Brian really was a darling. His positive outlook on life was always uplifting. Maybe everything would be all right.

If Charlie would have known how far from the truth those words were, she just might have turned around and gone home.

ಬಂಡ

"Jake...Jake? Are you there?" Jennifer's voice shouting through the intercom shook Jake from his daydream.

"Yes, I'm here, Jen. What's up?" he asked.

"Your ten o' clock is here. Shall I send them in?"

"Give me five minutes, Jen."

"Will do." She signed off.

Jake closed his eyes to get himself together. He'd been daydreaming about Charlie's comment on Saturday night. It seemed to him that she was still hung up on her deceased husband after all these years.

When he had noticed Charlie standing off to the side with a dreamy expression in her eyes while everyone else was saying good-bye, he thought she fit in so well with his family. Throughout dinner, he felt his connection with her had grown stronger than ever. Jake had been so sure Charlie was starting to warm toward him, especially when she would shoot him a smile every so often and hold his gaze purposely, as if they had been sharing a secret.

He'd wanted to know what she was thinking as she stood there. He'd wanted to know where her faraway look came from. Jake needed to know if that faint smile on her sexy lips had been due to the fact she enjoyed spending time with his family and especially with him. His heart had been so full of hope it had been a shock when she let slip that she was thinking about her husband. After that incident his night had turned sour.

Charlie was the master of emotional paper cuts. He walked away from her then like a wounded animal. He was in such a foul mood after her admission he could barely speak to her.

As he was leaving her house, he could have sworn he'd seen the look of desire in her eyes when she asked him to stay for coffee, but he convinced himself it was just wishful thinking on his part.

Jake didn't know how he could continue to fight for Charlie when his love was not being returned. He especially didn't know how he was going to compete with a ghost. He raked his fingers through his hair and let out a deep breath. How much more could one man take?

"Okay, Jen. You can send them in now."

ৠৈ ৠৈ

"Look, Steve, this has got to stop." Charlie spoke with a calm she didn't feel, annoyed at being ambushed yet again by the persistent man. This time he had caught her in the copy room making copies.

"Charlie, you won't regret going out with me. I will treat you like a queen," Steve said, taking Charlie's hands in his.

Charlie wrenched them out of his grip. "This is becoming embarrassing, Steve. How many times do I have to say no before you leave me alone? I'm sure this is embarrassing for you as well. Why do you keep asking me out when I keep saying no?" she asked warily. He really wasn't a bad guy. She could tell by the way he acted around the office. With the exception of Laura, most people enjoyed working with Steve. If she could only make him see how ridiculous it was for him to continuously ask her out, the better.

"I'm persistent in what I want and I want you," he said huskily.

"But I don't want you. Don't you hear yourself? You sound like a spoiled child," Charlie snapped, quickly losing her patience.

"You cut me to the quick. I'll keep asking until you give in. If you were to go out with me for one date, I promise, it'll be magic," Steve said smoothly, giving her the smile Charlie was sure he thought many ladies would fall to their knees for. She was tempted to laugh in his face.

The only magic Charlie wanted to see Steve performing was a disappearing act. "Steve, please stop. Take me on my word, and realize, I don't want to date you. I think you're a nice guy, but that's the extent of my feelings for you. We'll never have anything beyond a working relationship. You've asked me out at least a dozen times, and I've turned you down a dozen times, but you persist. If you keep asking, the answer won't change." Charlie tried to say it as gently as she could. If this joker said one more thing, she was going to let him have it.

"Charlie, you say no, but I know you'll eventually say yes. They all do in the end." He smirked arrogantly.

That did it. "Can't you get it through your thick skull I'm not interested, nor will I ever be interested. As a matter of fact, if you and I were the last people on earth, mankind would end with us," Charlie lashed out. She wasn't out to hurt the guy's feelings but enough was enough. Even she had her limits, and it was time for this office Romeo to get a clue.

Steve paled underneath his deep tan. He looked pissed, Charlie surmised. He probably wasn't used to rejection. "So I guess it's true."

"What's true?" Charlie asked nonplussed.

"You do prefer Jake. What's pretty boy got that I don't?" he demanded.

"What do you know about me and Jake?" Charlie's heartbeat sped up. Did Jake tell Steve what had happened?

"I have eyes. I know what happened in his office that day I saw you running out with the smell of sex clinging enticingly to your body." Steve must have realized he'd gone too far because his eyes widened, but the damage had already been done.

Charlie glared at him. "You're disgusting. Laura was right about you."

He paused. "Laura? What did she say about me?" Steve had a panicked look in his eyes.

"Ask her yourself," Charlie snapped. "Please don't bother me again, Steve, because the next time I'll be forced to take action."

"I'm sorry. I shouldn't have said what I did."

"But you did and now there's no taking it back. Now will you leave me alone?"

"If you preferred Jake, you should have said so in the first place."

She rolled her eyes. "Somehow I don't think that would have mattered to you."

He shot her a resentful look before turning on his heel and stalking away.

Charlie knew it was his vanity which drove him to continuously ask her out. She wasn't fool enough to think he was actually serious about her. Had she gone out with him the first time he asked, Steve would have lost interest by now. He'd get over it, and if he didn't that was just too damn bad. When she turned to leave the copy room, Charlie froze. Standing there with a smug expression on her face was Sandy the Mouth.

ഇൗങ

Jake was pissed. Everywhere he had gone in the building today, knowing looks followed. In the beginning he ignored them, but then curiosity got the better of him so he finally asked Jennifer what was being said around the office.

"Steve has a lot to answer for," Jake pounded his fist against Jennifer's desk.

"I wouldn't mind giving him a good smack myself. I shudder to imagine what he's done to that poor girl's reputation." Jennifer shook her head.

"I know. Steve can be a selfish bastard at times, but I didn't know he would stoop so low." Jake sighed. Steve had really gone too far this time and when Jake saw him, friend or not, Steve was going to get what was coming to him.

"You do realize what happened in your office was highly inappropriate," Jennifer reprimanded lightly.

Jake felt the color drain from his face. "I know, Jen. I'm as much at fault in this whole thing as is Steve." He sighed in resignation. "I know how inappropriate it was for me to do what I did, but he had no right to spread what happened all over the damn office. I never thought he'd stoop so low. It wasn't her fault. I was just...so..." Jake blushed.

"In love?" she guessed accurately.

"Is it that obvious?"

"You should have seen yourself before she came to your office that day. You were more nervous than a deer in a lion's den. Jake, I have two sons and two daughters, who are all older than you. Don't you think I would know a little something about this?" Jennifer paused for a moment. "You never did tell me about that scene in the lobby last week."

Jake figured she'd know soon enough anyway. Why not tell her? Taking a deep breath, he confessed. "That little girl you saw in the lobby was my daughter Christy."

"I know."

He gasped in surprise. "You knew? You never said anything."

"I didn't feel it was my place to say anything. I know you think I'm a busybody at times, but I figured you'd tell me about her whenever you were ready. She has your eyes, Jake, how could I not figure it out? Will you talk about it now?" she asked gently.

"It's a long story, Jen, and one I would rather not get into right now, but Charlie and I met a long time ago and our daughter was the result from that meeting. No one else knows about Christy other than my family, so I would appreciate you not saying anything around the office. There's enough gossip going around as it is."

"You know I won't, Jake. So what are you going to do about Charlie?"

"I don't know yet. I have feelings for her, but she doesn't feel the same."

"I don't know about that, Jake. Have you told her how you feel?"

"She has to know. I can't keep my hands off of her whenever she's around."

"All that proves is you want to go to bed with her. Now really, Jake, didn't your mother teach you better than that? Have you ever sent her flowers?"

"Yes." As soon as he said it, he blanched. He remembered the graphic message he had sent with the flowers. Was it possible Charlie thought he only wanted her for sex? He slapped his forehead. Perhaps that was why she had been so adverse to his suggestion of spending time with him. He would rectify that notion and soon.

అంఔ

"She is such a fucking loudmouth. If I weren't in HR, I would tell that bitch exactly what I think of her," Laura said fiercely.

"Laura, watch your mouth," Charlie censured, pointing to her daughter who was happily coloring at the coffee table.

"Sorry," Laura apologized quickly. "Well, I had to come over and let you know what was being said around the office."

"I appreciate it, Laura, but I kind of knew what would happen when I saw Sandy standing there listening to the whole conversation. The woman is certainly a nuisance but she will get her comeuppance one day. Karma is a son of a gun."

All day at work she had been the object of whispers and stares. Whenever she came upon a group, they would immediately stop talking. It was embarrassing to be on the end of office gossip, but she only had herself to blame. She shouldn't have snapped at Steve the way she had, regardless of whether he deserved it or not.

Now everyone knew about her and Jake, and the rumors were ranging from them making out in the elevators to them being caught in the boardroom having sex. If they only knew, she thought.

"So what are you going to do about it?" Laura asked curiously.

"Ignore it. It will eventually blow over."

"Girl, you are better than me. If I were you I would kick Sandy's behind. As it stands, I better not catch her outside of work or else I just might do it," Laura threatened.

Knowing her hotheaded friend, Charlie didn't doubt it.

Charlie shrugged. "What would be the point?"

"It would make you feel better."

"Temporarily maybe, but in the long run it won't accomplish anything. I just want to forget about the whole thing."

"Well, it's going to take a while for something this juicy to blow over. Didn't I tell you Steve was a piece of shit? Oops. Sorry about the language," Laura corrected herself. "Revenge seems to be his MO, no matter how misplaced," she finished bitterly.

Charlie gave her friend an odd look. This wasn't the first time she had made veiled references about Steve. "He wasn't intentionally malicious. He just let slip something that wasn't any of his business, although I felt like strangling him for doing so."

"If he hadn't been harassing you in the first place, none of it would have happened." Even Christy noted the bitterness in Laura's tone because she looked up at her with a frown before turning back to her coloring.

"I think you're biased where he's concerned."

"I have every reason to be. I warned you on your first day he was trouble. You should have listened to me."

"I think if I was firmer in the beginning it would never have come to this."

Laura narrowed her eyes. "You sound like you're defending him."

"I'm not. I'm annoyed as heck with him, but I can't lay the blame completely at his feet."

"Oh, but I can."

Charlie could hold her curiosity in no longer. "What did he do to you to make you hate him so much?" Charlie never mentioned Steve around Laura because it always raised Laura's hackles but she really wanted to know.

"Let's just say Steve and I will never be friends and that's fine with me. What happened between us isn't worth talking about." Laura's jaw set stubbornly.

"So there was an incident?" Charlie persisted.

"Let's not go there."

"Why not? I want to know."

"Okay, I'll tell you, if you tell me exactly what's going on with you and Jake. Is the rumor true?" Laura asked.

Charlie was caught in her own trap. She was saved from answering by the doorbell ringing.

"Now who could that be coming to visit around this time of night?" she said, getting up to answer the door.

She opened the door to see Jake's forlorn face.

Chapter Fourteen

"Jake!" Charlie exclaimed in surprise. "What are you doing here?" Her heart fluttered slightly. Damn. Why did this man have such an affect on her whenever he was near?

"I would like to talk to you. May I come in?" He looked uncertain.

"Oh, I'm sorry," she said, realizing how rude she was being by keeping him waiting outside, so she stepped aside to let him in. When Jake stepped into the light of the hallway, Charlie noticed Jake's swollen bottom lip. "What happened to your mouth, Jake?" Alarm spread through her.

Jake laughed without humor. "I had a little run-in with my ex-best friend."

"Steve? But why?" she asked.

"Don't you know? Haven't you heard what's been going around the office about you?" he asked in disbelief.

"Yes, I've heard them." She shrugged nonchalantly. "I don't care what people say about me at work. I never did. I'm there to do my job and that's it, not to make friends. Sure, I like getting along with my coworkers, but I won't lose sleep over them whispering behind my back. Anyway, I don't see why you would get into a fight over it."

"Don't you?" he challenged.

"No, actually I don't. Steve was indiscreet, but he wasn't the one who spread the rumors. I don't know him as well as you obviously do, but he doesn't strike me as the gossiping type— male chauvinist pig maybe, but not a rumormonger."

Jake seemed taken aback by her defense of Steve. His lips tightened. "Then how the hell did people find out what happened between us in my office if not from him? He was only other person who knew."

"He confronted me with the information, someone overheard."

"Who?" he demanded.

Charlie sighed not wanting to go into detail. It wasn't as though she were trying to defend Sandy, but it would have been pointless to continue on with something she rather forgot about. "I don't think it really matters."

"I think it does, not that it exonerates Steve. He had no business confronting you with what happened. If he hadn't, this person you're trying to protect wouldn't have had any ammunition to use against you."

"I'm not trying to protect anyone, Jake, I just want to put it behind me, and I can't do that if everyone keeps bringing it up. Look, I have company at the moment, but we're about to have dessert. If you'd like to stay and have some with us, you're welcome. I'm sure Christy will be glad to see you."

At the mention of his daughter, Jake cracked a genuine smile only to wince in pain.

"I'm going to get you some ice for that lip. It looks pretty nasty." Charlie looked up at him, concern taking over. Her thumb lightly brushed his injured lip. The intensity of his ice blue gaze seemed to burn into her. Heat coursed though Charlie as it always did when she was near him. Charlie quickly lowered her hand, stepping away.

"No, I'm okay. It looks worse than it actually is. You should see how Steve looks. He got much worse than a fat lip," Jake smirked.

"Violence is never the answer, Jake," Charlie reprimanded.

"If you ask me, it was a long time coming. Who's your guest?"

"Laura Tombega. You probably know her from work. She works in the Human Resources Department."

"Oh yeah, I know her," Jake said, omitting the fact Steve often referred to her as "Loose Laura", but he wasn't about to mention it in front of Charlie. He figured he was in enough hot water as it was.

"You sounded uncertain about that."

"Oh, I do know her, sometimes it takes me longer to match the name and the face. When I started my company, it was only myself and shortly after Jen and Steve. As MBF grew, it's become harder for me to remember everyone right away."

"I guess that's understandable. Come on in. Christy and Laura are in the living room. We're having chocolate pudding for dessert."

As Charlie had predicted, Christy was thrilled to see her father again. She rushed to him the minute she saw him and hugged his leg in a vise grip. "I missed you so much, Daddy," Christy greeted.

"I missed you, too, sweetie," he said, scooping her up. "Hi, Laura, how are you tonight? I hope I wasn't disturbing anything." Jake gave Laura a courteous nod.

"Not at all. Actually, we were just talking about you," Laura said slyly, sneaking a quick peek at Charlie's furious face. Charlie looked as if she was ready to commit murder.

"Oh yeah? What about?" Jake asked curiously.

"Oh, this and that." Laura smiled with devilment.

"Good things I hope."

"You could say that."

Charlie knew Laura was trying to stir the pot as usual, and she felt like committing murder that very moment. "Laura, why don't you come into the kitchen with me? I need help with the pudding."

"But Jake and I were talking. Besides, you didn't need my help before," Laura pointed out saucily.

"Well, I changed my mind," Charlie said through clenched teeth.

Charlie shot her friend the you're-in-big-trouble look. "Okay. Okay. Don't get your panties in a bunch," Laura said to Charlie before she turned to grin at Jake. "We'll be back."

Jake nodded absently. He was too busy listening to Christy chatter away.

In the kitchen Charlie turned to Laura. "What the hell was that all about?"

"Oh, lighten up, Char. I was just having a little fun." Laura grinned at her as if that explanation would fly.

Charlie wasn't amused. "Well, it isn't funny. He probably thinks I've been fantasizing about him or something."

"Well, haven't you been? I'm sure he already knows you have the hots for him." Charlie hated her friend's shrewdness at times.

"I don't know what you're talking about," Charlie protested.

"Yeah right."

"Okay. I do have the hots for him, as you so graciously put it. I want him badly. Now there! Is that what you wanted to hear?" Charlie practically shouted.

Laura grinned knowingly. "Whether it was what I wanted to hear or not, I'm sure Jake just heard you, too."

Charlie's face grew hot with embarrassment. She hadn't realized how loud her voice had risen. "Oh my God. Do you think he heard?" she asked in a panicked whisper.

"So what if he did? You want him and he wants you. You haven't confirmed any of those rumors, but you certainly didn't deny them either. Char, what's so wrong with admitting you want the man? He's drop-dead gorgeous, he's rich, and he's crazy about you."

"Crazy about me? I think he's crazier about getting into my pants." Charlie pursed her lips and crossed her arms.

"How do you know? Girl, when he walked into the living room, you should have seen the look on his face when he was looking at you. He looked like a lovesick puppy. By the way what happened to his mouth?" Laura asked.

"Too much testosterone."

"What?"

"Never mind. Look, I really think you're mistaken about Jake's so-called feelings for me."

"I don't think so, Char. Jake Fox is crushing on you in a big way."

"Well, even if it's true, I can't return his feelings."

"Why the hell not? Girl, if Jake Fox wanted me the way he obviously does you, I'd be on my knees kissing his hairy nut sack every day."

"Because I just can't," Charlie answered stubbornly. "And must you be so vulgar all the time?"

Laura grinned. "Not all the time. I have to sleep sometimes."

"Ha ha. Very funny. Not." Charlie rolled her eyes. "I meant what I said about Jake."

"You're not fooling anyone but yourself. You can't live in constant fear for the rest of your life."

"It's my decision. Look, I've already made up my mind about what I want from Jake," Charlie said with a determined gleam in her eyes.

"Well?" Laura prompted.

"I'm going to have an affair with him. You know how the saying goes, if you can't beat them...I mean, every time I'm near him, I lose all common sense, so I figure if I sleep with him voluntarily, my lust will eventually wane and then I'll be able to move on with my life—without him in it."

"What!?" Laura yelled, looking as if she couldn't believe what she had just heard.

"I'm going to have an affair with him," Charlie repeated.

"Get the fuck out of here." Laura looked at Charlie with a stunned expression on her face. "I can't believe I'm talking to the same Charlie Brown who waited for marriage in order to lose her virginity. Whoa. You've come a long way from that girl. Jake must have superdick if he's made you make such an about-face." Laura burst out laughing at the irony of it.

"Oh shut up, Laura." Charlie glared. "As I've stated already, I'm only going to have an affair with him long enough to work him out of my system, and when I do, things will go back to normal. I know I'll have to be friends with him for Christy's sake, but friendship is safer."

"Personally, I think you should be committed. Jake Fox is a catch, and you're nuts to let him slip through your fingers like this. What if your plan doesn't work?"

"It has to work," Charlie declared vehemently.

ഇ൝

Dessert was a tense affair. Jake kept shooting Charlie looks she found unsettling. Laura watched them both with a smug expression on her face. Christy was the only one oblivious to the tension. She was with three of her favorite people, her mommy, her daddy and her Auntie Laura.

Charlie was so strained by the time Laura left she felt like screaming. She let Jake give Christy a bath while she washed dishes. The whole day had been so surreal. First, her crappy morning, then walking into the office to be greeted by "The Mouth", and then her run-in with Steve. To top it all off, *she* was now the office bimbo. She knew she should have stayed in bed that morning.

Jake was another issue. He was acting as if he really did have feelings for her. On the one hand, she was a little annoyed he felt it was his right to go out and beat people up on her behalf, but on the other hand, it was actually quite gallant of him

God, I'm so confused.

"Hey, Charlie." Jake poked his head into the kitchen, breaking her out of her deep thoughts. "Christy is in her pajamas and she's asking for you. I've already read her a story."

"Okay, I'm just drying up the last dish. I'll be there in a minute."

Charlie entered the bedroom to find Jake sitting by Christy's bedside stroking Christy's hair. The tender look he gave his daughter made her heart twinge at the poignant scene before her.

"Hi." Charlie smiled at a sleepy Christy.

"Hi, Mommy. Daddy read to me."

"He did? What did he read?"

"Cinda-ela."

"That's nice. Did you say your prayers?"

"Yes." Christy yawned.

"Okay. Well, I guess it's off to sleep you go then." Charlie leaned over to give Christy a kiss on the cheek. "I love you."

"I love you, too, Mommy."

Jake followed suit and kissed Christy goodnight as well. "Love you, kiddo."

"Love you too, Daddy. Daddy, I wish you were here all the time," Christy said drowsily. She was losing the battle to stay awake.

"I do, too, baby." Jake's answer didn't sit well with Charlie. She hoped her daughter didn't get any ideas from that statement.

"I not a baby," Christy protested before drifting off to sleep.

Charlie and Jake looked at each other silently for several seconds until Charlie broke the silence. "Would you like to stay for coffee?" Charlie offered.

"Not really, but we need to talk."

Charlie agreed.

In the living room, Jake took a seat on the couch and Charlie sat next to him. "Your cologne smells nice." She smiled at him.

"Thanks." If he didn't know better, he would have thought she was interested in more than just talking. This was the first time she made an attempt to get close to him. Just being next to Charlie and inhaling her scent drove him crazy. He wanted to carry her to the bedroom and fuck her brains out.

"Charlie, I don't know where to begin," he said uneasily. This was going to be harder than he thought, especially with Charlie sitting so close to him, making his heart beat faster by her very nearness.

"Try the beginning," she said, devouring him with her eyes.

Jake shifted uncomfortably in his seat. His cock stirred. It was as if she were deliberately doing this to him, but he wouldn't be deterred from what he had to say, so he moved over, putting some space in between them. Charlie pouted, and Jake looked away nervously.

"Charlie, I'm really sorry about today. I blame myself," he blurted out, going for the safer topic.

"Why blame yourself? I was just as much at fault as you were. What happened in your office was inevitable, just like you said."

"You feel that way?" he asked in amazement. "You don't care about what's going around about you at work?" he asked again, not believing his ears.

"I was angry in the beginning, but as I was telling Laura, this will blow over. I don't care what they say about me."

"But I care, Charlie. I don't want you to be the subject of office gossip."

"Jake, if I don't care you shouldn't either. Now, I don't want to talk about it anymore."

"There's actually something else I wanted to talk to you about."

"Must we talk?" She looked at him with seductive eyes, scooting closer to him.

"Charlie, do you know what you're asking for," he asked huskily.

"Yes. I can't fight it any longer, Jake." She leaned over to touch her lips to his throat. The titillating feel of her lips against his skin was making his groin grow uncomfortably hard.

Jake went completely still as Charlie placed kisses against his neck and his jaw. The erotic charge she was creating made him groan. When she ran the tip of her tongue over the outline of his lips, he lost what little control he had been trying to maintain.

He grabbed her roughly in his arms and began to kiss her with an ungovernable passion that consumed them both. His tongue shoved its way through her parted lips. She tasted so good. He could search a million years but he knew no woman would taste as sweet as his Charlie. His Charlie. She belonged to him now.

Charlie twisted her head away. "Jake, let's go to the bedroom," Charlie suggested breathlessly.

Jake's response was a long, hard kiss. When he was satisfied, he stood and pulled Charlie with him, swinging her into his arms. Jake carried her to the bedroom where he proceeded to undress her as quickly as he could, dropping kisses on her satiny skin as he exposed it to his hungry sight. When Charlie stood nude before him, he tossed her unceremoniously on the bed, eager to sample each inch of her delectable body. There was not one part of her he would leave unattended by his tongue this night.

He began to rip off his clothes, impatient to join Charlie on the bed.

"Slow down, Jake." Charlie halted him. "I want to see your beautiful body. Take your clothes off slowly so I can enjoy the view," she ordered huskily.

Jake didn't know if he could hold out long with Charlie lying in bed, leaning back on her elbows looking like she had just stepped out of a teenager's wet dream. Her womanly, chocolate-dipped body was the most beautiful sight he had ever beheld. Her pert bounty of breasts jutted out temptingly, just begging to be sucked. She spread her legs ever so slightly so he could get a glimpse of her gorgeous pussy. The flash of the succulent pinkness of her treasure made come drip from his already aching cock.

He gulped, trying to keep himself from taking her right then and there. "Charlie, I need you, baby. Let me make love to you now," he pleaded. He rubbed his balls to relieve the pressure built up there. This was torture, pure and simple.

"Shh." She placed a finger over her lips and winked. "Please, Jake. For me." She pouted.

He sighed. When she pouted with those full sexy lips of hers, he could deny her nothing. He slowly removed his clothing.

Jake felt a sudden rush of desire as Charlie's eyes feasted on his body. His cock surged forward when he freed it from his boxers. Charlie licked her lips.

"You're so sexy, Jake. Mmm, I can already feel that big, beautiful cock of yours filling me. It's a monster," Charlie whispered. "Turn around so I can see all of you," she ordered.

Jake did, turned on by the way the woman he loved found him so desirable. Charlie slid off the bed and stood behind him before wrapping her arms around his waist. With slow, deliberate movements, she ran her tongue down the entire length of his spine, then nibbled at the tangy flesh, stimulating every nerve in his big trembling body.

Jake shuddered. He hadn't realized how erotic it was to be touched and kissed on his back. He let out a loud moan as Charlie slid to her knees and ran her tongue along one hard cheek. He shivered as she cupped and squeezed his buns in her hands, her fingers sending shockwaves throughout his entire being. She traced the curves and contours of his rear with her palm. Jake clenched and unclenched his fists, trying to control the raging fire Charlie ignited.

She pushed his legs further apart to gain access to his throbbing jewels. She lightly fondled his balls, tracing their hair-roughened surface. He thought his knees would give out. Jake was fast losing control but remained still. His breath came out in quick, shallow huffs. Charlie leaned forward and wrapped her lips around the throbbing tissue of his sack, sucking it gently into her mouth. "You taste yummy," she whispered against his flesh.

"Oh God!" he shouted. "Your mouth is amazing, Charlie," he muttered. He had never been touched quite like this before.

Jake gritted his teeth. He was so highly aroused by Charlie's hot, fervent mouth. With his balls still firmly in her mouth, Charlie reached between his legs to touch his cock, and that was when the fine line of Jake's control snapped. He could no longer take the delicious torture she administered. Jake pulled away from her, Charlie whimpered as his balls were practically ripped from her greedy lips. "I want more." She pouted.

"Lady, any more of that and I will finish before I even get started."

Jake turned around and yanked Charlie off her knees and then pushed her back on the bed where he immediately covered her body with his. He pulled her legs apart as far as they would go. "This is what you get for teasing me, woman!" Jake said before ramming his big, thick cock into her waiting cunt. He slid balls deep into her with just one stroke. Nothing compared to being inside of her.

"Do you like this, baby?" He wore a devilish grin on his face as he slammed into her.

"Oh. Yes, Jake. I love your big fat cock!"

"Do you like the way this big fat cock feels inside of you? Do you like your pussy being stretched by my prick?" he asked knowingly.

"Oh yes, Jake! Don't hold back. Fuck me! Make this pussy yours!" Charlie screamed, tossing her head from side to side.

Jake needed no further prompting to unleash all his animalistic passions upon her. He fucked her with reckless abandon, branding her with each and every thrust.

"Your pussy is so fucking good," he groaned as he continued to thrust his white shaft inside her ebony box. He couldn't get enough of her. Everything about Charlie turned him on.

"Your cock is so fucking good," she answered back, tilting her hips forward ever so slightly so he could push deeper still. The sensation was like nothing he had ever felt before. She bucked her hips against him to meet his thrusts.

Jake continued to pound into her with a vigor only Charlie could inspire within him. He felt his balls tighten. He grasped her thighs tightly and shuddered against her. As his seed shot up her sizzling passage, it triggered Charlie's own orgasm.

"Oh my God, Jake," she screamed.

Jake wasn't finished with her yet. He wanted some ass. He flipped her over on her belly, grinding her behind with his hardness. He parted her cheeks and began to rub his thumb over her puckered bud. Charlie stiffened.

"Jake?" Uncertainty wavered her voice.

"I want to fuck your ass, Charlie. Will you deny me?" He moistened his finger before inserting it into her behind. Charlie gasped.

"I've...never done it before." She sounded scared.

"You know I wouldn't do anything to hurt you. Say the word and I won't do it," he said as his finger worked slowly in and out of her bottom.

"That feels good, Jake, but I don't know if I could handle your cock back there." She still sounded uncertain.

"I won't hurt you," he whispered.

"I...oh God, Jake." She moaned as he slid another finger into her.

"If it hurts too much, tell me to stop and I will," he promised.

Charlie merely nodded. Jake removed his finger. With his other hand, he slid two fingers into her dripping cunt, and scooped out a generous amount of their mingled juices before rubbing it over her anus, slathering it for his entry.

"It may hurt a little at first, but it gets better," Jake warned. His dick was rock hard as it was poised to take her anal cherry. "Relax," he instructed when he felt her clench up.

He had wanted to do this to her since he first laid eyes on her magnificent ass. Her body was perfect. She only had to say the word and he would stop, but she only moaned. Jake watched her reaction, pleased she was as turned on as he was; Charlie's body trembled under his hand.

Jake thrust forward.

"Oh shit!" Charlie screamed.

Jake leaned over to kiss her neck and shoulders. "Do you want me to pull out?" he asked, although he would have liked nothing more than to ram her bountiful booty, her comfort was more important to him.

"I...I think if you stay still I will be okay," she whispered.

Jake kissed her cheek. "You're very brave, but I can't stay still for too long."

"I know," she said quietly. "Oh, Jake, it hurts a little but it feels so good." She sighed with content.

"Not as good as how my cock feels right now, baby." His hands caressed her round bottom.

Jake tried to remain still as long as he could but his dick had other ideas. He grasped her hips and began to pump gently at first. He began to feel a build up in the pit of his belly. The two lovers became lost in the crescendo of their passion. Jake continued to thrust relentlessly into her rear.

"Oh God, woman, what are you doing to me?" he groaned. Charlie's face was buried in her pillow. He could tell her climax was near by the way she shuddered beneath him. With one last powerful thrust, Jake shot his load up her ass.

"Oh fuck yeah," he yelled.

Charlie convulsed beneath him as she came with him. Reluctantly, he pulled his now semi-erect penis from the tight little hole of her butt and turned her over.

He gave her a long slow kiss before collapsing on top of her. With their bodies drenched in sweat they embraced, content to lie in each other's arms. Jake leaned over and kissed her tenderly. Nothing could compare to this moment. His heart felt as if it would burst with the love he felt.

"Where is your shower?" Jake asked.

"Through there." Charlie pointed toward the door at the far corner of the bedroom.

Jake slid off the bed and took Charlie's arm. "Let's cool off," he said, pulling her off the bed.

ฌงณ

Under the chilly spray of the showerhead, they began to soap one another. Jake took his time running his hands over her coffee-colored skin. As Charlie's hands washed his penis, it began to stiffen once more. Jake lifted her in his arms and thrust forcefully into her wet, soapy cunt.

Charlie wrapped her legs around his waist and her arms around his neck as he bucked in and out of her. "Yes! Yes! Yes!" Charlie screamed, reveling in the glory of their lust.

Jake buried his face in her neck as he possessed her. "I can't get enough of you, Charlie. I can do this all night." The erotic experience of their soap-slicked bodies sliding against each other was highly intense. Jake groaned loudly as he once again shot his load into her passage. Charlie shuddered against him when she reached her own climax. Once they were rinsed and dried off, Jake carried Charlie back to the bed.

Charlie was surprised when only minutes later Jake was hard again. He positioned himself over her and slid into her wet folds before he began to pump gently. She wrapped her arms around his neck, caught up in the beauty of the moment.

When Jake made love to her like this, she almost wished her heart was open to love again. The thought brought tears to her eyes so she clung tighter to him as he continued to move slowly in and out of her. Instead of concentrating on what she couldn't give him, she concentrated on the wonderful sensations coursing through her body. They climaxed within seconds of each other.

Jake fell to his side, and pulled Charlie within the crook of his arm. She rested her head against his chest, listening to the sound of his heartbeat. Jake stroked Charlie's back gently.

"Charlie?" Jake finally broke the silence.

"Hmm?"

"Look at me. I want to tell you something."

She lifted her head, instantly alert by the seriousness of tone. "What is it, Jake?"

"I've wanted to tell you for a long time now, but I was just too scared to tell you up until now."

"What? Tell me, Jake."

"I love you, Charlie, and I want you to marry me."

Chapter Fifteen

Charlie's jaw dropped. She must have heard him wrong. She had to have because there was no way Jake had just told her he loved her. Not only did he confess his love for her, he had actually asked her to marry him. No. She had definitely misheard him.

"Say what?" she asked in disbelief when she finally found her voice.

"I love you, Charlie. I have for a long time. Hell, I think I probably fell in love with you the very first time I saw you. Nothing would make me happier right now than for you to consent to be my wife. Please say you will," he said with eagerness.

Charlie pulled out of Jake's arms and looked at him. She was stunned. She didn't doubt his sincerity but she couldn't take this sudden declaration of love. "Jake, we never talked about love," she said warily. Oh dear, what was she going to do now? Love was not supposed to be a part of the equation. "You don't really mean what you're saying. You're just caught up in the moment." She patted his chest lightly.

"Don't patronize me, Charlie." He sat up abruptly. "Of course, I mean it. I've never told any other woman I loved her. I don't use that word lightly so I would appreciate it if you wouldn't tell me how I'm feeling right now. I know how I feel and I love you," he said passionately.

Charlie went completely still. All this time she had thought Jake had only wanted a physical relationship with her. How could she have been so blind? She had been so busy trying not to fall in love with him herself she hadn't noticed Jake falling in love with her. Had she known how he felt about her, she would have run the other way.

Knowing Jake loved her put things into a different perspective. She would have to disabuse him from any thoughts of his love being returned. Loving him back was just not a gamble she was willing to take.

"Charlie, say something," Jake said with anxiety.

"Jake, I don't know what to say."

"Say you'll marry me and make me the happiest man alive. We'll have a big wedding with all our family and friends there. Christy can be the flower girl...my nieces and your friend Laura can be bridesmaids. My family will be thrilled," he said with an excited gleam in his eyes. He had this all thought out.

"Whoa. You're going too fast. First of all, I didn't say I'd marry you. Second, I don't love you."

Jake paled. "What?" he asked with widened eyes, looking as if he couldn't believe she was rejecting him

"I don't love you, Jake," she repeated, trying to be as gentle as she could.

He looked at her with pain-filled eyes. "You practically threw yourself at me. I thought you loved me, too." He sounded on the verge of tears. He took deep breaths as though he were hyperventilating.

"Jake, are you okay?" Charlie asked with genuine concern. It hadn't been her intention to hurt him but, then again, she didn't know she would be put in this situation. "Jake?" she asked again uncertainly. He had lost all color in his face.

Jake took several minutes before he answered her. Anger contorted his handsome face. He leaped out of bed, startling Charlie by his sudden movement. He pulled her roughly against his chest by her forearms. She gasped in fear at the blaze in his ice blue eyes. "You're lying!" he said vehemently.

"I'm not, Jake. I don't love you. I'm sorry but it's the truth," she said tearfully.

"You do love me. I know you do." He shook her with each angry word.

"Jake, let me go. You're hurting me," she ordered.

Jake looked down at her with a dark brooding look before he let her go. Charlie fell back against the bed. She rubbed her arms in order to get the circulation flowing once more. "I'm sorry. I didn't mean to do that to you."

"It's okay," she said quietly, recognizing the pain reflected in his eyes.

"No, it's not okay. I had no right to manhandle you that way. I abhor violence against women."

"You're right, you didn't, but I understand. I know you didn't mean me any harm."

"I didn't but damn it, Charlie, how can you say you don't love me when we just finished making love the way we did. We didn't just fuck; we made love!" He raised his voice.

"Lower your voice, Jake, before you wake Christy up." Charlie said the only thing she could think to say. She didn't want to have this conversation right now, and actually not at all.

"You didn't care about waking Christy when you were screaming my name, begging for my cock," he accused brutally.

Charlie blushed. "Jake, it was just sex," she argued.

"It wasn't just sex, or at least it wasn't for me. I told you I loved you and you tell me it's just sex?"

"Jake, I'm sorry, but I don't love you. I'm sorry you got the wrong impression but it was just physical," she said with tears in her eyes. She wanted so badly to tell him she loved him but she just couldn't allow herself to.

Jake sat back down on the bed.

"Charlie, I love you. I don't care if you don't love me back. Marry me and I promise I'll spend my every waking minute making you happy. Maybe in time, you will grow to love me, too. Please, Charlie. Please say yes," he pleaded, taking her in his arms, planting kisses all over her face.

Paul had promised the same thing but now he was dead. Charlie pushed against his chest. "No, Jake. I can't."

"Why can't you? Please tell me, Charlie."

Charlie looked at him. How could she tell him that if she allowed herself to love him, she would be in constant fear of losing him, and if she did lose him, how could she go on living?

"I just can't, Jake," she said, tears falling freely down her face.

"Is it because you are still in love with your husband?" he asked.

"Jake, I...yes. It's because I'm still in love with Paul. No one will ever take his place in my heart," she whispered.

Jake paled. "So where does that leave us?"

"There is no us. There's a physical attraction and that's it. We can't get married but there's no reason why we can't still be lovers."

Jake gave her a long hard stare. "I asked you to marry me because I love you. I worship the ground you walk on. I want

211

you as my wife, yet, you'd rather just be lovers. Not lovers really, but fuck buddies, because that's all it would be if there's no love. Your offer is insulting and degrading. I won't be your stud." He slid out of the bed.

Charlie watched as Jake grabbed his clothes and pulled them on. "Jake, you won't... I mean, you won't let this affect your relationship with Christy will you?" she asked tentatively.

"You must really have a low opinion of me, Charlie."

"No, I don't," she said hastily.

"You obviously do, or you wouldn't have implied such a shitty thing. I love that little girl more than life itself and I won't stop seeing her just because her mother wants to use me like some man-whore she can dismiss at the snap of a finger."

"That's not true!" Charlie protested.

"Isn't it? Look, I need to get out of here. I know I said I'd have a support check for you today but I got a little sidetracked. I will mail it to you, so you'll have it this week. Don't forget, I have Christy for the weekend, so is it okay if I pick her up Friday night?"

Charlie nodded mutely. What could she say? She could see how hurt Jake was but her fear would not allow her to go to him and throw herself into his arms as she longed to do.

"Well, this is it then. There's no way you will consider marrying me?" he asked stiffly. Charlie shook her head tearfully.

He nodded. "Okay. I'll respect your wishes. I do want you to be happy, Charlie, and I'm sorry you're still grieving over your loss. If you need me for anything, don't hesitate to ask," he said before walking out the door.

Charlie sat in the middle of her bed when Jake left. Tears rolled down her cheeks, before she broke into loud, body-shaking sobs. Jake loved her, yet, she sent him away. She knew she had hurt him, but she ended up hurting herself far more.

৯০০৪

"Jennifer, cancel all my meetings for the rest of the week. I'm going to take a few days off," Jake said as he walked into his office the next day.

"My, my. Mr. Workaholic is taking some time off?" Jennifer asked in amazement.

"Please, Jen, I'm not in the mood. Please just cancel all my appointments." He sighed heavily.

"What's wrong, Jake? You sound frustrated."

"Nothing I care to get into right now."

"Okay. I'll cancel those appointments right away." She knew when to back off.

Jake went into his office and closed the door. If he didn't have an important meeting today, he wouldn't have bothered coming in. As it stood, he didn't know how he was going to get through the rest of the day. Charlie had taken his heart and ripped it to shreds.

Fortunately, he had a million things on his desk to attend to so he was thankfully able to throw himself into his work. At least work was the one thing in his life that wasn't out of whack. Jake was so engrossed with what he was working on he was surprised when the intercom buzzed. He frowned when he looked at his watch. It was just before noon. His meeting wasn't for another couple of hours and he didn't have any other appointments scheduled.

"What's up, Jen?"

"Steve is out here. He'd like to see you, Jake," Jennifer announced.

Jake frowned. The last person he wanted to see right now was Steve. "Tell him to go away," he growled, not caring whether Steve wanted to see him for work-related reasons or not. Jake didn't want to see that rat's face. He sat back in his chair as he recalled the events of yesterday.

When Jennifer had told him what was being said around the office and from where it had come from, Jake saw red. He stormed out of his office and strode down the hall to Steve's, like an angry avenger. The wind was taken out of his sails when Steve's personal assistant Janice informed Jake Steve had gone for the day.

Not able to leave right away because of an important meeting with a client later on, Jake impatiently waited until his meeting was over to leave. He drove straight to Steve's house. Steve's car along with another car was in his driveway. Jake figured it was probably a woman. How like Steve to heal his wounded ego with a session of sexual aerobics, Jake thought with disgust. He hammered on the door impatiently.

"Steve! Get your ass out here!" Jake called.

"What's the commotion? What are you doing here? I have company upstairs," Steve asked opening the door.

"You know why I'm here and the only bastard around here is you. How could you, Steve?"

"What are you talking about?"

"How could you do what you did to her? Don't play dumb. I shouldn't have to spell it out to you," Jake shouted at the top of his lungs.

Jake advanced on Steve and before he knew what happened, Jake's fist slammed into his face, knocking him on his ass.

"Get up, you son of a bitch," Jake growled, ready to give Steve more.

Steve's ire was now raised. He quickly got up and charged at Jake. Jake tried to sidestep Steve's fist but Steve landed a solid punch to Jake's mouth. A rage that had been building up since the afternoon was unleashed as he pounded Steve in the face, and then punched him again.

When Steve dropped to the floor again Jake kicked him in the ribs. Steve lay motionless on the floor and for a second, Jake was scared he may have gone too far. The feeling was short-lived when Steve turned over and stared at him with angry green eyes. "We've never come to blows over a woman before. Don't you remember our motto? Bros before hoes." Steve wiped the blood from his mouth.

"Shut your fucking mouth. Don't you ever talk about Charlie like that again! She is not just a pussy. She's the woman I love, and the mother of my child." Jake yelled. Steve looked at Jake as if he had been hit again. "Yeah, that's right. Charlie and I have a daughter together, a beautiful little girl, so if you ever refer to my daughter's mother as just a ho again, I'll fucking kill you," Jake threatened.

"What the hell are you talking about? How can this be?" Steve was dumbfounded.

"When Charlie started working for the company, I was stunned. When you were talking about her, I instinctively knew she was the same Charlie Brown I met over three years ago. I told you I knew her but you chose not to believe me. I should have handled things differently but that makes no difference now." Jake paused to rake his fingers through his hair. He didn't really feel like explaining all this to Steve but Jake figured Steve should know where things stood between him and Charlie. "That day in the office when you saw Charlie running out, you got pissed at me. I would have explained the entire situation to you right then and there but you were sulking like a little bitch and you then refused to talk to me."

Steve stared at Jake, trying to take this all in. "Where does a daughter fit into all this?"

"I found out Charlie had a daughter as a result of our previous encounter. I knew she was my daughter the minute I saw her. I won't go into further details, but there you have it. I'm in love with Charlie and I have been for years now. I intend to ask her to marry me, so if you so much as say her name in that tone of voice..." Jake broke off.

Steve finally got up. "Why the hell didn't you tell me all this?" Steve sounded hurt. "I'm supposed to be your best friend."

"Because I know you, Steve. If I would have told you to back off or if I tried harder to explain I'd known her from years back, you would have seen that as a challenge. You would have gone after her anyway. I never minded the friendly competition before, but Charlie was different. And when you caught us in the office together, you were giving me the cold shoulder. When exactly did I have the chance to tell you after that, Steve?"

Steve had the good grace to look embarrassed. "But we're best friends." He rubbed his swollen face.

"Correction. We were best friends. After what you did today, I don't even want to know you. Charlie's reputation is mud all over the office and you're partly to blame. If you didn't work for MBF, I would tell you to stay the hell out of my life, but as it stands, I don't want you to say anything to me unless it's MBF related," Jake finished coldly, looking his former friend up and down before he strode out the door.

"Jake, I don't think he's going to go away," Jennifer said, interrupting him again.

"Please, Jake." Steve's voice came from the intercom.

What the hell? Knowing Steve, he wouldn't go away until he had his say. Jake rubbed his temples.

"Okay, Jen. Send him in."

Chapter Sixteen

Steve walked into the office sporting a nice shiner. One side of his face was covered in black and blue bruises. Knowing how vain Steve was, Jake was surprised Steve had even bothered showing up for work looking the way he did. Jake didn't care about his appearance half as much as Steve did and he himself would have stayed home for a few days until his face looked normal.

"You have five minutes," Jake grumbled, taking a look at his watch indicating to Steve he was dead serious.

"May I sit down?" Steve requested humbly.

Jake raised an eyebrow. This was a departure from the usually cocksure Steve. "Suit yourself." Jake shrugged. "But don't get too comfortable. You've already wasted thirty seconds." He leaned back in his chair and stared at Steve, stony-faced.

"Jake, I don't know where to begin," Steve started uneasily. Jake didn't say anything but he did look at his watch again. Steve paused as though trying to find the right words to say. "I'm sorry, Jake," Steve apologized solemnly.

Jake cocked one brow. In all the years he had known Steve, his friend rarely said he was sorry, but there was no way he was about to make this apology easy for the son of a bitch. "Now that you've said what you had to say, you can leave. As you can see, I have a lot of work to do."

"Jake, if your friendship didn't mean so much to me I would walk out the door right now but I'm not going to give up easily. Look, I know I was a dick. There is no excuse for my behavior. I know I shouldn't have acted that way with Charlie. If I had taken her first no as an answer instead of persisting, none of this would have happened. My ego was crushed, and I was irked to lose out to you. She didn't deserve that."

"Damn straight she didn't," Jake said through clenched teeth.

"Like I said, I had no excuse for what I did. I know I overreacted when I saw Charlie rushing out of your office. God knows, I've swiped women from under your nose on numerous occasions yet you and I never let it come between us. Then when the shoe was on the other foot, I couldn't handle it." Steve paused. "I'm sorry you felt you couldn't confide in me about Charlie. I haven't been a good friend lately, and I deserved what happened yesterday. I promise I'll do everything in my power to make sure all the gossip going around the office about Charlie is squashed. I understand you don't want to be my friend anymore, but if you decide to forgive me, I'll be around," Steve finished, getting up to leave.

Jake sat motionless. His emotions were in turmoil. He was still pissed but he and Steve had been best friends for eighteen years. Steve's behavior was still reprehensible but Jake at least understood.

"Steve, wait," Jake called out as Steve was walking out the door. Steve turned around. "I appreciate the apology."

"Yeah?"

"Yeah. Have a seat." When Steve did so Jake continued. "I should have set you straight from the beginning, so I'm just as much to blame in this whole fiasco as you are." Jake sighed as he rubbed his throbbing temples.

"So how is Charlie taking all this?" Steve asked curiously.

"Surprisingly well actually. I'm more upset about this whole thing than she is. She said it would all blow over."

"That's really classy of her. I knew she was a classy lady when I first saw her, unlike that *puta,* Laura, she calls a friend. That's one of the reasons I guess I was so attracted to her. She's not like the other women I've dated," Steve explained.

"She's very classy," Jake agreed, choosing to ignore Steve's comment about Laura. Those two would have to work out their own issues.

"So where do you two stand? When are you going to pop the question and when do I get to meet your little girl?"

"I'm sure you'll get to meet Christy eventually. She's a great kid. As for Charlie, I already asked her last night."

"And?"

"She said no."

"What?" Steve asked incredulously.

Jake shrugged. "She doesn't feel the same. She's still in love with her husband," he said more calmly than he actually felt. It was painful to talk about it.

"Isn't he dead?"

"Yes, and he has been for some time now. I can't compete with a ghost, but I swear, if that bastard was alive, I would punch his heart out," Jake said, fiercely jealous of the man who Charlie still loved above all else.

"Whoa, you don't need to go beating any more people up." Steve shook his head.

"Don't worry. I've hung up my boxing gloves."

"So you're just going to give up? On Charlie, I mean."

"Short of kidnapping her, what do you suggest I do? She'd rather have a physical relationship with me than be my wife. Do you know how degrading that feels?"

Steve thought for a moment. "There has to be some reason for that. She doesn't seem like the type to sleep around, unlike that friend of hers." Steve shook his head.

"Don't start that again."

"Start what?" Steve asked innocently.

"You know, but look, Charlie has made her decision and I have to accept it. It hurts like hell but I'm going to have to let go of the dream," Jake said raggedly.

"I'm sorry, man. Is there anything I can do to help?"

"Yes, actually there is. I'm going out of town for a few days. I'll be back to the office on Monday but I want you to take care of any fires that pop up. I'll keep my cell phone on if you need to reach me."

"Where are you going?"

"I think I'll head to my condo at the shore. I need some time to think."

"Okay. No problem. I'll hold the fort down for you."

"Thank you. Well, I really do have to get some of this stuff done before I leave today. By the way, what will you tell people when they ask what happened to your face?" Jake grinned for the first time that day.

"I'll tell them I got mugged." Steve grinned back.

෮෧

Charlie sat home feeling miserable. She couldn't get thoughts of Jake out of her mind. She had lied when she told him she was still in love with Paul, but she had only told him that to protect herself. Oh, her love would never die for Paul, but she was no longer in love with him. It was hard to stay in love with someone who was no longer there.

The crushed look in Jake's eyes when she told that lie tore her heart out. If she didn't love him, then why was she in so much pain? On Tuesday, she received a letter in the mail from Jake. Ripping the envelope open, she found a check. She put it aside to read the note he had sent along with it. The note was short and concise, written as if to a business associate.

Charlie, here is the child support check I promised. I know we didn't discuss an amount but this check should bring me current for all the missed months. However, if you feel the amount is insufficient, we can discuss it when I pick Christy up on Friday. I will be out of town until then. Jake.

When Charlie actually saw what the amount of the check was, she nearly fell over. The check was nearly as much as Charlie's annual salary. She knew Jake had been serious when he said he wanted to take care of Christy financially, but she didn't know he would give her such a grand amount that was more than enough. It didn't surprise her, however. Over the past months, she had gotten to see the kind of person he was. He was a good man.

He loved her, but how could she have accepted his proposal when she knew she would have lived in a constant state of paranoia. She would have worried every second of the day and her paranoia would have eventually run him off. She couldn't do that to herself and she couldn't do that to Jake.

By midweek, Charlie felt as if she'd been through hell and back. She lay awake at night not getting much sleep, and when she did manage to nod off, she ended up dreaming of Jake's hurt face when she'd rejected him. On Wednesday morning as she sat at her desk trying to concentrate on a report she needed to finish, she was surprised to hear Steve's voice. She stiffened, not wanting to deal with him when her week was already shitty.

"Can I talk to you for a moment?" he asked. Gone was the cocky office Romeo from Monday. His face was black and blue, and Charlie couldn't help but wince a little at the show of Jake's temper on her behalf.

"Okay," Charlie said warily, not knowing what he was going to say to her. If he tried anything, she was going to tell him to get lost.

"I just wanted to apologize for the way I acted. I should have taken no for an answer when you first said no, and I certainly shouldn't have cornered you the way I did. If it's any consolation, I put the word out that any gossip as a result of said incident will be immediately dealt with by me. I'm not asking you to forgive me because I know what a tall order that is, but I just wanted you to know how I felt."

Charlie was surprised. She initially thought Steve was a pain in the ass, now he was showing her a completely different side to him.

"You're right, Steve. You should have left well enough alone, but we won't mention it again. Okay?" She hadn't exactly forgiven him but she was impressed he had the balls to admit when he was wrong.

Steve turned to leave but stopped at the door. "Jake really loves you. Please give him a chance," he said, and then walked away. Charlie sat there in stunned silence.

By noon Friday, Charlie heard through the grapevine of Sandy's firing. Apparently she was fired for a poor job performance, or at least that was the official reason. Some people speculated she had a falling out with her cousin who had gotten her the job in the first place. No one was sad to see her go.

When she arrived home, Charlie prepared Christy for Jake's visit. Charlie was so tense she felt any little thing would set her off. Her nerves were shot at the thought of seeing Jake when he came to pick up Christy. How would he act around her? How would she act around him?

One thing was certain. Christy was excited at the prospect of spending the weekend with her father. She talked about nothing else all week. This would be her first weekend away from Charlie. Charlie had even taken her shopping for child-size luggage to take for her weekend visits with Jake. Christy loved it.

He arrived right on time. Christy bounced up and down when Charlie let him in. "Daddy!"

Jake gave Charlie a nod, barely acknowledging her presence. She hadn't known what to expect, but she didn't think he'd give her the cold shoulder. He saved his smiles for Christy. "Here's my little girl. Are you ready to go, kiddo?"

"Yes. I wanna see the bears."

"She's been talking about going to the zoo since I've told her about it. She likes bears," Charlie explained.

Jake spared her a moment's glance, which was a huge difference from what she was used to from him. "Well, I'll make sure we see them. Are there any no-nos you want to go over before we leave?" he asked coolly.

"Well, I usually have her in bed by eight and make sure she doesn't eat too much junk food. You already have all my numbers in case something happens so I guess that's it really. When should I expect the two of you back?"

"I'll drop her off on Sunday around noon. Is that okay with you?"

It cut her how he spoke to her as though she were a stranger, but this was what she wanted wasn't it? "That's fine.

Uh...I wanted to thank you for the check, although it's probably more than I need."

"Nonsense. I'm sure you can put it to good use. If you want to discuss it, can we do it later? I left the car running."

"Oh, okay. You did purchase a car seat for Christy, right?"

"Yes. I got one this week per your instructions."

"Well, that's all right then," she finished lamely for lack of anything better to say. Charlie gave Christy a kiss on the cheek. "Be a good girl for Daddy okay?"

"Okay," the child agreed easily.

Jake looked at her with indiscernible expression in his eyes. "We'll see you on Sunday, Charlie."

"Okay. Jake," she called to him as they were about to walk out the door.

He turned to her, impatience in his expression. "What?"

What did she have to say to him? Now that she'd made her decision, why was it so hard to stick with it? "Nothing. I'll see you Sunday."

He nodded.

When they were gone, Charlie felt desolate. She only had herself to blame.

ഗ്രൂ

"Uncle Jake!"

His head shot up as one of his nieces, Kammy, demanded his attention. Christy sat eating an ice pop. He'd brought ice cream for the girls, and they all sat at one of the tables with their treats. After taking one bite of his ice cream sandwich, Jake put his aside, his appetite nonexistent. "What is it, sweetheart?"

The redheaded girl sighed with exasperation. "I was trying to get your attention for a long time. You were daydreaming."

"Was I? I'm sorry. What did you want?"

"We're finished with our ice cream, can we see some more animals? You said you'd take us to the monkey house."

"Wait until Christy is finished and we can go."

"She is finished," Kara pointed out.

Jake looked down to see Christy licking what was left of her pop. She'd gotten most of it on her shirt and his pants. "Geez," he muttered, grabbing napkins to wipe his daughter off. He should have been paying closer attention, but his mind was elsewhere.

What should have been a fun day for him, Christy and the twins, was turning out more miserable by the minute, and it was all Charlie's fault. After she'd delegated him to being the stud in her life, he hadn't quite recovered. Even the time away he'd taken hadn't help.

He'd come to the conclusion that he'd have to get over her, but why did it hurt so much? Jake wiped the sticky film from Christy's face and hands. "Ow, Daddy. I don't like that," his child protested, making him realize he was being rougher than he'd intended.

"I'm sorry, sweetheart." He kissed her cheek and resumed the cleaning up, this time being more careful. Yet another thing he could blame Charlie for.

"Are you okay, Uncle Jake? You've been acting funny all day?" Kammy eyed him shrewdly.

He sighed. "I guess I've had a lot on my mind. I'm sorry if I've been more distracted than I should be."

"What are you distracted about?" Kara asked.

Jake laughed at his twin inquisitors. "What is this? Twenty questions?"

"Well, you're usually really fun," Kammy answered and then turned bright red when she realized how her words may have sounded. "Sorry, but it's true."

She was right. Whatever his problems with Charlie were was between him and Charlie. He shouldn't allow it to affect this outing. Even if it took the performance of his life, he'd make sure the rest of the day went smoothly for the girls. Later when he was alone, he'd figure out how to start living without Charlie.

Chapter Seventeen

The next couple weeks were stressful for Charlie. Although the office gossip had cooled considerably, she was still miserable. Jake no longer pursed her, but Charlie couldn't help feeling something was missing. When he'd dropped Christy off that first weekend, she'd invited him in for coffee, but he'd declined. The only thing he wanted to talk about was arranging for Christy's next visit with him.

It shouldn't have hurt, but it did.

Charlie picked at her lunch, not really feeling up to eating.

"Okay. Spill it. What's wrong, Charlie?" Laura demanded. She'd invited Charlie to lunch because they'd both been busy at work lately. This was the first time in a couple weeks when their schedules actually meshed.

"What's there to tell? I've been keeping busy."

"How's the grand love affair?"

Charlie groaned inwardly knowing her friend was going to bring the subject up when she had invited her to lunch, but she still wasn't prepared for it. "Can we not talk about it?"

"I think we do need to talk about it. I hope you don't take what I say next the wrong way, but you look horrible. You look like you've lost weight and you're wearing a miserable expression on your face. Please tell me what the matter is. Does it have anything to do with the grand love affair?"

Charlie sighed, knowing how Laura could be relentless when she wanted to be. "There is no grand love affair."

Laura frowned. "What do you mean? I thought you'd decided to have an affair with Jake."

Charlie shrugged. "When I apprised him of the plan he wasn't of the same mind."

"What happened?"

"Jake asked me to marry him and I turned him down. I told him I'd rather have a no-strings-attached affair."

Laura, who had been in the middle of taking a sip of her soda, spit it out on the table. "What? Did I just hear you correctly?" She grabbed her napkin and blotted the mess she'd made.

"Yes, you heard me correctly."

"Are you daft? You turned down a marriage proposal from Jake Fox. Wow, you are officially bonkers."

"Please stop. You're not making me feel any better."

"I'm sorry, but I just don't get it. Jake's a great guy who's apparently crazy about you and Christy. That you could turn him down is beyond me."

"I think it's for the best."

Laura shook her head in obvious disbelief. "How is it for the best when you're obviously miserable and you're depriving your child of a full time father?" She took a deep breath. "I'm not trying to judge you but—"

"Well, you're doing a pretty good job of it," Charlie snapped, losing her patience. When she'd agreed to have lunch with Laura it wasn't to be beaten over the head with the foolishness of her rash decision.

"Don't play the injured party here. I'm your friend, and as your friend it's my job to tell you when you're being a butthead. What did Jake say about your grand scheme?"

"He was angry."

"Justifiably so I would say."

"He hasn't said a word to me since, that wasn't related to Christy. As a matter of fact, he's supposed to be picking her up tonight. He's taking her to the circus. She's looking forward to it," Charlie babbled to stop from breaking down.

"It hurts, doesn't it?"

"I don't know what you're talking about."

"I think you do, Char. You've fought so hard to not fall in love with him, but it ended up happening anyway. And now because of your brainiac decision, you may have lost any opportunity you may have had with him."

"I don't love him!" Her voice rose louder than she meant it to, drawing stares from the other diners.

"If you say so."

"I do, so can we please drop the subject."

Laura reached across the table and grabbed Charlie's hand. "I'm not trying to be a pest, but I'm only bringing this up because I care about you."

"I know you do, Laura, but trust me to know my own feelings. I do appreciate your concern, but can we just let it go?"

"If that's what you want."

"It is."

Laura gave her a skeptical look. "I just hope you know what you're doing."

So do I, Charlie thought.

୫୦୦୪

Charlie was furious. She knew Jake was upset with her, but he could at least have granted her the courtesy of calling her to tell her he'd be running late. Jake said he would be there before eight to pick Christy up, but when ten o'clock rolled around there was still no sign of him. Charlie grew angrier with each passing minute.

Christy was especially upset, crying as Charlie bathed and put her to bed. "Where's Daddy?" she asked Charlie between sobs.

"I don't know, honey. Daddy is just running late."

"Daddy won't come?" Christy asked tearfully.

"When you wake up, he should be here." Charlie kept her fingers crossed on that one. *Damn you, Jake.* She had been so sure Jake was sincere about spending time with Christy so where the hell was he?

Eventually, Christy drifted off to sleep and Charlie tried to phone Jake to see what the deal was. She tried his home phone and his cell phone. She received no answer on both lines. When she saw him again, she was going to give him a piece of her mind. Christy had cried herself to sleep, and it was all Jake's fault. You just couldn't play with a little kid's affections like this.

By midnight Charlie finally decided to go to bed herself. As she was getting undressed the phone rang. If it were Jake, he was in for it she thought.

"Hello?" She answered the phone aggressively thinking it was Jake.

"Charlie, is that you?" A female voice anxiously asked on the other end. The voice was familiar but Charlie couldn't quite place who it belonged to.

"Yes, who is this?"

"It's Moira Fox." Jake's mother? Why in the world was she calling at this time of night?

"Hi, Moira. Is everything okay?"

"No. Everything is not okay. Jake's been in an automobile accident. They're saying he won't make it through the night." Moira began to sob through the phone.

"Oh my God!"

"Will you please come? Bring Christy with you. Bill and I want close friends and family around before he goes," Moira said between sobs.

"Of course. What hospital is he in?"

"Fairfax Memorial."

"I'll be there in a half an hour."

"Thank you, Charlie.

Charlie collapsed to the floor after she hung up. She hadn't even told him she loved him and she was doomed to lose him anyway.

ഇൻ

The family was waiting together in the lobby of the critical care unit. Charlie went immediately to Moira's side and hugged her tightly.

"Charlie, I'm so glad you and Christy could make it," Moira said, smiling through the tears glistening in her eyes.

"How did it happen?" Charlie asked.

"He was just leaving our house actually. He stopped by after working late at the office. Jake left our house around seven because he said he was going to go pick Christy up for the weekend. Apparently midway between our place and yours he was blindsided by a drunk driver. Why do people drink and drive? Now, I'm going to lose my baby." She broke into noisy, heart-wrenching wails. Bill Fox came over and hugged Moira. His eyes were bloodshot as if he too had been crying.

The entire room was filled with a somber-looking crowd. The entire Fox clan was there, kids included. Steve was there, and a few other people Charlie didn't know. The family who had been laughing and joking only a week before was now shattered with grief.

"What's she doing here?" Helen asked, charging toward them, red eyes shooting daggers at Charlie.

"I called her here, Helen, so don't you dare start anything, missy," Moira warned.

"Oh, I'll start something with her alright. After what she did she has a lot of nerve to show her face right now." Helen advanced on Charlie as if she wanted to hit her. Fortunately, Jason was close by to grab his wife before anything happened.

"I'm sorry, Charlie. She's a little distraught. Emotions are running high right now," Jason explained apologetically. He turned to his wife. "Helen, let's go get some coffee," Jason suggested. Helen glared at Charlie one last time before allowing her husband to lead her away.

"We're really sorry about that, Charlie. She didn't really mean it. We love Helen but sometimes she thinks without speaking," Bill apologized.

"It's okay. Can we see Jake?" Charlie asked anxiously.

"The doctor is allowing only one person at a time to see him. We've already seen him. Carl is in the room right now. He should be out any minute. You can go next. We'll keep an eye on Christy for you," Bill said.

Charlie took a seat with Christy in her lap. She cradled her daughter close to her. Silent tears coursed down her face. She hadn't felt like this since the night Paul died, but only now, the feeling was ten times worse because she was finally able to admit to herself she loved Jake and now it was too late.

If she could turn back time, she would have said yes when Jake proposed. Even if she knew she only had a short time to be with him, he would have at least died knowing how she felt about him.

Carl came out to the lobby. He was wiping a tear from his eyes. "Whoever's next, can go in," he said taking a seat next to his wife.

Charlie looked over to Moira and Bill for reassurance. Moira nodded. Charlie took a deep breath and stood up with Christy in her arms. Christy looked up with a glazed look in her blue eyes Charlie attributed to sleepiness. "Don't cry, Mommy. The man said everything would okay," Christy whispered.

Charlie looked at her daughter oddly. "What man, Christy?"

"The man in the blue shirt."

Charlie looked around. There was no man in the lobby wearing a blue shirt. Obviously Christy was delirious from lack of sleep. "I hope everything will be okay, honey." Charlie leaned over to give Christy a kiss on the cheek. She handed Christy to her grandpa who directed her to Jake's room.

Charlie wasn't prepared for the sight she saw. Jake lay on the bed, broken and bruised. He had a bandage wrapped around his head, and he had bruises and cuts all over his exposed skin. He was connected to several machines and he looked so pale. Charlie walked over to his bedside.

She began to cry softly. Her Jake, her beautiful perfect Jake lay in the hospital bed so helpless. "Jake, if you can hear me, this is Charlie." Charlie stole a nervous glance at the EKG machine, which was steadily beeping away—for now.

"Jake, I'm so sorry. I'm so very sorry. I lied to you, Jake. I lied about still being in love with my husband. I mean, I'll always love him but not the way I love you. I love you, Jake. Don't you die on me."

She got angry. "Don't you dare leave me and Christy. She needs you. I need you." Jake lay there silently. "Did you hear me, Jake? Wake up! Wake up you son of a bitch and live! Live, because if you don't, I'll die too!" Charlie broke into body shaking sobs. How could God be so cruel? Jake didn't deserve it. "It should be me, God!" Charlie shouted heavenward.

Just then a nurse walked in. "Ma'am, you're making way too much noise in here. I'm going to have to ask you to leave."

"Please. I'll be quiet," Charlie begged, not wanting to leave Jake's side.

Just then Charlie heard a sound she'd only ever heard on television and movies. She turned to the EKG machine in time to see it flatline.

Chapter Eighteen

Jake trudged toward the light and its warmth. It seemed to beckon him forward. He thought he heard someone talking to him from a distance, but he was probably imagining things. Jake was nearly there when a tall, dark figure blocked his path. "I can't let you go in there," the man said with a shake of his head.

"Aren't I supposed to go there? I feel like I'm being called there. Please move out of my way." When Jake made a move to walk around him, the stranger also moved.

"I'm sorry, but I can't. Don't you know where that tunnel leads to?"

Jake shrugged. "Should I care?"

"I think you should, considering that tunnel takes you to the other side."

"The other side? What in the world are you talking about?" Who was this man and why was he trying to stop Jake?

"The other side of life I mean."

Jake paused. "Do you mean...if I walk into the light I'll be dead?"

"That's exactly what I'm saying. You don't want to go in there."

"What...what happened to me?"

"You were in a pretty nasty car accident."

"So you mean...."

"Yes, your life is hanging in the balance. This is actually your subconscious, but trust me, going into that light will end your life."

Jake narrowed his eyes. "Who the hell are you?"

The stranger grinned. "Hell has nothing to do with my mission, but I can't let you walk into that light."

"Why do you care?"

"Because I made a promise to someone very special a long time ago, and I intend to keep it. You can't go anywhere."

"Why not?"

"To keep my peanut happy. Besides, you have so much to live for. At this very moment, your friends and loved ones are gathered in the hospital praying for your recovery. You wouldn't want to let them down would you?"

Peanut? Was this guy crazy? He snorted. "I bet Charlie isn't out there."

"Actually she is. Didn't you hear her speaking to you earlier?"

"All I can hear is the beautiful music playing in that light over there."

"You're not even trying to fight, are you?" The man shook his head in what looked like disgust.

"What do I have to fight for? The one thing I believed in is gone."

"So because of that you're just willing to give up? That's rather selfish of you."

"You wouldn't know anything about it."

"I wouldn't? I doubt that. I know a lot about disappointment actually. I'll never have another chance at reclaiming the woman

I love, but you have that opportunity and I'll be damned if I allow you to throw it away."

"Opportunity? What opportunity? She's already made it clear I'm just a glorified sex toy to her."

"Maybe she had her reasons for doing what she did, but you'll never find out what those reason are if you walk into that light. Are you willing to abandon your daughter so easily? She's a precious little thing. She'll need her father in her life, don't you think?"

At the mention of his daughter Jake realized how selfish he was being. "You're right. I guess I wasn't thinking clearly, but I feel this strong pull toward it. It seems to be sucking me in."

"This is where you have to fight. You have to figure out how badly you want it."

"I do want it, for my daughter's—and Charlie's sake."

The man smiled. "That's more like it. Give me your hand.

Ⅎℛ

"No!" Charlie screamed. The nurse rushed out of the room, returning immediately with a doctor and another nurse.

"Ma'am, you're going to have to leave while we attempt to resuscitate the patient," the nurse said as she gently guided Charlie out of the room. When Charlie was outside the door, it shut firmly in her face with a decisive click.

Charlie watched helplessly through the glass in the door as the team tried valiantly to save Jake's life. She couldn't move. She felt her world had crumbled. She watched for several seconds before her legs decided to cooperate. She didn't want to be the one to tell the family, but she had to. This was obviously her punishment for not telling Jake how she felt.

She walked numbly back to the lobby. She caught the anxious look on Moira's pale face, and her heart sunk further. "Charlie what's wrong? Has something happened to Jake?" An alarmed look crossed Moira's face. The family immediately surrounded her.

"They are trying to resuscitate him right now as we speak, but he flatlined," Charlie reported numbly.

"No! Not my baby. Not my baby!" Moira collapsed against Bill, who looked as if he needed someone to catch him. The room broke out in cries of anguish. Steve sat in the corner of the room with a stunned expression on his face. The children were huddled together with tears in their eyes.

The only dry eyes in the room belonged to Christy, who seemed to be in her own little world. Charlie stood in the center of the room wishing this were all a nightmare. How in the world was she going to explain to her child her daddy was dead?

Charlie looked at her daughter, who was looking around at everyone as though she were trying to make sense of everything. She couldn't help but wonder why Christy was strangely calm. She hadn't even complained after being woken up so abruptly. Her daughter climbed down from her chair, holding her cherished doll "Baby" Jake had given her. Christy walked over to Charlie and tugged on her pant leg. "Mommy, don't cry. The man said Daddy is okay. He said he would hold Daddy's hand," Christy said.

Charlie looked dazedly down at her daughter. What the heck was Christy talking about? Charlie leaned over and scooped her daughter up and clutched her to her chest. Charlie's body shuddered with sobs as she held and rocked Christy.

"Mommy, the man says it makes him sad to see you cry. He says don't cry 'cause Daddy is okay." Christy looked at her with tears forming in her eyes.

"What man?" Charlie demanded, raising her voice. Christy cringed at Charlie's raised voice and began to cry herself. Charlie felt lower than low. She hadn't meant to yell, besides, Christy was all she had left in the world. She walked over to the nearest chair and sat down with Christy on her lap. "I'm sorry for yelling, honey, but what man do you keep talking about?"

"The man with the blue shirt. It has footprints on it," Christy sniffed.

"Where is he?" Charlie looked around her, but saw nothing.

"He's with Daddy, holding his hand. He was sitting in the car with us Mommy."

Charlie froze. Was this her daughter's way of dealing with grief—making up imaginary friends? "Christy, there wasn't anyone in the car with us."

"Uh-huh. He sat next to you," Christy argued stubbornly.

"Christy—"

Just then, the doctor who had been in Jake's room walked out into the waiting area. Charlie held her breath, waiting for fateful words she knew the doctor would say. The room fell silent and she knew the rest of the occupants were just as anxious as she was. She braced herself for the official words.

Dr. Reynolds cleared his throat officiously. "We were able to resuscitate him," he began. Loud sighs of relief broke throughout the lobby. "As I stated before, we didn't expect him to make it through the night, but his vitals are reading much stronger now than they originally were when he was brought in. That in itself is a miracle but he's not out of the woods yet, ladies and gentlemen. He took a pretty hard hit on the head so even if he awakes there could be some brain damage. The next twenty-four hours are going to be the most critical, but I think if he makes it past that point, he'll pull through."

"Oh thank God," Moira said with tears streaming down her face. Charlie stood up with Christy in her arms and went over to hug Moira. As a mother, Charlie knew exactly how Moira was feeling. Had it been Christy in the same predicament, she didn't know what she would do with herself.

"See, Mommy. I told you," Christy gloated.

"You sure did, honey. I guess we have your friend to thank," Charlie said, playing along, still not believing some mysterious man was talking to her daughter.

"What's she talking about?" Bill asked curiously.

"She says there's a man in a blue shirt who has been telling her Jake would be okay. She's been saying it since we got here," Charlie explained.

Bill looked at his granddaughter curiously. "May I?" he asked Charlie for permission to take Christy. Charlie nodded. Bill lifted Christy into his arms but the rest of the family who had heard snippets of the conversation gathered around them curiously. "Can you tell Grandpa about this man?" Bill asked Christy.

"He was in the car with Mommy and me. He gave me a hug. He said Daddy is okay, and to tell Mommy not to cry." The room was silent.

"What else did he say?" Bill prompted.

"He said don't worry. He will hold Daddy's hand to make sure he won't go away," Christy said. Where was she getting all this from, Charlie wondered?

"Where is this man now?" Moira asked.

"He's next to Mommy." Christy laughed as if it were the most obvious thing in the world. Everyone gave Christy a strange look. "There's no one there, honey." Moira pointed to the empty space beside Charlie.

"Yes, there is!" piped in a little voice behind them. The voice belonged to Helen and Jason's second youngest son, five-year-old Caleb. Everyone turned to the little boy. "Nana, he's standing right there beside Auntie Charlie. Can't you see him? He's a brown man, and he's wearing a light blue shirt." Caleb pointed to the apparently empty space next to Charlie.

All the adults looked uneasily at each other.

"Caleb, what did Mommy tell you about lying," Helen scolded, coming forward to take her son's hand.

"I'm not lying, Mommy," Caleb said indignantly. "He's standing right there. His shirt has footprints all over it with a ram in the front," Caleb described.

Charlie froze. No. It couldn't be. "Caleb, can you recognize letters yet?" Charlie asked.

"Of course he can. My son is no dummy." Helen glared at Charlie.

Charlie ignored Helen and knelt down in front of Caleb. "Are there letters on his shirt?" she asked the little boy. Caleb nodded solemnly. "What color are the letters?"

"White."

"What do they say, honey?" Charlie prompted.

"Oh come on. These kids are obviously tired, they must have talked at some point and they're sharing the same hallucination," Helen dismissed.

"Pipe down, Helen. I would like to hear what Caleb has to say." Bill chided lightly.

"What do the letters say?" Charlie asked again.

Caleb turned and looked up at the empty space beside Charlie as if he were in a daze. "U-N-C," Caleb read proudly.

Charlie passed out.

ॐ

Charlie came to on the couch in waiting room with someone fanning her face. A nurse was standing over her. "What happened?" Charlie asked, shaking her head.

"You gave us a bit of a fright but I think the events of the day have just overwhelmed you. I suggest you go home and get some rest. It will be a while before Mr. Fox regains consciousness," the nurse advised.

Charlie shot up. "No. I'm not leaving," Charlie protested with a determined gleam in her eyes.

The nurse looked like she wanted to argue but thought better of it. "Well, you're in for a long wait."

"I don't care."

"Suit yourself, but take care of yourself, or we will have to admit you too," The nurse warned before going off.

When the nurse was gone, Moira came to Charlie's side. "Charlie, you scared us for a second." Moira knelt down to feel her brow.

"I'm fine. I think I just need some air," she said.

"Okay. I'll walk with you."

"Where's Christy?" Charlie looked around.

"Carl took the children down the hall to the vending machine to get something to drink. Don't worry. She's in good hands. Come on." She helped Charlie off the couch.

When they stood outside of the hospital doors, Charlie felt a little better. She hated the smell of sickness that saturated the hospital.

"Are you feeling better?" Moira asked.

"Yes, much better. Thank you. Moira, I appreciate you being so nice to me," Charlie said.

"Why shouldn't I be? Don't let Helen get to you. Her bark is far worse than her bite." Moira shrugged off the incident.

"I wasn't thinking about her actually, although I wish we had gotten off on better footing."

"Well, Helen is quick to judge a lot of times, but she's a good girl. She'll come around. Now, tell me what happened in there. When Caleb said those letters, you looked as if you had seen a ghost before you passed out."

Charlie shivered. "I didn't but Christy and Caleb apparently did," she answered slowly.

"What?" Moira asked, looking confused.

"They described my husband's favorite shirt. He always wore that shirt. I put that old shirt in storage before I moved to this area, so how could they possibly know about it? I never talked to Christy about my husband, and Caleb...well, he obviously wouldn't know anything about it."

"Oh my. It all sound so very twilight zone to me."

"I know. It's so weird but they say angels do exist and I don't think I knew anyone who deserved to be an angel more than Paul. If he is an angel, this sounds like something he would do."

"What do you mean?"

"He would find a way to reassure me everything is okay. He was always looking out for me." Charlie smiled. Her heart swelled fondly, knowing Paul seemed to be giving his blessing to love Jake. Why else would he be there holding Jake's hand as Christy had put it?

"He sounds like he was quite a guy. You must have loved him very much," Moira observed.

"I do. I mean I did...well, I will always love him. I'm not in love with him anymore, though. I couldn't have asked for a more special man in my life. He touched so many people when he was alive," Charlie said wistfully.

"But?"

"But I also know he wants me to be happy, and the fact Christy said he was holding Jake's hand, it's as if he's trying to save Jake to make me happy."

"Will it make you happy?"

"Yes. It would make me very happy. I love Jake very much. I was so scared of loving again I lost sight of the gift I was given. I had such a loving relationship with Paul, I thought I would never find it again, but then Jake came into my life and things changed. I think that's why I fought so hard. I was falling in love with him, but in the back of my mind, I thought if I allowed myself to give into those feelings, I would lose him like I lost Paul. I know that sounds silly but it's how I felt," Charlie explained.

"It doesn't sound silly to me at all. I knew we were kindred spirits when I met you. I was scared to love at one time, too. Believe it or not, the road wasn't easy for Bill and me," Moira confided.

"Really? But you two seem so in love." Charlie was incredulous.

"We are now. As you can see, Bill is still a very good-looking man. You should have seen him when he was in his twenties. He was...what do you young people say? A hottie I think. Yes, that's it. Bill was quite a hottie. We formally met at a civil rights march although we went to the same school. I just never had the courage to approach him before then because he was the big man on campus. He had a bit of a reputation for being a ladies' man. Even back then I was losing the battle with my weight and I wasn't exactly prom queen material, so when Bill showed an interest in me, I couldn't see what he saw in me. He could have practically any girl on campus, but he liked lil' ole frumpy me. I was scared to love him because I wasn't beautiful and I thought he would eventually leave me for someone who was all the things I felt I wasn't."

"I think you're beautiful." And Charlie meant it.

Moira smiled and patted the younger woman on the cheek. "That's sweet of you to say, dear."

"But it's true and your husband is crazy about you. Anyone can see that."

"I know that now, but the point is, it took something big for me to wake up and realize life is much too short for what ifs."

"What happened?"

"Oh nothing of this magnitude but it was enough to make me realize what I fool I was being. You see, Bill was accepted to two law schools after graduation, Columbia University on the east coast, and Stanford on the west coast. He asked me to marry him. I turned him down so he chose Stanford. When he left, I was devastated. I moped for weeks until a good friend of mine talked some sense into me. I hopped on the next flight to California, and when I found him, I got down on my knees and asked that man to marry me," Moira finished proudly.

"You asked him?"

"I sure did and I don't regret a single minute. Bill has been a wonderful husband and father. He's brought joy to my life every single day since we've been married."

Charlie was humbled by Moira revealing such an intimate detail of her life to her. "Thank you for sharing that with me."

"No problem, dear. After all, you'll be my new daughter if Jake pulls through this."

246

"Jake will pull though this. I know he will," Charlie said with a certainty she hadn't felt earlier. She knew her guardian angel was looking out for Jake.

Chapter Nineteen

Nearly a week later, Charlie drove to the hospital after dropping Christy off at daycare. She still couldn't believe the events of the past week. Everything seemed to mesh into one big blur. Jake did pull through with no signs of brain damage, much to her and the Fox family's relief. Thankfully, the only damage he seemed to suffer was a couple of fractured ribs and a broken arm, but they would heal.

The only reminder he would probably keep from the accident was a scar along his temple where the doctors had removed glass fragments. In time, that too would eventually heal until it was barely noticeable. Charlie knew it could have been much worse.

At the insistence of Jake's attending physician, a strict visiting schedule was implemented so as not to tire the patient. Although she was never alone when she went to see him, Charlie took some time off from work so she could be available if Jake suddenly needed her. There was always a family member, a friend or someone from work already there when she went to see him.

Jake always seemed happy to see her but there was a bit of reserve in his eyes that made Charlie wonder if this accident had perhaps changed Jake's feelings as well. The thought made her heart ache. She figured it was no more than she deserved if he stopped loving her.

Charlie walked into Jake's room to find him alone. Here it was. This was her opportunity to tell him how she felt without interruptions.

"Hi, Jake." Charlie smiled nervously entering the room.

Jake, who had been vacantly staring out the window, turned his head toward her with tired eyes. "Hi, Charlie. Have a seat."

"How are you feeling today?" She sat in the chair next to his bedside, taking a deep breath. What she wanted to do most was throw herself at him and beg his forgiveness, but she had to take things easy—for now.

"I'm feeling much better than I did yesterday, but my arm itches like a son of a bitch and if I move a certain way, my side hurts. I'm not due for another round of Percocet for another hour," he complained miserably.

"I'm sorry to hear you're uncomfortable. If there's anything I can do to make it better, I will."

"Thanks, Charlie, but I will be okay. So I see you're taking some time off," he observed.

"I couldn't work knowing you were here, Jake."

"You didn't have to do that, Charlie. I'll be okay." Jake shrugged nonchalantly.

It was now or never. She had to tell him now. "Jake I—"

"So where's—" They both laughed because they had started to speak at the same time. "You first."

"No, you please," Charlie said to buy herself some more time. She didn't realize how hard this was going to be.

"I was going to ask you where Christy was."

"I dropped Christy off at the daycare for a couple of hours. She missed her friends and I thought she needed a little break from the hospital. It's been a rough week for her." Charlie hesitated and then added, "It's been a rough week for me as well." She finished, looking at Jake with probing eyes.

"Has it really?"

Charlie was about to answer him when the door opened.

"Jake, you're up. That's good I was—oh, you're here," Helen finished rudely as she saw Charlie sitting at Jake's bedside.

"Yes, I'm here. How are you today?" Charlie asked, clenching her jaw to hold her temper in check. She didn't want to start anything with Jake's sister, but there was only so much she could take. All week Charlie had put up with rude remarks and angry glares from Helen. Charlie was not easily riled, but her patience was wearing thin.

Helen looked as if she didn't want to answer but she finally did after another glower to Charlie. "Fine," Helen said, her tone short. She then sat down on the other side of Jake's bed and took his hand. Helen chatted on, rudely ignoring Charlie.

Now that Helen was there, Charlie knew she wouldn't get a word in edgewise. She sat there for a few minutes while Helen dominated the conversation. Jake tried to include Charlie, but Helen would take over if Charlie even attempted to speak. After this went on for several minutes Charlie stood up. "I have to go, but I'll be back to visit you, Jake," Charlie said during the first break in conversation.

"You don't have to go." He reached for her with his good arm only to end up jarring his ribs. He winced in pain.

"Be careful, Jake," Charlie said with concern. "I will leave you two alone. I'll bring Christy by the next time I visit."

"When will you be back?" He almost seemed as though he were upset she was leaving so abruptly, but there was no way she was going to stay with him another minute without knocking his sister into next week.

"Maybe in a day or two. You need your rest," Charlie finished firmly.

"Can't you come back tomorrow?"

"For God sake, Jake, if she wants to go, let her." Helen rolled her eyes, exasperation in her voice.

Charlie turned to Helen. The little bit of control she had been holding in concerning this woman was threadbare. She would have loved to give Helen a nice smack, but didn't want to cause a scene at the hospital that would upset Jake. She wasn't, however, going to put up with anymore of Helen's taunts.

"Helen, I'm not sure what I did to you personally to warrant your rudeness. I have tried to be nice but you have been a nasty bitch. You're lucky I don't believe in violence or I'd ram my fist down your throat. Because you're Jake's sister I would like us to be civil to each other at least, but if you ever again talk to me like you have been, I just might break my no violence rule." Charlie turned away from Helen's stricken face.

"I'll see you later, Jake." She smiled at him before walking out the door.

"The nerve of that woman," Helen huffed. "Really, Jake, just because she managed to pop out your child, who she hid for all this time, doesn't mean she can just ingratiate herself with the family. You should have seen the way Mom and Dad were treating her."

"How did Mom and Dad treat her?" Jake asked, wanting to strangle his sister. He couldn't blame Charlie for going off on Helen. He'd always told Helen her mouth would get her in trouble one day.

251

"Like she was one of the family. Oh, she put on a good show as if she cared, but I know it was just an act. Then she made up some ghost story just to be the center of attention. To make matters worse, she involved the kids," Helen seethed. Jake had tuned Helen out at the word ghost.

"That woman needs a good slap across the face," Helen declared, bringing him back to their conversation.

"That woman has a name. It's Charlie, use it."

"I would sooner call her something else."

"Are you finished?" Jake put up with a lot where his sister was concerned, but the disrespect of his daughter's mother was one thing he wouldn't tolerate.

"I could go on all day about that woman."

"But you won't because I will not listen to you anymore."

"Jake—"

"Can it, Helen. You know what? You can be a real jackass sometimes. What right do you have to treat her that way?"

"How can you ask me that after what she did to you? She's lucky I don't scratch her eyes out."

"Helen, you're lucky she didn't kick your ass. What happened between Charlie and me is none of your business. No matter what you think you know about the situation, don't you ever talk about her like that again. She's the mother of my child and I love her," Jake warned his sister.

Helen snorted. "You love her? Even after what she did?"

"Helen, I know your heart is in the right place but you don't know Charlie. Maybe if you got to know her, you would realize she is not as bad as you think. Truth be known, I haven't been an angel in this entire ordeal."

Helen's jaw dropped as if she couldn't believe he had spoken to her that way. "Jake, I just want you to be happy, and from what I've seen, Charlie has made you miserable. Even when I walked in here you had sort of a sad look in your eyes. Do you think I can stand back and say nothing?"

"As difficult as I know it is for you to keep you mouth shut, that's exactly what I'm asking you to do. I'm asking you this, as your brother, to be nice to Charlie and if you can't be nice to her, please be civil."

"No way!"

"For me, Helen. You claim you are mad at her because of the way she treated me, but you don't seem to care very much for my feelings right now. I'm asking you to do this one thing for me. If you want me to be happy then prove it. Just lay off, okay?"

"And if I don't?" she challenged.

Jake sighed. "We've always been close, Hel, and I would hate to lose that closeness by not visiting you anymore."

"You wouldn't!"

"I would hope you don't test me on it."

"You can't be serious."

"I have never been more serious about anything in my life. When you speak against Charlie, you're speaking against me," Jake said, wincing in pain as he tried to reposition himself in the bed. He wished the nurse would hurry up with his medication so he could get some sleep.

Helen folded her arms mutinously before she spoke. "Fine. I'll be civil, but not for her sake. I'm doing it for you and that adorable little girl of yours," she said stubbornly.

"That's all I ask," he said leaning back against the bed.

"So where do you two stand?"

"I don't know. I really don't know."

ഇരു

That night as Charlie was tucking Christy in, she asked, "Can I see Daddy soon?"

"Sure. We can see him tomorrow." Charlie knelt to kiss Christy's cheek.

"You haveta kiss Baby too," Christy ordered, holding up her doll. Charlie chuckled softly, bending over to kiss the doll held so tightly in Christy's arms. Heaven forbid if she forgot to kiss Christy's favorite toy. Charlie suspected Christy loved her doll so much because it had come from her daddy.

"Mommy?"

"Yes, sweetie?"

"I miss Daddy."

"I miss him, too," Charlie answered truthfully.

"Can he come live with us?" Christy asked innocently.

"I don't know but I hope so. I would like that very much actually. Mommy will try her best to make it happen, okay?"

Christy nodded her head, seeming to accept this answer. "Mommy, the man wanted me to tell you somethin'."

Charlie stiffened. Was Paul right here with him at this very moment? "Is he here now?"

"No. He had to go home."

"Where is his home?"

"Heaven."

Charlie's eyes misted with tears. She had always known Paul would end up there, but it was nice to have her suspicions confirmed. "What did he say, honey?"

"He said 'be happy, peanut'," Christy giggled. If Charlie had doubts before, she had absolutely no doubt in her mind that she had a special guardian angel. She waited next to Christy until she fell asleep. Charlie walked out on the patio and looked heavenward.

"Thank you, Paul." Tears coursed down her cheeks. He had kept his promise to her.

℘∞℘

Jake was released from the hospital the following week. His parents picked him up. He was anxious to get back to work. There were so many loose ends he had to tie up. At least if he was working he could forget about how much he loved Charlie and how little she loved him. It tore him apart, to think she only wanted him for sex. If he could, he would sever all ties with her so he could move on with his life, but he had his daughter to think of.

He loved Christy more than life itself and would always be in her life, but it would be tough dealing with Charlie and pretending to feel an indifference toward her he didn't feel. On the car ride home from the hospital, he stared aimlessly out the window.

"Jake, are you okay, honey? You've been awful quiet?" his mother asked.

"I'm fine. I'm just thinking about work. I have a lot of stuff to do at the office and I was hoping to go in tomorrow," he replied. That wasn't exactly a lie. He had been thinking about work.

"Are you crazy, son?" his father roared from the driver's seat.

"No. I just have a lot of stuff to attend to."

"There is no way we're letting you go back into work so soon after your accident. We've already discussed this; you're going to convalesce at our place until the doctor says you can go back to work," his mother stated firmly. Her tone suggested the subject wasn't up for discussion, but Jake wasn't going to let the conversation end.

"Mom, my employees depend on me. I have some important meetings scheduled."

"Don't argue with your mother, Jake. I'm sure Steve is capable of handling things for you while you're out," Bill interjected.

Jake sighed. He felt like he was ten years old again. "What the heck am I suppose to do? I can't stand staying still for very long."

"Steve was nice enough to bring your laptop to us. You can use that, as long as you don't overdo things, and we're throwing a party for you tomorrow. A sort of welcome home celebration," Moira answered.

"A party? Mom, I don't want a party. Can't you cancel it?"

"No. Carl and Helen are bringing their families. We've invited some neighbors who have asked after your well-being, and Charlie and Christy are coming. When I talked to Christy on the phone the other night, she sounded very excited about the party."

At the mention of Charlie's name, Jake perked up. "And Charlie? Did she sound excited?" Jake asked anxiously.

"She sounded pleased," Moira answered.

At that moment, the thought of a party didn't sound so bad. Charlie sounded pleased? Did he dare to hope? He had already gotten his hopes up with her before, only to have them cruelly smashed. Doubts assailed his mind. Maybe his mother had said that Charlie sounded pleased to make him feel better, but then again, she could have been telling the truth.

She did visit him in the hospital. He wondered what would have happened if they'd had some time alone when she had come to visit him in the hospital. He was almost positive she was going to tell him something the one day she had come to visit and Helen had interrupted. Jake wished he had the answers because he didn't think his heart could take another beating right now.

♏♏

As Charlie drove to the Foxes' for the party she was bristling with anticipation. Tonight would be the night to tell Jake what was in her heart. Moira welcomed Charlie and Christy when they arrived. Christy leaped out of Charlie's arms, gave her nana a kiss and went in search of Jake.

"She's been so excited about the party. She's talked nonstop about it."

"Well, it's a pretty exciting thing to have Jake back with us. It was a little touch and go there for a while." Moira shuddered as if she were recollecting that night a few weeks ago.

"I know. I don't think I could ever go through something like that again."

"The twins have been waiting for Christy to arrive. Those two are little mothers in training and someone else has been asking when you would arrive." Moira smiled.

"Who?"

"Jake, silly. Who else?"

"He has? In the hospital he seemed so...distant. He was friendly but a little distant."

"He's hurting, Charlie. He loves you, but he won't make the first move. Why didn't you tell him what you told me at the hospital?" Moira asked with a bit of censure in her tone.

"Because we were never really alone. He always had a visitor."

"That's no excuse. You're scared. I know how you feel. Remember, I've been there. When I proposed to Bill, he was in the middle of a lecture. I did it in front of about two hundred students. There are about forty people here, give or take a couple, so you march yourself in that living room right now, missy, and tell my son how you feel," Moira commanded with all the fierceness of any Army general.

"Yes, ma'am."

Charlie squared her shoulders and walked off to find Jake. He was in the living room sitting on the couch with Christy on his lap. Some family and guests whom Charlie didn't know surrounded him. She made her way through the crowd to stand in front of him. "Hi, Jake," Charlie said nervously.

"Charlie," he acknowledged with reserve still in his eyes.

"Christy, why don't you go find your cousins to play with while I talk to your daddy?"

"But I just got here," Christy argued.

"Please? I think Kara and Kammy were looking for you."

At the mention of the twins, Christy jumped off of Jake's lap. "Bye, Daddy!" And she raced off.

"That kid is a little Benedict Arnold. She shows absolutely no loyalty to her old man." Jake shook his head.

Charlie grinned. "When she gets tired of them babying her, she'll be back. May I?" She indicated the empty space on the couch next to him.

"Sure. What did you want to talk to me about?" he asked cautiously.

"I wanted to talk about us."

"Us? According to you, there is no us."

She flinched at the reminder. A hush fell over the curious onlookers who surrounded them. She wasn't going to back down. "I was a fool, Jake. I was so scared to love you I ended up hurting you and myself, as well. I messed up, Jake, and I'm asking you to forgive me and I'm asking you to be my husband."

Their audience let out a collective gasp. By now, people who had only been pretending to listen before were openly listening.

"What?" Disbelief filled his piercing gaze.

"I love you. Will you marry me?" Charlie repeated. Her face was hot with embarrassment and her heart was pounding so loudly she was sure everyone could hear.

The incredulous look on his face told her he still didn't believe her. She wished he would say something because she was growing more worried by the minute. What if he no longer had feelings for her? If that were the case, she didn't know what she would do with herself, but it was no less than she deserved.

"Is this a dream?" It was obvious he couldn't believe this was happening.

"If it is, then we're both dreaming." She laughed nervously as he grew silent again. *Please let him love me.*

"Jake?" Charlie didn't know how much longer she could sustain herself under his intense scrutiny without breaking down.

"For Pete's sake boy, say yes." Bill's loud voice boomed through the crowd.

Jake looked up, noticing for the first time they had an audience.

"Say yes," someone else called out.

He nodded his head numbly.

"Is that a yes?" Charlie smiled, some of the tension draining out of her.

"Yes." He finally found his voice.

"Come here." He pulled her to him with his good arm and kissed her with a hungry passion, which she eagerly returned. He pulled back slightly. "This isn't a dream," he whispered then his lips found hers once more.

A burst of applause went through the room. Christy came running over to them. "Mommy, now can we all live together?"

"Yes. Definitely," Charlie answered, pulling Christy up on her lap.

"Oh boy," Christy shouted. Everyone laughed at Christy's enthusiasm.

"Oh boy is right." Jake was grinning from ear to ear. His eyes were filled with unshed tears. Before he could say anything else, people began to rush forward to congratulate them.

Jake's parents came forward to kiss the three of them.

"Finally," Moira said.

The entire Fox clan walked over to Charlie to welcome her into the family. Even Helen offered her congratulations, although she still wasn't overly warm in offering them.

Jake turned to Charlie and kissed her gently on the lips.

"I need to be alone with you." The soft whisper in her ear sent goose bumps along her arm.

"Come home with me," Charlie replied.

৩০৫৪

It was another hour before the three of them could leave the party. Jake informed his parents he was going home with Charlie and that she would take care of him. There was no argument from them. The Foxes smiled knowingly to each other, remembering what it was like when they were younger.

Later that night after putting Christy to bed, Jake and Charlie lay cuddled close together. They were unable to make love because of Jake's ribs, but they were both content to lay naked side by side, stroking each other's bodies.

"Charlie, what changed your mind about us?" He cupped a perky breast in his hand, rubbing his thumb over her hardened nipple.

She moaned softly at the feel of his hand on her sensitive skin. She clasped her hand over his to pull it away. She could barely think when he touched her like that.

"When I heard about the accident, I wanted to die. I realized what a fool I was being. You see, I lied to you about my husband, Jake. I'm not in love with him anymore. He'll always be special to me, but he's gone and I have to move on with my life. I was just so scared of loving you because I didn't want to be hurt again," she explained.

Now that she was finally confessing this to him, she felt guilty. Charlie felt awful that it took a terrible car accident in order for her to realize her foolishness.

Jake stroked her cheek. "Charlie, why couldn't you tell me this before? We could have worked through this together. I thought you hated me."

"I never hated you, Jake. I hated myself at times for being such a coward, but never you. I love you. I was just too scared to tell you. To my way of thinking, I just couldn't put my heart on the line like that again. When I lost Paul it nearly destroyed my life, but in the back of my mind, I knew you posed a much bigger threat to my heart than Paul ever had. Besides, in the beginning, I thought you only wanted me for sex."

"Of course you know now, that that isn't true. Yes, when we make love, it's like magic, but that's only a small part of what I feel for you. I didn't realize it then but I believe I fell in love with you on the night we first met."

"After a one-night stand?"

"It was more than that and you know it. Love is a funny thing. Sometimes it grows with time, but sometimes, as in our case, it's instant. You felt it too but you weren't ready to accept it yet. I never got over you leaving me the way you did. I tried to forget about you by dating other women, but when I was with them, all I could think about was you." Jake tilted her chin and planted a gentle kiss on her lips.

"You did?"

"Yes."

"Oh, Jake. I'm so sorry for running off like that. I was so confused. I was still caught up in my grief and I had all these feelings that were surfacing for you, I didn't know what to do so I took the coward's way out. I ran," she recounted, ashamed of her actions.

Jake kissed her as if to say all was forgiven. "Everything is okay, now that we're together." He lowered his head once more, deepening the kiss. "Do you have any idea how intoxicating you are, Charlie? From the moment I laid eyes on you, I wanted to taste your sexy lips, and when I finally did, I didn't want to stop."

Charlie touched his face. How she loved this man. "You always say the most wonderful things. I don't think I deserve you," she said humbly.

"If anything, I don't deserve you. I don't think I really started to live until you came into my life." He paused to laugh. "I should write greeting cards, shouldn't I?"

"Umm, don't give up your day job. God, I'm horny," she admitted. Being so close to him like this was wreaking havoc on her body.

Charlie felt Jake's erection pressing against the back of her thighs. "Let me help you with that." Charlie smiled wickedly. Charlie rolled over and gently pushed Jake back against his pillows.

She slid down to his side until she was eye level with his throbbing shaft. She gently took it into hand and began to pump gently. Jake moaned loudly, thrashing his head back and forth.

Charlie leaned over to stroke the velvety tip with her tongue. His body tensed under her mouth as he released an impassioned groan. "Do you like that, Jake?"

"You know I do," he answered through gritted teeth. She smiled, lifting her head and seeing his passion-glazed eyes. It pleased her to know she had this effect on him. She could tell he was fighting for control to remain completely still by the way beads of sweat broke out along his forehead. His control was really tested when she lowered her head once more, wrapping her mouth around his cock and slowly beginning to bob her head up and down.

"Oh God, Charlie. I want to fuck you so badly." He spoke the words through clenched teeth.

"When you heal, I'll hold you to that." She smirked before devouring his cock. She sucked him into her greedy mouth, enjoying the feel and the taste of him. Her cunt was damp with desire. Just knowing she was responsible for making him so hard was nearly enough to get her off. The sense of her sexual power was heady.

Every so often Jake would make small sounds of pleasure in the back of his throat as Charlie continued to suck his cock. "Oh baby," he muttered over and over again. Feeling daring, she began to take more and more of his cock into her mouth, practically swallowing it whole down her throat.

He screamed out, "Oh God, Charlie, I'm going to come!"

Charlie continued to suck his cock in and out of her mouth until he stilled, and spurted come down her thirsty throat. She slurped his essence down, drunk off the high of his flavor.

She released him before sliding next to him. Charlie then kissed him on the neck. "That was amazing, Charlie." Jake returned the kiss.

"You're amazing." She smiled at him.

They lay, side by side, not saying a word for several moments until Jake broke the silence. "Charlie, when I was unconscious in the hospital, I heard your voice."

"Really? You never said anything. And you scared me to death when you flatlined."

"I remember exactly what happened, but at the time, I thought it was just a dream. It was as if I was in limbo, but I saw a light. The light was so warm and welcoming I started walking toward it. That's when I heard your voice, but by then, I think I was too far away to hear what you were saying. I thought maybe I had imagined it so I kept walking toward the light. But then I was pulled back by a man in a Carolina Tar Heels T-shirt. I don't know why that particular detail sticks out in my mind, but it just does."

He paused briefly, looking as though he was trying to remember what happened next. "He told me it wasn't my time, and I had to keep his peanut happy. I'm not sure what he meant by that, but I started to walk away from the light. When I turned to ask him who he was, he was gone. I don't remember anything after that except waking up in the hospital."

Tears began to stream down Charlie's face. It seemed she had been doing a lot of crying lately. "What's wrong, baby?" he asked, alarmed by her tears.

"It was Paul. He saved you. He brought you back to me."

A puzzled expression crossed his face, so Charlie explained all the events in the hospital and what Christy had told her.

Jake gave her a funny look.

"Are you serious?" He didn't sound convinced.

"Yes. I know it's hard to believe, I mean, I hardly believe it myself."

Jake was silent for a moment. "But there seems to be no other explanation for it though."

She had gone over it in her mind several times but could come up with no other explanation either. "I guess not."

"I feel like a jerk."

"Why?"

"All the uncharitable thoughts I had about him. The guy must have been a saint.

"Believe me, he was not perfect, but he was a good man." Charlie smiled, remembering Paul fondly.

"And it seems I have a lot to thank him for."

"So do I. He gave us another chance at love."

Epilogue

"If you ask me, he looks like a wizened little old man," Jake joked.

"How dare you. My baby is the most beautiful baby ever born, besides Christy of course," Charlie argued. "And anyway, he's the spitting image of his father so what do you say about that, smarty-pants," Charlie pointed out. She cradled their three-hour-old son against her breast. The baby suckled her nipple hungrily, making grunting noises as he fed.

"Greedy little devil isn't he?" Jake grinned proudly. "A boy after my own heart." He leered at Charlie devilishly.

"Jake, you're too much." Charlie chuckled, pulling the baby away from her breast so she could burp him. She touched one of his curly brown locks gently. He was indeed the spitting image of his father. Charlie had a feeling as their son got older he would have to beat the ladies off with a stick. She placed him over her shoulder and gently patted his back.

"He is something else, isn't he?" Jake reached over to stroke his son's back, as though tracing the little form to memory.

"Yes, he certainly is," Charlie smiled.

Jake leaned over to kiss his wife of a year. "I love you so much, Charlie. Each day with you is like Christmas, but I think this little guy, along with our little angel, are the greatest gifts you could have given me."

"I love you, too, Jake. So much." Her heart burst with love. She smiled as she thought back on their past year together.

Charlie and Christy had moved into Jake's large estate house in Springfield shortly after their engagement. Jake had insisted on a speedy wedding in Vegas. He didn't want her changing her mind, but neither the Foxes nor the Browns were having it. Their parents had wanted a big grand event so Charlie and Jake compromised, deciding on a small church wedding with friends and family. It took two months to throw everything together, but with Moira and Delores working with fevered diligence, things went off without a hitch.

Christy was the flower girl. Helen and the twins were bridesmaids. Laura served as Charlie's maid of honor. On Jake's side, Caleb and Dylan served as ring bearers. Jake's other two nephews Jason Junior and Mark were groomsmen while Steve and Carl shared the honor of best man. Boy, did the sparks fly between Steve and Laura, but for the most part, they managed to behave themselves for the majority of the day.

The ceremony was beautiful and poignant. Jake and Charlie recited vows they had composed from their hearts. There was not a dry eye in the entire church.

The reception was held under a tent in Jake and Charlie's backyard. Everyone had a good time. No one seemed to notice when the two of them slipped off to be alone. They honeymooned in Fiji for two weeks while Christy stayed with the Foxes.

They both decided she should stay home to raise Christy, and Jake began to delegate more and more work for Steve to do so he could spend more time with them. It soon came to the point where Steve was doing so much around the office, Jake made him a full partner at MBF.

When Charlie announced a few months into the marriage they were expecting their second child, Jake was ecstatic. He had made it clear he was thrilled he would be there for the birth of their second child.

They both cried when the doctor announced they had a healthy baby boy. Charlie smiled as she remembered Jake crying harder than her.

The baby let out a loud belch. "I think the little bugger is finished for now." Charlie laughed. Jake took his son out of Charlie's arms so she could adjust her gown.

"Christy was a little disappointed she couldn't come, but she was excited when I told her she had a little brother. She said she would draw a picture for him." Charlie smiled while Jake relayed the phone conversation he'd had with their daughter.

"Jake, thank your parents again for watching her. They have been a big help through this entire process."

"Believe me, they're having a blast. They say watching their grandkids helps them stay young."

"My parents say the same thing. I can't believe they're finally going to sell that house on wheels and settle down in the area." No one could be happier about that bit of news. Her parents were getting on in years, and Charlie worried about them roaming the country without any permanency.

"Who can blame them, when they have the world's greatest grandkids as an incentive?"

"I think you're a little biased." Charlie laughed.

"You better believe it." He gave their now sleeping son a kiss on the forehead. "So what do you think Steve and Laura are going to say when we tell them they're to be the godparents of this little bundle of joy?"

"I think they'll love it. They both spoil Christy half to death as it is."

"Yes, but will they behave? You know how they can barely stand being in the same room," Jake pointed out. "Remember how they acted at our wedding?

"They'll behave or they will have me to deal with," Charlie said fiercely.

"Speaking of our little bundle of joy, what should we name him?"

"How about Jacob Junior?" Charlie wasn't too crazy about it, but she'd been so sure they would be having another daughter, she hadn't come up with a boy name she liked.

"No, I was thinking along the lines of Paul."

Charlie looked at Jake, her heart swelling with love. His generosity made her heart skip a beat.

"Really?"

"Yes. Without Paul, there would be no us," he said.

Charlie leaned over to her sleeping son.

"Happy birthday, Paul," she said.

Just then Paul opened his eyes, seeming to approve of his new name.

"I think he likes it." She smiled, feeling content.

"I think so, too. Paul it is then." Jake smiled back.

"Jake, I love you."

"I love you, too, Charlie Fox."

About the Author

To learn more about Eve Vaughn, please visit www.evevaughn.com. Send an email to Eve at eve@evevaughn.com or join her Yahoo! group to join in the fun with other readers as well as Eve! http://groups.yahoo.com/group/evevaughnsbooks

Look for these titles

Now Available

The Life and Loves of April Johnson

Coming Soon:

Reinvention of Chastity